SHADOW BOX

This one is for the tattooed lady
PC

First published 2016 by Walker Books Ltd
87 Vauxhall Walk, London SE11 5HJ

2 4 6 8 10 9 7 5 3 1

Text © 2016 Peter Cocks
Cover design by Tom Sanderson

The right of Peter Cocks to be identified as author of this
work has been asserted by him in accordance with the
Copyright, Designs and Patents Act 1988

This book has been typeset in Palatino and Pahuenga Cass

Printed and bound in Great Britain by Clays Ltd, St Ives plc

British Library Cataloguing in Publication Data:
a catalogue record for this book is available from the British Library

ISBN 978-1-4063-3431-9

www.walker.co.uk

SHADOW BOX

PETER COCKS

WALKER
BOOKS

"I don't need a friend who changes when I change and who nods when I nod; my shadow does that much better." Plutarch

PROLOGUE

Brockley was the last place Donnie had expected to wind up.

He'd known the suburb by name most of his life, it being only ten minutes by car from where he'd spent his childhood – a childhood punctuated by thick ears, bloody noses and petty theft. Brockley had always sounded rural to his ears, and compared to the Docklands, it was. It was a steep climb up the hill from New Cross, past a park with a view across London and through a few leafy streets. But Brockley was a place no one of his acquaintance ever went; you just drove through it, cutting up through Lewisham or New Cross with a view to ducking down to Peckham or Forest Hill to do a deal. A late-night route through anonymous backstreets of terraced houses, where you could be almost sure you wouldn't get a tug when you were driving with a skinful. There were no pubs in Brockley. Actually, that was an exaggeration. There were one or two; the kind of places populated by builders covered in plaster dust discussing the price of copper pipe with plumbers who tutted and sucked their teeth between gulps of lager. And there was a new one he'd seen, they called it a microbrewery, full of tits eating "pulled pork" off a plank of wood. But there were no destination boozers where you would bump into a face or two.

Really, that had been the trouble since he'd got back from Spain. With his payoff from the Spanish job, he'd found a riverside flat in Woolwich, not far from Dave Slaughter. Everywhere he went he'd bump into old muckers who had known him long enough to recognize him beneath the tan and the moustache. He couldn't go into the Plume of Feathers on the side of Greenwich Park without someone slapping him on the shoulder, buying him a vodka and asking, "Awight, Don?" or "Back from the old Espanol, then?"

From their admiring looks, it was clear to him that the rumour that he had done the big hit on the Costa had spread.

When he'd tried to stay in Eltham for a while, it was worse. The wannabe hoodlums had tugged their forelocks in respect to the man who was reputed to have assassinated Patsy Kelly in Spain.

On the orders of Patsy's own brother, Tommy.

A major betrayal of one Kelly brother to prove his loyalty to the other.

Donnie never acknowledged the rumour. To be known as a Kelly hitman, as he had been for years, gave him kudos enough.

Pulling off a big hit on someone within the family elevated him to legendary level – but it was not something for which Donnie wanted to be famous.

So Dave had found him this new place in Brockley, a modern development two minutes from the station. And as soon as his tan had begun to fade, Donnie grew back some short grey hair and a stubbly beard, ditched the earring and wore a Baker

Boy cap whenever he left the flat.

The place had changed since he'd last been here: a couple of delis and coffee shops signalled a new kind of inhabitant, drawn by cheapish housing and the overground line to the trendy bits of Dalston and Shoreditch.

Trendy? Donnie didn't get it. Both places were shitholes, to his knowledge. Neither did he get the wispy blokes – dressed like bent lumberjacks with bushy beards, armfuls of tats, big specs, skinny trousers and handbags – who walked past his apartment to get the train every day. What did they do? They all seemed to have money. Computers, Donnie guessed. Internet stuff.

No job for a man.

Since he'd been back, Donnie hadn't done much work as such. He'd banked a bit of money from the Spanish job, though not as much as he'd have liked. The big payoff always seemed to elude him.

There was the little hit he had done the other day, of course. Nothing challenging: a simple gun to the back of the head on the doorstep. A Russian geezer, tailed to a posh house in St John's Wood, silenced Beretta slipped out of his holdall, tap on the shoulder…

Bang.

Job done, then home in time for lunch.

5 k in the bank. Not enough to retire on, but kushti.

A good freelancer, ex-SAS or whatever, could probably demand 10 k, but Donnie now felt he had a little more job security: the flat, the firm behind him again.

5 k was fine for a killing, with fringe benefits.

Today was shaping up like most days. He smoked a fag and drained several mugs of strong tea while reading The Sun *and*

9

flicking between daytime TV programmes. The news passed him by unless it was to do with armed robbery, and there wasn't much of that any more. Most crime was on an industrial scale now, or done on the money markets with a computer. Donnie had never had any need for a computer; he used his phone for the little contact he made with others. He'd had almost no concern at all for the outside world since he'd come back from Spain.

He had mixed emotions about his time over there. It had started off all right; he'd met a decent bird and that. But then, as these things had a habit of doing, it all went tits-up. Donnie acknowledged to himself that he'd lost the plot a bit. He'd been overcooking it on the nose candy, which always made you a bit mental. Sure, he was under pressure from the firm to choose sides and, first up, he'd gone the wrong way.

It was not a mistake he would make again.

Now it was not so much a case of staying on the straight and narrow, it was more about keeping his nose clean and doing what he was told, following orders, leading more of a regular life. Apart from anything else, Donnie was tired of racing around.

At 12 p.m. he stretched a black leather jacket over his bulky shoulders, pulled the cap down over his forehead and walked down to the station. Five minutes and one stop later, he was out in the familiar smog of New Cross, feeling more at home among the traffic and chaos, enjoying the stale beer smell as he swung open the door to the pub.

He was sipping the top of his second lager and watching the racing results when his phone rang.

"R. Swipe," Donnie said.

"Don?" the voice replied.

"Dave?"

The ritual was a familiar one, played out whatever self-invented alias Donnie came up with, most of them well tried and tested.

Half a minute later Donnie finished the call. He sighed inwardly at Dave's command and within five minutes he'd necked the rest of his lager, flagged down a cab and was on his way up to Greenwich Park.

He found Dave Slaughter in the car park, sitting in a shiny navy Mercedes looking out across the panorama: the O2, the river, the tangle of cranes and new developments. Donnie got into the passenger seat and inhaled the leathery smell of the spotless interior.

"It's all changed, innit?" Dave observed, looking at the oddly shaped towers and spires that had replaced former London badlands.

"All changed," Donnie concurred. "So, wassup, Dave?" he asked, though he didn't really want to know the answer.

Dave turned and looked at him. "You know Paul Dolan's case's gone to the High Court?"

Donnie's mind clunked into gear: Dolan, another Kelly family hitman, had been nabbed when Tommy Kelly had been arrested.

"What's 'is chances?"

"None. Irish prick," Dave said.

"Good," Donnie said. Neither of them liked Dolan. "So?"

"Guvnor wants to see you," Dave replied.

"Thought I was on light duties." Donnie sighed. A prison visit to Tommy Kelly didn't bode well.

"No such thing on this firm, Don."

Donnie had kidded himself that after the big one on Patsy Kelly he would be put out to pasture for a while. He looked out of the steamy car window, his clear view of the panorama now blurred.

"Two words, Don," Dave said. "Eddie Savage."

Bollocks, Donnie thought.

ONE

The smack in the mouth came from nowhere.

I saw stars and tasted blood.

The sensation was a familiar one. I steadied myself and, blinking through the tears that had sprung to my eyes from my flattened nose, launched myself off the back foot, throwing a right at the coked-up Essex boy who thought he'd have a go. My fist connected with cheekbone and my opponent staggered back. I used my advantage to leap forward and throw another punch, hard on the jaw, twisting his head round and dropping him to the wet pavement. I jumped on top of him and grabbed a handful of Superdry, pulling his head up, fist poised for another punch to his face.

"You had enough?" I shouted.

A small group had gathered around us outside the pub.

"Leave it, mate," a voice came nervously, stopping just short of pulling me off. "Leave it."

13

I dropped Essex Boy's head back onto the ground, climbed off him and wiped the blood and snot from my nose.

"He hit me first," I pleaded with the crowd, noting the expressions on the faces of two girls who had stopped to watch. I realized how alien this casual brutality was to the average passer-by, and how horrifying.

The man who had spoken helped my attacker to his feet and propped him against the lit window of the pub. He was groggy; drunk, or woozy from my assault. I looked from face to face, friendless. I had nothing to explain, so I turned and walked away.

I dabbed my bleeding nose as I trudged through the drizzle, wondering why it had happened again. I was getting into situations like this far too often. Several times in the last few months, scraps like this had kicked off in or outside pubs in the back streets of London's West End, my night-time stomping ground. Every night seemed to be a bad dream of dark bars and clubs, of shots that tasted like cough medicine, girls the colour of furniture polish with boyfriends who looked like gay cage-fighters, snorting coke in the bogs and getting lairy to the constant thud of machine-like dance music.

It was driving me mad. Perhaps it was my moody swagger as I walked into places where I knew nobody; I rarely went to the same place twice to avoid familiarity. Perhaps it was my dead-eyed stare as I drank lager and people-watched. Whatever it was, my mood seemed to bring out the aggression in others, who thought I was staring at them, their orange girlfriends or their pints.

Enough to make them confront me, or follow me out and have a pop.

Then there were the trendier places, full of posher, hipper kids, smiling inanely and dancing like sweaty puppets to endless House tracks, gobbling up Es like sweets. The drugs were everywhere I went, and given that my brother had died an addict and my last girlfriend had been killed as a result of a bad cocaine deal, I was still totally anti-narcotics. I don't know why I even went out – I was always out of sync wherever I was – but of the two, I preferred the prickly tension of the Essex boy clubs to the goony ambience of the ecstasy bunnies.

Really, I knew what it was. I felt dead inside; the lager and the buzz of aggression were the only things that made me feel alive. I was drinking too much, from boredom and to blot out the events that still scarred my mind.

I didn't like being Eddie Savage. I was getting out of control. I needed help.

Tony Morris became a regular visitor to my flat.

I knew what he was trying to do. After my experiences in Spain I had hidden myself away: attempting to overcome the trauma of the car bomb that had been meant for me and had killed my girlfriend; trying to rewire my memory and lose the character of Pedro Garcia, my cover identity over there.

Tony was hoping to rehabilitate me. I had refused therapy – I felt I'd had enough to last me a lifetime. I knew what was wrong with me, anyway; I had been scarred and traumatized by getting involved in organized crime

15

while working undercover for Tony's – and, I suppose, my – legit organization.

I'd nearly been killed twice in as many years, and I was still in my teens.

In my view, the best way to recover was not to do it any more.

But Tony had different ideas.

"You can be helpful, mate," he said. "Just by keeping your eyes open when you're out, seeing who's selling what to who."

"You never see anyone dealing cocaine, Tony. It's all done quietly in bashed-up Beemers in supermarket car parks."

"Not so much the coke these days. It's the synthetics we're bothered about, the Es and MDMA. Any spod with a chemistry degree can knock out pills in a garage. Volume, low risk, high profit: that's where the organized firms get interested."

"What firms?"

"Eastern Europeans working over here, Russians, Irish. Most of them are already shifting moody fags through corner shops. Knocking out pills is an easy and more lucrative step up."

Tony was always casting me nuggets of information, to see if I'd take the bait. To get me back to work. Usually, I wasn't interested. But he also told me that Tommy Kelly wanted to see me. As bait goes, Tommy Kelly was quite a fat maggot. I gave it a millisecond's consideration, but … no.

"What good could it do me?" I asked. The head of the

Kelly crime family had liked me and, as far as he was concerned, I'd turned him in. I'd got close to his daughter, his pride and joy, just to be able to spy on him. I'd nailed his son and got them both a life stretch. Tommy Kelly was hardly going to greet me with open arms and let bygones be bygones. So I continued to say no to Tony, and after a while he stopped asking.

But Tony was a sneaky bugger. It was part of his job. He would drop by in the evening with a couple of cold beers and reminisce about the work I'd done for the organization. He would praise me and big up my results, reminding me how close they'd got to cracking the cocaine syndicate in Spain on my intel. Although whatever he said, there seemed to still be tons of it in London, as well as plenty of E, so the gear was obviously still getting through.

But, Tony pointed out, good intel is never wasted. It joins up other dots.

Other times he'd call round in the morning. "Let's get you out in the fresh air," he'd say. We would walk through the central London parks, stopping for lattes, watching girls go by. Tony would give them marks out of ten, but I'd lost interest. We'd talk about this and that, and nothing in particular. Gradually, I began to feel a little more normal. It was like having a dad; someone who made me feel safe again. I got to know Tony, who had never given much of himself away, a little more. He had been in the background in my life for as long as I could remember, an old family friend. I never knew quite what his connection to us was.

He told me he had joined the army when he was about my age and had done a tour of Northern Ireland, where he had become involved in military intelligence. His fleshy face and indistinct looks meant that he rarely stood out, which was useful. I have never known anyone less conspicuous than Tony Morris. I would quite often lose him when we were out and about, unable to see him in a group of three or so people in Regent Street. Tony could disappear in an empty room.

A useful skill in this line of work.

"What did you do in Ireland?" I asked.

"Counter-terrorism," he said. "The IRA was powerful back then, and political. Now it's more or less another organized crime gang: they're not so bothered about religion and politics, more about trading arms and controlling drugs. Back then they were passionate about the cause. They'd blow up a town full of people to make their point ... and they did, in Birmingham, Manchester, London – even Ireland itself."

Tony had explained the backdrop to the Troubles to me before. Of course, I'd known from the news for as long as I could remember that there had been things going on in Ireland, but the details, the fact that the Catholics wanted an independent republic while the Protestants were loyal to the Queen, seemed almost lost in the mists of time.

"Steve went over there, right?" I asked. Tony nodded.

I remembered hearing some of my brother's debriefings after his death. Steve had been over there a few years before, trying to infiltrate an IRA cell. Before me, Steve had been recruited by Tony in a deal to get him off a drug rap. He had ended up dead at the hands of the Kellys.

"So what did *you* actually do there?"

I was straying into an uncomfortable area for Tony. He was naturally secretive. He scratched his head and looked at the ceiling.

"I managed to stop a big bombing in central London," he said finally. "Rush hour, Kings Cross tube, would have killed hundreds and trapped hundreds more. Not only would the body count have been the biggest London had seen, but the city would have ground to a halt. Total chaos was what the IRA planned."

"Nicely done."

"Thank you," Tony said. "I nearly got caught, though. I had to be spirited out of Northern Ireland overnight. I was becoming a bit conspicuous. We were deeply embedded in the IRA and I became a suspect."

"So what happened?"

"I knew the IRA had their suspicions about me and I was asked to go and see a bloke called Padraigh Lynch. He was in charge of their punishment squads."

"Punishment squads?"

"Yeah, they would dish out retribution to anyone they felt wasn't following the rules. They would kneecap a fourteen-year-old for shoplifting, fire a 9 mm into a kid's ankles for breaking into a pub."

"Rough justice," I said.

"It got rougher," Tony said. "The last IRA informer on my watch was hung upside down in a garage, beaten, burned with fags and had his shins smashed with iron bars until the bones poked through…"

I winced. "Shit."

"They kept him like that until he confessed. When the police – the RUC – eventually found his shallow grave, his captors had finally executed him with two bullets to the back of the head. And do you know the worst thing? He was no informer. He was innocent, an IRA man through and through, and just a kid." Tony paused, shut his eyes momentarily. "And it was me who dobbed him in to Lynch to divert attention from myself."

He opened his eyes and a change of expression came over Tony's face.

"'Dere was no way Michael O'Neill could stay in the old country."

It was as if Tony, boring, featureless Tony, had channelled a different personality. A convincing one at that.

"That was your cover? Michael O'Neill?"

He laughed, shrugged. There really was more to Tony than met the eye.

"So, when I started with the service back here, I was kept on the Northern Ireland case as it was my area of expertise. And when Steve started to work for us, I trained him up to pick up some of the pieces."

I did a mental calculation. "That must have been a few years later?"

"A few," Tony agreed. "But all the leads were still up and running, a couple were brown bread but I was able to place Steve right where all the action was. And by that time, Tommy Kelly was helping out the IRA too. Steve hooked up with the Kelly firm through the Irish connection, and as you know, the rest is history."

"Steve did well, didn't he?" I wanted to hear good of my brother, who I had worshipped for so much of my childhood – before he lost the plot.

Tony nodded. "Yeah. He did some good work, but you know Steve, he was a bit of a wild card. The Irish began to suspect quite quickly, so we pulled him out."

"And that's when he started working on the Kelly business?"

Tony nodded again. He looked me.

"I know you think the sun shone out of Steve's arse, mate. But you're the better agent."

I shook my head. "I cock up all the time, Tony."

"We all cock up," he said. "It's not an exact science. Your cock-ups are as useful as a lot of other people's successes." Tony had the knack of making me feel that everything I'd done so far was child's play in terms of the big picture, but that at the same time I was useful and doing well. He gave me a sideways glance.

"So what about going to see Tommy?"

"I've told you I am not going to visit Tommy Kelly," I said. "No way."

TWO

A week or so later, I found myself in the back of a darkened car with my new case officer, Simon Sharp, headed towards Belmarsh high security prison.

Sharp was in his late twenties, with cropped blond hair and a face that wouldn't have looked out of place in a boy band. He was a little taller than me, but wiry.

I looked out of the window at the familiar puzzle of roads that formed the Blackwall Tunnel approach.

"Nervous?" Sharp asked.

I would have been lying if I'd said no: my mouth was bone dry and my stomach was in a tight knot. If I'd eaten, I would probably have vomited.

"A bit," I said. I looked at his knee jigging up and down, and guessed that he wasn't exactly relaxed either. But as far as I knew, he didn't have history with the man I was about to visit.

"Did Tony tell you Paul Dolan's appeal has come up?"

He hadn't. The last time I'd seen Dolan was a couple

of years ago on the Thames, the night they arrested him and Tommy Kelly on my tip-off.

"He hasn't got a hope in hell," I said.

"You never know, if Tommy Kelly's pulling the strings."

"Even if he could pull strings from inside, I think he'd be pulling them for himself, not Dolan. Have *you* met Tommy?" I asked.

He shook his head. "No, but I've done my homework, and pretty hairy reading it makes. They reckon you're the expert in the field."

I shrugged, flattered that my case officer was deferring to me. "I guess I got closer than most."

He paused. "What's he actually like?" Sharp looked at me. The enquiring note in his voice revealed a trace of an accent that had otherwise been carefully concealed.

I tried to recall Tommy Kelly. It had been a while. "If you forget everything you know about him, you could mistake him for a prosperous builder or a car dealer," I said, then reconsidered. "No, actually that makes him sound naff. He's classier than that, knows all about art. Dresses well. In person he's warm, good manners..."

Sharp raised his eyebrows. "Interesting," he said. "I get the feeling you almost like him."

I looked out of the window again, at the industrial wasteland of Woolwich speeding by, and acknowledged to myself that in a strange way I did have a reluctant liking for the old villain.

"The prodigal returns," Tommy Kelly said.

The man waiting for me in the scruffy interview room

in Belmarsh did not look quite as polished or expensively dressed as I had described to Sharp, but he had managed to make his prison kit look dapper. The sandy hair was paler, shorter and not as shiny as when I'd last seen him. He'd aged quite a bit.

"So, Eddie Savage back from the dead, eh? I must be losing my touch."

"Hello, Tommy," I ventured. My voice cracked with nerves. I stood in front of him like a right plum and continued to stare.

He smiled at my nervousness, and I caught a glimpse of repairs made to his teeth. Repairs to damage that I had personally inflicted. He gestured to a chair opposite him at the table. The room had scuffed vinyl floor, plastic chairs, a mirror. I was grateful to sit down; my legs had been shaking from the moment I was processed through security and allowed into the inner sanctum of HM Prison Belmarsh.

On a nod from Tommy, the prison warder left the room. However he had changed, there was no disguising the air of authority that still hung around Tommy Kelly. It wasn't every Category A prisoner that could call an audience with someone from the outside, then dismiss the screw. It made me more nervous. This was a man I'd seen shoot his own best friend in the head at point blank range.

He crossed his arms and looked at me. The look wasn't unkind or menacing, but it was one I had seen before: searching, locking on to my eyes. I tried to hold contact, but couldn't.

"So we still don't know who you really are, do we,

Eddie Savage?" he asked. I said nothing. "Though we do know you're a pretty sneaky little operator," he continued.

I held my silence. I really didn't know what to say, or how or why I was here.

"Cat got your tongue, son?" he asked. "I remember you as quite chatty, especially round my wife and daughter."

The mention of Sophie pricked my conscience, and I looked up into his questioning face.

"How did you know I was alive?" I asked.

"I know everything," he said, smiling. "Surely you know that?"

I didn't reply.

"I may be in here, but I have eyes and ears everywhere." He nodded towards the mirror, clearly two-way, that was fixed to the wall at eye level. "All of them sitting behind the mirror know that, and there's not much they can do about it. They think it's better that I speak freely and they can sweep up what crumbs I drop them." He gave a little wave of his fingers at the mirror and smiled at me, the old, confident Tommy coming to the surface.

"I'm sorry to hear about your brother," I ventured.

Tommy's cheek twitched. If he was about to ask me something, he thought better of it. He nodded instead.

"I know what it's like to lose a brother," I continued. I was gaining a little confidence; I felt sure that he didn't know much about my time in Spain. Although his man Terry Gadd had clearly been on my case by the end, I don't think my cover had ever been blown.

"So, Eddie Savage," he said. "How have you been?

25

You seem fit and healthy, but when I look at your eyes I can see that you're not a happy bunny."

I looked at the floor, avoiding his searching gaze.

"How would you like to work with me again?"

"*What?*" I was incredulous. My case officer and God knows who else were listening to this: Tommy Kelly trying to recruit me from inside Belmarsh under their noses.

"I thought we worked quite well together until, well…"

"Until you got caught out?" I suggested. He smiled.

"You really think you were responsible for sending me down, boy?" He shook his head. "You may have wrong-footed me a couple of times, but there was someone bigger and dirtier behind that sting. Don't flatter yourself: Tommy Kelly doesn't get brought down by a kid."

I felt slightly put out. While there had clearly been other fingers in the pie, I had played a significant part in Tommy's capture and conviction.

"You haven't answered me, Eddie," he said. "About working for me?"

"Of course I won't work for you."

"You don't know what the job is," he pointed out.

I guessed he had *some* idea of who I might be working for. He had known I was still alive, and through his lawyers, or the police, the word had filtered through to Tony Morris's government intelligence department. But I wasn't going to spell it out for him. Neither did he seem to expect me to.

"I trust no one," he said. "Not even my closest friends and associates, and I certainly don't trust you." He jabbed a finger at me. "But of all the fuckers I don't trust, you are the only one I can trust with this job."

"What is the job?" I asked, intrigued. I looked up at him and his expression had softened. He slid a postcard across the table to me.

"I want you to find Sophie."

THREE

Sophie.

Her name, spoken by her father, brought my mind back into sharp focus.

South London on the way back from Belmarsh went by in a blur, images, places and events from my time with Sophie Kelly replaying vividly in my brain.

It was as if my suppressed memories had been rebooted. I stared at the postcard Tommy had palmed me. The picture was of a non-specific sunset. I turned it over. The blurred postmark was from somewhere in Spain, the message simple: *I'm OK, Dad. Hope you are. Love you. S xxxx*

Sophie was clearly up to speed at giving nothing away. The thought that she was alive somewhere, right now, gave me a buzz. In the seat next to me, Simon Sharp nattered on, clearly excited about his first view – albeit from behind a two-way mirror – of Tommy Kelly. He seemed almost starstruck, eager to know details about the Kelly family business. He quizzed me all the way into town, not stopping until we arrived outside a fish restaurant in Soho.

"Lunch?" he asked. Sharp ran a long finger down the dishes on the menu, settled for scallops with black pudding and a grilled Dover sole. Then he took out his briefcase and opened a dossier of photos. "Tony thought you might like to see these," he said.

They were of Sophie Kelly – surveillance pictures taken on a long lens. They looked like paparazzi shots from a celeb magazine: Sophie and her mum sitting outside a restaurant; Sophie in a white bikini, sunbathing on a yacht and putting on sun cream; Sophie walking out of the waves, topless. I felt a pang of protective indignation, they were like those "snooper" pics you see of footballers' wives on the front of tabloid newspapers.

I swallowed hard and placed the pictures face down on the envelope.

"Where were these taken?" I asked Sharp.

"Miss Kelly's been travelling quite a lot," he said. "Once the guvnor got nabbed, she and her mum went straight to Majorca to the family villa. It was the obvious choice. Probably where the card came from."

It crossed my mind that while I had been in the south of Spain infiltrating the circle of the *other* Kelly brother, her Uncle Patsy, Sophie might have only been a short boat trip away.

"That's where the first of the pictures were taken, about a year ago. I was assigned to keep an eye on them. I was out there anyway, keeping tabs on one of the nightclub syndicates."

"Tough gig?" I asked.

Sharp shrugged. "Bit like being on the night shift. You start about 6 p.m. round the bars, and then you hop from club to club, keeping an eye on who's selling what to whom. Have a few drinks, chat to people. You know the score."

"Sure," I said. "Tiring. It messes with your body clock, doesn't it?"

"I'm pretty much a night owl anyway," Sharp said. "But those places aren't really my scene. I'm sure you know the ones I mean."

I did. It took me back to 24-Hour Square in Benalmádena, and the clubs: the endless house music and drunken girls staggering around – and worse – in the street. It reminded me of hanging out with Gav Taylor. Took me back to the bar in Benalmádena where I'd stabbed him in self-defence, notching up my first killing. I'd "done my one" and didn't feel too proud about it.

"I'd start a bit earlier in the day," Sharp continued. "Keeping the Kelly villa under surveillance, following Sophie and Cheryl if they went out to a restaurant."

"Did they know they were being watched?" I asked.

"I'm sure they did, eventually. They'd committed no crime themselves but they were paranoid that with Tommy out of the way someone might have a pop at them, so they moved on pretty quick."

"How did they seem?" I asked, eager for information about Sophie.

"Edgy, obviously. I managed to get close enough to them for a bit of small talk. I said I was a designer doing up some apartments for Russian clients."

"Didn't that make them suspicious? They have quite a few Russian friends, or at least Tommy does."

"If it did, they didn't bat an eyelid. The Russians are everywhere now; they're taking over. Of course, I was hoping they might have been a bit more forthcoming and dropped a name or two, but they're cagier than that. They became a little more relaxed with the wine, and once Cheryl could see I wasn't trying to hit on her daughter."

A defensive instinct rose in me.

"Lovely, isn't she?" he said. "A real warm, classy girl."

I nodded. Whatever might have happened between me and Sophie, I still had a soft spot for her. Very soft.

"Then one day they didn't turn up."

"Where did they go?"

"It's more a case of where didn't they go," Sharp said. "They sailed out of Palma Majorca, then stopped in Ibiza. That's where the bikini shots were taken. Terry Gadd has a place tucked away there. He can't use it, so Cheryl and Sophie holed up there for a month or so."

"Where's Terry now?" I asked.

"Good question," Sharp said. "He's slipped off the radar. We suspect Turkish Cyprus. Easy to get lost, no extradition treaty."

"What about Sophie and Cheryl – when did you lose track of them?"

"Someone else watched them in Ibiza. For me to have followed them there would have been too obvious. Then I got the nod when they packed their bags and left Gadd's place."

31

I picked at the plate of whitebait I had ordered and resisted the urge to turn the photos back over.

"They got on a yacht from Ibiza, registered to a Russian company that we think is an offshoot of a larger firm owned by an oligarch called Alexei Bashmakov. Ring a bell?"

"I've met him," I said. Sharp nodded; it must have been on my file. I had been there when Tommy Kelly hooked up with him in Croatia. Tommy had sold him a moody Francis Bacon painting for a fortune, plus a huge consignment of cocaine disguised in wax champagne bottles.

"Anyway," he said. "I chartered a small boat from a holiday company out of Palma and picked up a sighting of the Kelly girls as they crossed south of Majorca. It's difficult to keep track of a boat when you're out in the open water because you're easy to spot, so we kept half a day behind them, relying on satellite surveillance. Our last report was in a marina on the south coast of Sardinia. We kept an eye on the boat, but by the time we got an agent down there the boat was all locked up and there wasn't a trace of Sophie or Cheryl.

"Where do you think they've gone?" I asked. I lost interest in the cold plate of small fish in front of me.

"Anyone's guess," Sharp said. "They could have been driven overland, then gone up to Italy. They could have found somewhere pretty and isolated there. Puglia, Tuscany... Italy's so rural and full of Brits they could easily have hunkered down. Or they could have gone to Rome and flown almost anywhere in the world. Or they could have changed boats and headed off towards Greece via Cyprus, and up the coast to eastern Europe."

Suddenly I wanted to find Sophie.

"Do you have a clue?" I asked. "Are you putting me on her case?"

Sharp pursed his lips and signalled for the bill.

"Probably," he said. "We'll talk to Tony, see if he has one of his hunches."

Simon Sharp picked up the photos again and cast his eyes over them before putting them back in the envelope.

"Don't worry," he said, smiling and handing it to me. "She's not really my type."

I looked around at the rest of the restaurant's clientele and realized that she probably wasn't his type at all.

FOUR

Tony Morris always played shit music.

I picked up a scuffed CD cover from the car's foot-well and looked at the tracklist. It was a *Now That's What I Call Music* compilation from a couple of years back, already way out of date. They were either poppy urban acts – Rihanna, Alesha Dixon – or winners and runners-up from one TV talent show or other – Olly Murs, Leona Lewis, One Direction. They were names that had barely registered on my psyche. The background to my life had been flamenco and Spanish club music for a while, and since I'd come back I'd found it hard to even listen to my iPod for fear of igniting unwelcome memories.

"Spoken to your mum recently?" Tony asked.

I hadn't for a while. Calling the old girl always made me feel an awkward mixture of guilt and a longing for one of her roast dinners. It was my brother's and my fault that she'd had to move so far away. But she was settled in the Midlands and I didn't want to rock the boat.

I found it easier to lock off the needy emotions I felt when I thought about her.

"Not for a bit," I said. I stared at the CD cover and pretended to read it.

"You should," he said. "She misses you. Worries about you."

Sensing my discomfort, Tony left it there. He adjusted the volume on the car stereo and caught me wincing as the electric crackle of Lady Gaga singing "Telephone" with Beyoncé started.

"Gotta keep up to date, mate," he said, grinning.

"These are well past their sell-by. *Lady Gaga*, Tony?"

"I probably *would*, given half a chance." He leered, his chunky hands tightening on the steering wheel. "You seen the video? Starts off with a load of half-dressed birds in a prison…"

"Pervert," I said.

I didn't really mean it, I was just falling in with Tony's laddish banter, his attempt to jolly me along. The conversation lulled and my mind slipped a gear.

"What thoughts do you have on Sophie Kelly's whereabouts, Tony? Are you sending me after her?"

Tony stared straight ahead along the motorway for a moment. He indicated, overtook a heavy lorry then pulled back into the middle lane.

"We're following several lines of enquiry," he said, cautiously.

"I know," I said. "Simon Sharp told me that much."

"We haven't got much at the moment, mate, so I don't want to give you false hopes, or send you out thinking we're heading in a definite direction."

"Give me *false hopes*?" I was taken aback. "I haven't got any hopes, Tony. I hate to remind you, but since you recruited me I've been shot twice, beaten up more times than I can remember, stitched up on a drugs sting. I've also killed a man barely older than me, lost one girlfriend and watched while another was blown up in a car bomb meant for me." I began to warm to my theme. "Ever since then, I've been stranded here in London like Johnny No-mates, hanging around in shit clubs doing my best to avoid drugs that might, just *might*, make me feel better about it all for a while. So instead, I get beered up, end up in fights and wake up alone, trying to remember what happened before I do it all over again the next night. It's shit. So, no, I don't really have many hopes, as such."

Tony was quiet, keeping his eyes on the road.

"You've had a tough time, Eddie," he said finally. He didn't usually "Eddie" me. I was more often "kid", or "mate". "You've been dropped in at the deep end. I just don't want to throw you straight back in again when we're not entirely sure where this one's leading. I don't want you to think that going off after Miss Kelly like a knight in shining armour will be all hearts and flowers."

"When did anything to do with the Kelly family end up all hearts and flowers?" I laughed. "The hearts usually have bullets through them and the flowers end up on their graves."

"Nice," Tony said. "Poetic."

"And one thing I want to know, Tony, is why are you doing what Tommy Kelly wants? Is it usual to put someone like me on a mission under instruction from someone like him?"

"It's not strictly kosher, I'll give you that, but we tend to operate outside the normal boundaries, as you know. For us, I'm sorry, but Sophie herself isn't all that important."

I smarted. I had assumed it was a missing persons case – one person being every bit as important as another.

I guess it depends on who your dad is.

"We're not doing this for Tommy Kelly or his daughter; we are doing it *in spite* of Tommy and *because* it's his daughter. We're an intelligence agency: it's the route that leads us to her that's the interesting bit, what the investigation might bring us on the way. Sometimes you have to dance with the devil, and on this one, he's calling the shots."

As ever, Tony muddled the phrase.

"So, what if I call the shots? What if I say I'm not going to do it?"

Tony sounded like he was trying to convince me, but he knew he had me by the nuts.

"One, we think that Sophie Kelly, wherever she is, will not be there of her own free will. Anyone who knows Tommy knows that the girl is his weak spot, it's the only thing that makes him vulnerable. He may not show it, but he will do anything to assure her safety. Two, I think you still feel something for her…"

It was true. The mention of her name made my stomach lurch, still produced a feeling that reached all the way to my toes.

"So don't tell me you wouldn't do what you could to make sure she's safe."

He was right. Sophie Kelly filled the void I had that passed for feelings. She was a love that I had known – and now missed.

"Also, three, if Tommy Kelly sets you off on a mission, his name will open doors for you, offer you some protection. We can back you up against anyone who threatens you, but if you've been given the carte blanche by Mr K, plenty of others will treat you with kid gloves."

"Lucky me," I said bitterly. "Once again, under the protective wing of Tommy Kelly."

"And me," Tony chipped in. Tony's protection hadn't always been that good in my experience, but given the choice between him or Tommy Kelly… "Listen, bottom line is, Sophie is a big piece of bait for anyone who wants leverage on Tommy. So you'll be the sprat sent to catch the rabbit."

Tony may have mangled the phrase but his meaning was clear enough. I didn't like the idea of being the bait. To use another cliché, I felt I was being pulled into another mess, hook, line and sinker. I opened my mouth to argue, and Tony took his eye off the road for a second to look at me. I didn't see the car that overtook us, fast – just a flash of black.

Then there was a bang, and Tony shouting "Fuck!" as he tried to regain control of the wheel, twisting sharply left and narrowly missing the back of a container lorry before we hit the verge and went over.

Gravel scraped the roof, the windscreen shattered and then, finally, the sound of sirens.

FIVE

Donnie hated prison visits at the best of times.

They brought back memories of his own spells at Her Majesty's pleasure: the endless boring days; the permanent underlying aggression; the terrible food and the stench of "slopping out" – clearing up your own shit and piss as they'd had to do in his day.

Being a big bloke with a reputation made matters worse. Either you were surrounded by toadies – weaklings in for fraud, scared to death, who would suck up on a daily basis with gifts of fags, hoping to ensure your protection – or you were honour-bound to be the one to bash up the nonces and kiddy fiddlers when they came in, to make sure they were put on the special unit out of the way of the good, honest criminals like Donnie and his colleagues. Worse, you were a target for the up-and-coming villains and hard men who thought they could have a go to secure their reputation on the wing. There would be the surprise crack on the back of the head from a cosh made out of a chair leg wrapped in scraps of nicked roofing lead. If you managed to stay upright, you had to muller the assailant into oblivion to maintain your own rep and keep the other "have a go" boys down.

Any of these put you at higher risk if you were just trying to keep your nut down, do your bird and hope for parole in eighteen months.

Donnie's mind drifted back to the showers in Wormwood Scrubs a few years back. He had already been on a five-year stretch for grievous bodily harm when some herbert had decided to try it on. Shivering and damp and naked in the changing room, Donnie had felt the tap on his shoulder and turned to find a fist smack in his face, breaking his nose. Even for the hardest bastard, a surprise busted conk was almost impossible to recover from, and Donnie had reeled back as his attacker jabbed soapy fingers in his eyes, brought a knee up into his crown jewels and crashed another right-hander into his jaw.

The man was shorter than him, but squat, with a thick neck and shoulders like a bull. He was well known to Donnie: Roy Francis, an enforcer for another firm, the north London Noble family – or "No Balls", as the Kelly firm referred to them. Francis had been giving Donnie the needle for weeks, looks across the dining hall, snide comments in the exercise yard, usually because of some real or imagined slight or insult, or word from the outside that there was friction between the two firms that could be carried on inside the prison.

Donnie had fallen to his knees, blinded by watery eyes, as further heavy punches had rained down on his head and ears. Through his blindness he managed to grab a stocky ankle and twist Francis to the ground, making him slip on the wet floor. His attacker had made the mistake of coming at him with bare feet and Donnie managed to clamp his jaw round Francis' last two toes, biting down hard until he felt flesh give and bone crunch.

Francis's screams had alerted the screws, but some, either from fear or enjoyment, would let these rucks play out until most of the aggression had gone from the fighters. Donnie's eyes cleared a little and, while the other man was writhing in pain, he jumped on top of Francis with a knee drop across his throat, grabbed his opponent's ears and pulled hard, cracking the other man's head back across the changing room bench. Finally, he brought his massive head down into Francis's nose, causing a spray of blood to cover both their faces.

As the eight assembled warders eventually wrestled Donnie against the changing room wall, he caught sight of himself in the mirror: eyes swollen like rotten peaches, a mask of blood and scratches covering his face and smashed nose, blood and drool pouring from his mouth and down his chest.

He looked like a monster. He was a monster.

Being attacked had cost him several weeks' solitary and pushed his parole back another year – a year in which Donnie pledged to keep out of mischief and never go back inside, swearing he would shoot himself sooner than serve another stretch.

Now he swerved prison visits if he could; he always got the sweats that they would keep him in. But, of course, when Tommy asked to see you, you went.

The inside of Belmarsh smelled like a prison, but the wing to which Donnie was escorted was much posher than anything he was used to. With shiny lino floors and bright lighting, it felt more like some kind of day centre.

Tommy smiled and held out his hand to shake, but he didn't get up from the plastic chair.

"Don."

"Tommy."

Donnie found it difficult to make eye contact with the guvnor at the best of times, but this was the first time he'd been face to face with Tommy since he'd assassinated his brother Patsy in Spain.

"Good to be back from the Costa?" Tommy asked.

"Yeah. Thanks. Settled back in OK." Donnie sniffed nervously, wiped his knuckle across his nose and looked at the floor.

"Don't be awkward, Don," Tommy said. "It's me. Tommy. You done good over there. Very handy. It was all getting a bit out of control."

Donnie had always assumed that the order to kill Patsy had come from Tommy, but that made it worse. He found it awkward to look in the eye the man who was capable of ordering the slaying of his own flesh and blood. And paying Donnie for doing it.

"So, how you getting on with business, Don?"

"You know, keeping out of mischief. Doing a bit of this and that for Dave." Donnie shrugged, tried to divert attention away from himself. "Dave said Dolan's up for appeal? D'you think...?"

"Don't be a numpty, Don. His only way out's in a box and I'll make sure of it."

"S'what I thought." Donnie nodded.

"Good," Tommy said. "Anyway, I've got a little errand for you. A bit of unfinished business."

Donnie's heart sank, but he tried to look interested.

42

"Remember the kid who went out with Sophie?"

Donnie nodded: he remembered the name Dave had told him; remembered shooting him in a flat in Deptford.

"Well, he's back."

Donnie raised scarred eyebrows. "Back? Dave mentioned 'im, but I thought..."

"Didn't we all, Don? But a little bird told me he's still around."

Donnie felt embarrassed. He was being told, he felt, that he had cocked up a job. The sense of failure that always lurked close to the surface of Donnie's shallow depths broke out as a patch of sweat under his armpits.

"So, what can I do to help, Tommy?" Donnie asked.

"Dave will give you the full SP but, long and short of it, I want you to keep a close eye on Eddie Savage."

SIX

"It was a blow-out," Simon Sharp said.

Sandy Napier sat on the other side of the desk and looked closely again at the report.

"Forensics have been over the vehicle with a fine-tooth comb. The tyre was bald on the inside and the tracking was out, which can't have helped," Sharp continued. "There was also debris found on the road near by, which may have contributed. The engineering boys have been given a bollocking."

Tony rubbed a hand over his stubbled jaw. He hadn't shaved for a few days; the dressing on the side of his face prevented it. I had got off quite lightly: mild concussion, cuts and bruises and a painful lump on the side of the head. We had been in and out of casualty within a few hours and were driven back to HQ in Beaconsfield.

"It just feels too much like a coincidence," Tony said. "Me and him on the way here, black car... I've been doing this job long enough to know when something feels wrong."

"We've checked every angle, Tony," Sharp insisted.

Napier nodded. "I know how it looks, but the motorway cameras have been checked. The black BMW was legit, registered to a Mr Khan in Edgbaston. He wasn't even much over the speed limit. That's all there is to it. He wasn't responsible for you crashing, it was a tyre blowing out at speed, pure and simple."

I could see that Tony was having none of it. Whether it was deliberate or a complete accident, he didn't like the omen.

"So we need to get you back on track, Mr Savage," Sandy Napier said. "I hope you don't mind me saying, but you've put on a few pounds."

It was true. I hadn't exactly kept up a fitness regime in Spain, and since I'd been back, apart from the odd run round Regent's Park I'd been a bit of a couch potato.

"We'll get you back down to fighting weight," Napier assured me. "Also we want to train you up in a few surveillance techniques. Be handy. Good to have you back, Savage."

I felt a little swell of pride. Kind words from Napier were as rare as rocking horse manure.

"Thank you, sir," I said.

Half an hour later, Simon Sharp finished eating and went back to his desk, leaving me and Tony alone. Lunch was canteen spaghetti bolognese. The tomato sauce was too acidic and the dried parmesan smelled a bit vomity. I'd learned to add a pinch of sugar and a splash of milk to tomato sauces to take out the sharpness. And to use fresh parmesan.

Sharp had left half of his, but I was hungry. So was Tony, judging by the slurping noise as he sucked the pasta in and the trickle of orange sauce that stuck to his chin.

"He doesn't eat much," I said, nodding at Sharp's plate.

"Got his figure to think of; you might take a leaf out of his book." Tony grinned at me and winked, then helped himself to some of Sharp's leftover spag bol.

I paused for a minute. I wanted to ask Tony about Sharp but wasn't sure how to approach it.

"So, Simon's on my case now, full time?"

"Sure," Tony said. "That OK?" He wiped the last of the sauce from his chin with a paper serviette and belched.

"Yeah," I said. "Fine. He seems cool."

"He's a good agent," Tony said. "Bright as a whip. Got degrees in rocket science and ancient Serbo-Croat, or something."

"Yeah, he's smart. Is he...?"

Tony looked up at me from the bowl of rhubarb crumble that he had swapped for his empty pasta plate.

"Is he what?"

"Is he gay?"

Tony nodded. "Sure. Got a problem with that?"

"No, of course not," I said. I didn't. "I just wanted to know."

"Good," Tony said, between spoonfuls of crumble. "Because he's the best man for the job. He was Ian Baylis's protégé. Baylis took him under his wing, trained him up: languages, surveillance ... he's an all-rounder."

Baylis had been *my* original case officer. He hadn't

exactly taken me under his wing. We'd disliked each other on sight.

"Sharpie kept an eye on you in Spain from time to time."

"Really?" My case officer on the Costa had been Anna Moore. I'd got a little too close to Anna, which I suspect is why I'd had a new handler assigned to me.

"You wouldn't have seen him, though. He disappears like a fleeting shadow. He spirited your girl Juana back to your apartment the night it all kicked off in Benalmádena."

"I knew someone from our firm must have looked after her, but I never saw anyone."

"Sharp's good, I told you."

"Didn't save her, though…"

Tony raised his eyebrows to silence me. I felt a hand on my shoulder. I hadn't seen Simon come back to the canteen or heard him approach.

"We need to get on, Eddie," he said. Everyone at HQ seemed to have reverted to "Eddie", my original cover name. Tony dismissed me with a flick of his fingers as he chewed his crumble.

I followed Sharp to the office we were to share while I was here. It was very tidy: everything was stacked in neat piles on the desk. A Mac laptop glowed on Sharp's desk; a screensaver with a *Wizard of Oz* film poster was the only bit of colour in the room. He rebooted the screen, which opened to Facebook.

"We're going to do some very basic surveillance to kick off."

"FB?" I asked.

"It's made some of our work very easy. The link-ups you can get through a few Facebook trawls deliver the kind of basic intel you could have only dreamed about a few years ago. We're working with the Facebook people so we can access all users. You got your laptop?"

I opened my Mac and fired it up. My screen showed the purple swirling pattern that came ready loaded. I didn't like personalizing my desktop and was surprised that Sharp did; I thought it gave too much away.

"I'm going to send you a new email address to log on to Facebook," Sharp said. "You will use it only for this case. It will supersede any other addresses you've had. You can cache anything else you want to keep on a portable hard drive. Of course, the archives here will always have back-up."

Sharp typed in an address and pressed send.

A new window opened on my desktop: an internal message from Sharp. I opened it and read my new email address: kieran.kelly@gmail.com

"Kelly?" I asked, incredulous. "Kieran Kelly? What the...?"

SEVEN

"You're joking," I said to Tony. "Kieran Kelly? What are you thinking?"

Tony was tilted back in his office chair, sipping coffee, weaving a ballpoint in and out of his fingers.

"New cover. Sharpie's idea," he said, and winked.

Sharp brought up some Photoshop images on his laptop, pictures of me that had been altered. He pointed to one of them. "If you look at the basic shape of your face, it is not a million miles away from the shape of Tommy or Patsy Kelly's. We've run a DNA check and you do share a few of their Celtic genes, probably Irish, so you are roughly within the same food group, so to speak."

"What are my other genes?" I asked. I was interested, knowing little about my background beyond my mum.

"You're a mixed bag," Tony said. He grinned. "A bit of a mongrel, but it's the Mick bit we're looking for."

Sharp laid mugshots of Tommy and Patsy Kelly over the photos of me, stretched and squeezed them in

Photoshop until the size and shape roughly matched that of mine. Then he began making the layers of the other faces more translucent until they were just ghosted over my own. I could see a new person emerging. He rubbed out some bits and airbrushed others.

"Your eyes are already grey-blue, which is close enough," Sharp said. "We can redden up your hair a little without making you a complete ginge, maybe put a bit of wave in it."

"Steady," I said. My hair had reverted to its natural dirty blond, straight as an arrow.

The Photoshop picture on the laptop was still recognizably me, but had an unmistakable look of one of the Kelly brothers about it too.

"You're Kieran Kelly, Patsy's son from an earlier relationship."

"I'm Patsy Kelly's *son* now?" I shook my head in disbelief. "How does that work?"

"It all stacks up pretty well. I've put a watertight cover together for you," Sharp explained. "Patsy's no longer around to disclaim you, and because Tommy wants doors opened for you, he'll back the story up if necessary."

"It's really another layer of protection," Tony continued. "No villain's going to question you if you're family."

"So not content with having me infiltrate the most dangerous family of villains you could hope to meet, you now want me to actually *be* a Kelly?"

Tony looked at Simon Sharp, who nodded.

"Yup. 'Bout the size of it," Tony said.

* * *

"Hello, handsome."

I opened my eyes and looked in the mirror to see Anna Moore standing behind me. It had been a while. She'd got me out of Spain the day the car bomb killed Juana. I hadn't been in any kind of mood to talk at the time.

I wasn't in the mood right now, either, but it was a distraction from the scratching pain on my arm.

"I thought I'd come and see how your makeover's going." She cocked her head to one side and studied me in the mirror. "Nice job, Sharpie," she said. She and Simon Sharp stood back and admired the work that had been done so far. It was fairly subtle, I have to say. My hair had been dyed a little darker and redder and cut into a choppy crop. Some wax had been rubbed in and tousled about, making me look a bit rougher and borderline chavvy. A few freckles had been henna-dyed across my nose and cheeks, breaking up my normally clear skin. My eyebrows had been reshaped and dyed and, sitting there, bare-chested with a gold chain round my neck, I could have mistaken myself for one of the Kelly family, a boyish amalgam of Tommy and Patsy.

The pain in my arm got momentarily worse and I winced as the buzzing went to a higher pitch. Anna leant in to look as the tattooist stretched the skin taut across my bicep with a latex-gloved hand.

"Don't be a wuss," Anna joked. "You've been through worse."

I *had* felt worse pain, admittedly, but although the insistent scratching of the tattooist's needle burned, what hurt more was submitting voluntarily to being permanently marked as a member of a crime family. Tony had said it could be lasered off at a later date, but in the meantime, the image that was emerging from the bloody mess on my arm identified me as one of theirs. I remembered seeing the same on Jason Kelly's arm among the Celtic bands and Ninja flashes: a green shamrock and a harp, fake membership of a club to which I didn't want to belong.

Half an hour later, with my bare arm wrapped in cling film to protect my fresh tat, I went through my new identity on paper. The birth certificate looked genuine enough:

Name:	**Kieran Patrick Kelly**
Date of Birth:	**15.03.1997**
Place of Birth:	**Bexleyheath, Kent**
Father:	**Patrick Ronald Kelly**
Occupation:	**Builder**
Mother:	**Maureen June Kelly (née Carter)**
Occupation:	**Housewife**

I knew what a multitude of sins the occupations "builder" and "housewife" covered in the Kelly family.

As Kieran Kelly I had gone to primary school in Bexley, then the family had moved to Spain. Patsy and Maureen had divorced soon after and "Kieran" had gone back to live with his mother in Kent. For a Kelly, Kieran had lived a pretty anonymous and blameless life.

"All make sense?" Sharp asked. He passed me a driving licence and passport made up with my new photo.

"Sure," I said. The cover was so simple, and the

disguise not a million miles away from how I looked anyway, that it was completely convincing.

Having spent nearly two years getting close to the family, it was a surprisingly easy step for me to actually become a Kelly.

EIGHT

EIGHT

The pub was one of the oldest on the Thames, supposedly the place where the Mayflower set sail for America.

Donnie remembered it from his childhood. The jetty hung over the muddy riverbank at Rotherhithe. As kids, they'd fight around in the mud for the coins, clay pipes and other treasures that had been dropped by generations of drinkers. He leant over the rail now, ignoring the rain, and looked down at the greasy shore forty years on: rubber tyre; shopping trolley; plastic water bottle. Where the water lapped, the bloated body of a dead rat lay on its back, yellow teeth gnawing at thin air.

"I'm going inside, Don," Dave Slaughter said. "I'm drenched."

Donnie flicked the stub of his cigarette down into the water, where it went out with a hiss.

They headed upstairs to the private bar for lunch. Donnie scanned the menu, moving his lips as he read.

"What is pulled pork anyway?"

"Dunno, Don, but I know when someone's pulling mine," Dave laughed. "Hurry up."

Both had the ribeye steak with chips. Dave, rare. Donnie, well done.

"So: Eddie Savage," Dave said.

"Does Tommy think I buggered up?"

"Probably." Dave raised an eyebrow. "A bit. But then you've done better since, so that's redeemed you in his eyes."

Donnie felt a queasy relief as he swallowed the best part of a pint of Guinness. No matter what Tommy Kelly said to your face, you could never really tell where you stood. Dave was the most reliable barometer of how you were regarded by the boss.

"You'll need to do a bit more, though," Dave told him. He carved a huge, bloody slice off his steak, speared a dozen chips and rammed them into his mouth.

"He said I got to keep an eye on him," Donnie said.

"Bit more to it than that," Dave said. Of course there was. "Miss Sophie's been on the missing list for over six months and she's done it in good style. We've had not so much as a peep from her or Cheryl."

"Ransom thing?" Donnie asked.

"There's been rumours," Dave said. "Red herrings, mostly. Any villain who knows she's missing might have a go at extracting a few quid from TK. But Tom's no mug, he knows it would be the easiest thing in the world to hand over a mil in ransom in exchange for his daughter, and he doesn't think anyone would dare. He thinks it goes bigger than that, and although he don't show it, that's what's making him sweat."

"So, what about the Savage kid?" Donnie asked.

"Tommy knows he's like a frickin' terrier where Sophie's

concerned. Plus, whoever the kid's working for will be helping him with information in tracking her down."

Donnie tried to keep up.

"So hang on, who is the Savage kid working for? The Old Bill?"

"Don't be daft," Dave laughed. "It's some intelligence set-up."

"And Tommy's using them to help find his daughter? It don't sound right." Donnie shook his head.

"It's very smart. From inside, the guvnor is manipulating intelligence to get them to find his daughter when he can't. Any information they gather on the way isn't likely to harm the firm: they pick up something that points at us, we chuck 'em a googly about someone else. Disinformation. Intelligence works both ways, Don. Tom's getting them to work for us without giving nothing away ... apart from a large drink to one or two of their operators."

Donnie wrestled with the idea of Tommy working alongside a legitimate agency.

"How do I fit in?" he asked.

"It's mostly a watchin' and waitin' job for you, Don." Dave smiled. "You just stick close to the kid. Shadow him. Follow where he goes, who he talks to, keep tabs."

"How will I do that?"

Dave took a photo from his pocket and handed it to Donnie.

"He's changed a bit," he said. "Disguised his'self, or someone else has. Probably got an alias, but we're on it." He passed another across the table. "There's also this other bloke..."

Donnie looked at the photo, taken on a long lens, of a slim young man outside a Spanish restaurant. He was talking *and drinking with Cheryl and Sophie.*

"This bloke was spotted a couple of times, hanging around Sophie and Cheryl in Spain. We're not sure which side he's batting for. Watch out for him, and all."

"How do you know this stuff?"

Dave tapped his nose. "A bit of 'insider trading'."

"Wouldn't it be better to put someone on it who don't stick out so much?"

"It's your job, Don. You're pretty low-profile when you need to be. Besides, I forgot to mention, you keep track of Eddie Savage until he finds Sophie..." Dave stabbed the last piece of meat on his plate, used it to wipe up the rest of the bloody juice and shoved it into his mouth. "Then, when he does find her," he said, chewing, "You grab Sophie, put her somewhere safe and finish what you started: you blow Eddie Savage's fucking brains up the wall."

NINE

"That's her," Tony said.

I watched a dark-haired indie chick dressed in scruffy denims, lumberjack shirt and a leather biker jacket cross the road. Pretty, in a hipster girl way, but serious-looking.

I held the Nikon up to my eye and squeezed the shutter button, firing off several shots in quick succession before ducking back into the depths of the transit van where we had been holed up for the past two hours. I checked the shots. I had managed to get a clear profile of the girl as she turned to cross the road.

"Any good?" Tony asked. I showed him. "Not bad for a beginner."

"Worth waiting all that time for?" I asked. My buttocks had gone numb from sitting in the back of the surveillance van.

"That's nothing," Tony said. "Sometimes you can be staked out all day and night and still not get a shot."

We watched the girl continue up the Kilburn High

Road and then turn left. Sharp started up the van and followed her, turning into the same side street. I fired off a few more shots from the rear window as we drove past, then Sharp put his foot down and we headed back to base.

I uploaded the images onto my laptop, zoomed in and cropped them, then sharpened them up.

"You've got a knack for it," Sharp said, admiring my work. I had only recently picked up a camera and had been shown which buttons to press by one of the spods. I was also given a crash course in Photoshop, enabling me to manipulate the images and clarify them. I printed out a few on A4 and pinned them to the wall.

"Hannah Connolly," Sharp said.

I typed the name into Facebook and, several down the list, there she was.

"Before social networking it would have taken months to gather the amount of information you've got here," Sharp said. "It's good to know how a real camera works, you need a long lens for surveillance, but your iPhone's just as good most of the time. Ten years ago, it would have taken a day in the darkroom to do what your phone can do in a few minutes. It's got more memory on it than it took to put a man on the moon. We're lucky."

I took it on board. I'd watched plenty of spy films: Bond, Bourne and all that. With voice recording, video and SIM cards, I guessed we didn't need a tape recorder hidden in a suitcase any more. Steve Jobs had sorted it all out for us.

I scrolled through photos of Hannah Connolly. Even

those that were available without friending her gave a fairly clear impression. She looked quite bohemian: thick fringe, dark eyeliner, nose ring, tattoos on her wrists. Her clothes were art-studenty, and most of the pictures were taken in pubs and bars and at gigs. I scrolled through her likes, at a glance a mix of bands that I hadn't heard of, clubs that looked like the kind I hated and political groups I didn't give a stuff about.

"Shall I send a friend request?" I asked.

"Not so fast," Sharp said. "We don't know if she's friendly yet."

"What's our interest in her?"

"That's for you to find out," Sharp said. "Tony's passed down a bit of intel that's flagged this girl up, among others. She's someone you can get at, right age. Might need to find a few new interests…"

"This anything to do with Sophie Kelly?"

"Don't think so." Sharp shrugged. "Tony thinks it's too early to go after Sophie. He doesn't want to appear to jump when Tommy says jump. So this will keep you busy for a bit, help you to get into character."

I felt the first pang of frustration; I hated it when even the people I was working with, or *for*, didn't give you the complete picture. Or didn't want to. It was a feeling that aroused another familiar, anxious sensation in my stomach.

"So how am I supposed to find out about this girl?" I asked, cautiously.

"First things first," Sharp said. "We're going to send you on a course to polish up your photography. It's something you have in common."

TEN

I hadn't realized why they were so keen for me to learn photography until I turned up at the art school in central London a week later.

I had been registered on a part-time course under the name Kieran Kelly.

It was good to be back in the centre of town, and it was bustling on a Tuesday afternoon. I'd eaten pizza in a cheap Italian in Soho where lots of students hung out: a boho place on Bateman Street with a big painting of a mermaid on the wall. The customers were a young, trendy lot in narrow trousers and vintage clothes that they had clearly spent some time thinking about. Each tried to look a bit more arty than the last. There were plenty of tats, and some had bushy beards. The guys, I mean.

I felt a bit square in rolled-up chinos and sailing shoes, so I made a quick detour into a vintage shop in Covent Garden, where I bought a retro tweed jacket with some of the money that Tony had lined me up with.

The class was on the third floor of the art school. I lugged my camera bag and portfolio up the stairs to the studio.

A dozen or so students milled around looking at each other's pictures. Some painfully cool students were looking at some fashion shots. One of the girls gave me a quick up and down before turning back to look at another print.

Perched on a stool in the corner by herself and checking the back of her camera was Hannah Connolly.

I didn't want to be caught looking at her, so I plonked my folio down on a desk, unzipped it and made a show of organizing my own photos.

I had spent a week with Sharp putting a credible set of images together. My interest was documentary photography and photojournalism, we had decided. We had driven off to a seaside town on the south coast, where I took shots of broken-down buildings, empty amusement arcades and lonely looking people protecting themselves from the wind in seaside shelters.

Technically they weren't too bad, and everyone agreed that I had a pretty good eye. Subject-wise I thought they looked a bit corny, but Sharp decided that Kieran Kelly is quite serious-minded, and he helped me write a mission statement about my photos.

I set out to record some of the more desolate areas of "Broken Britain": areas of high unemployment, high immigration and closed down high streets. Places where people feel isolated...

It went on like this for a couple of sides. By the time you finished reading it, you would think that Kieran Kelly had quite a social conscience but not much of a sense of humour. I had schooled myself in photography from the depression of the 1930s, World War II and the 1950s. I got quite bored of looking at black-and-white pictures of coal-dust-covered workers, stressed soldiers and men in flat caps and baggy trousers, but it certainly set the mood for the kind of pictures I was to be taking.

"Good shot," a voice said from behind me, the Irish lilt unmistakable.

I turned to find Hannah Connolly looking over my shoulder at a photo I had taken of a Staffordshire Bull terrier walking past a wall in Margate on which the slogan KOSOVANS OUT had been graffitied.

"Cheers," I said. "I was worried about getting bitten."

Hannah nodded, serious.

"Documentary stuff your thing?"

"Yeah, photojournalism, reportage…"

"Me too," she said, unsmiling.

"You Irish?" I asked, stating the obvious.

"Genius," she said, without sarcasm. "Hannah."

"Kieran," I said. "Where are you from?"

"North," she said. "I was at uni in Belfast. I did my foundation over there."

"My family are Irish, but they all live here. I've never been, but I'd like to."

"You should," she said. "Reconnect with your roots."

"Are they showing?" I asked, putting a hand through my hair to make the lame joke obvious.

"Something terrible," she said. And for the first time, Hannah Connolly smiled.

ELEVEN

"Mike Oxlong," Donnie said. It was the closest he ever came to making a joke.

"Don?" Dave said.

"Dave?"

"Don't muck about, Don," Dave said. "Dolan's out."

"Dolan's out?" Donnie repeated. They were both quiet for a moment.

"'kin hell," Donnie said.

The news that Paul Dolan was out of prison was not good. Many of the Kelly firm felt that he had let Tommy down when he was collared. Dolan had been caught in the boat with Jason Kelly when the three of them had tried to make a getaway down the Thames. Most people thought the Savage kid had dobbed Tommy Kelly in, but others, Dave included, always suspected that Dolan was up to something. It was in his genes.

He was Irish, for a start, and although Tommy and the rest of the Kelly family made a show of their Irish background, Paul Dolan was a real, dyed in the wool Paddy. He'd been brought up *at horse fairs and started a life of crime early on, nicking scrap metal and winning prize fights. He had been in the notorious Maze prison and had IRA ancestry that went back to the 1920s.*

All these credentials made him a folk hero on his own turf and a public enemy to the Irish authorities.

Donnie and Dave had never really trusted him for not being one of theirs, but he was hired by the firm because of his reputation as a hard man, and one who combined his killer tendencies with connections and a native intelligence.

"What does Tommy think?" Donnie asked.

"Think? He's bleeding livid. Paul Dolan's done less than two years of a fifteen-year stretch – put the appeal in and got off on a technicality. The guvnor's appeal's going nowhere at the moment, so he's doing his nut – changing lawyers, the lot."

"So where's Dolan now?" Donnie asked.

"Fuck knows," Dave said. "Snidey bastard's given everyone the slip."

"Paul Dolan's been released," Sandy Napier said tightly.

I'd been called to a meeting in Napier's Whitehall office.

The last time I had seen Paul Dolan was when he was arrested. As far as I was concerned, his and Jason's boat had been intercepted on *my* intelligence. My superiors, and Tommy Kelly himself, were of a different opinion. While Tony Morris had left me in no doubt as to how critical my intel had been in bringing Tommy and his son to justice, there was a lingering suspicion that, somehow, Paul Dolan had manoeuvred an internal stitch-up.

I still had an abiding image in the back of my mind of Dolan, when he was led away down at Long Reach, winking at me.

I hadn't known what it meant then, and I didn't now, but there was something in that gesture that made me feel complicit; that while he acknowledged I'd turned Tommy in, we were both part of a bigger secret.

I kept my thoughts to myself as Sandy Napier huffed and pushed around sheets of paper. A secretary was printing out more information from her computer at another desk.

"It's a complete cock-up," Napier said. "It leaves us with egg all over our faces."

Tony and Sharpie looked at their shoes. It was difficult to make eye contact with Napier when he was unhappy; he looked as though he might bite.

"Dolan was our collar, and a big one. I can only think that someone, somewhere, is jealous of our success and got behind the appeal." He rubbed his hand over gingery bristles.

"So do we have any further idea where...?" Tony ventured.

"Not a bloody clue," Napier snapped, looked daggers at him. "We have this picture of him leaving prison. Then this is where you come in, Tony, or, I might say, *should* have come in."

I heard Tony sigh. Napier clearly thought he was at fault. I picked up one of the printed sheets. A surveillance photo showed a man walking towards a car. The image was a little blurred and I could barely tell that it was Paul

Dolan. The physique was about right: medium build, dark hair, a fighter's posture. But, to be honest, it could have been anyone.

"He got into this car. We tailed it, of course, for several miles back towards London, and then something happened," Tony explained to me.

He slid another sheaf of pictures across the table: the same car in a service station. The printout told me that it was Clacket Lane Services on the M25 the day before. The dark-haired man was standing by the car, smoking.

"They go in and order a McDonalds – Big Mac Meal," Napier said, with his usual attention to detail. "Take their time eating it, clearly not feeling under any pressure..." He glanced through his eyebrows at Tony again. "Then they pull in for fuel. Dolan gets out and goes into the shop, where we lose sight of him. After he fills up, the driver goes in to pay, then comes out two minutes later with what appears to be Dolan, stumbling in front of him."

Napier swung the screen of his computer round so that we could see the time lapse of the man leaving the service station in jerky close-up. He clicked on the mouse and zoomed in. I compared the man in the new picture with the one outside the jail. The hair seemed bigger and blacker, but the clothes were the same.

"Our chaps tail the car into London and, when they get to South Norwood station, it pulls over and Dolan gets out. The car pulls away fast, so we have the choice of following Dolan, who appears to be about to get on the train, or following the car and the driver."

"So our guys go after Dolan," Tony said.

"They went after who they *thought* was Dolan," Napier snapped. "Only to find that the man is a traumatized salesman who has been forced to wear a wig and another man's jacket."

I looked at the photo again: a wig.

"The poor guy had only been having a crap in the services and comes out to find himself locked in and held at gunpoint by two Irishmen while he is forced to swap clothes with one of them and then drive all the way to London with the other," Napier said.

"So, meanwhile, the real Paul Dolan is hiding out in a lav on the M25?" Sharp asked.

"Either that, or driving happily in the salesman's car into central London," Napier replied. "And we've completely effed-up. Tony, you should have had a team of twenty forming a circle round a man like Dolan. From the M25 he could have gone in any direction: Gatwick's only twenty minutes from there."

"We were caught out, Sandy. We didn't get wind of his release until a couple of hours before, and we don't have the staff – you know how stretched we are. He's got about a dozen aliases and passports," Tony said. "Slippery bugger could be anywhere. We need to draw him out."

"Apart from our own failings," Napier said pointedly to Tony, "my feeling is that we have been stitched up by the Met." Napier always seemed convinced that the regular police were trying to wrong-foot the service, as if they were as much our enemies as the villains.

"I don't want to sound stupid, sir," I said. "But surely

if Paul Dolan's been released, you can't charge him with anything anyway. To all intents and purposes, he's innocent."

"Paul Dolan? Innocent?" Napier asked, incredulous.

And all three of them laughed out loud as I felt my face redden.

"We didn't *want* to bring him in," Tony clarified. "We just wanted to keep a tab on him. Where someone like him goes on their release is important, and we fell at the first fence."

I felt foolish as I left the office and walked down the cabbage-smelling corridor with Tony and Sharp.

"I thought I was supposed to be going after Sophie Kelly," I said, a little narked.

"You are," Tony said. "But Dolan's release has landed me in the doo-dah and delayed the search for Miss Kelly a little. You just keep on doing what you're doing and we'll keep an eye on the bigger picture."

Tony patted me on the shoulder; not for the first time since I'd been recruited, he made me feel like a kid.

TWELVE

A few days later I got a call.

Anna Moore. First thing in the morning. Never good, but worse when it's not a college day and I fancied lying in till 11.

"Napier wants you back in, Eddie," she said. No "hello handsomes" today.

"When?" I asked.

"Now."

I squinted at the G-Shock beside my bed. 7 a.m. Ouch.

Ten minutes later I was in a cab towards Trafalgar Square, and not long after that, knocking on the heavy oak of Sandy Napier's door as Big Ben chimed the half-hour near by.

"Sit down, Savage."

Simon Sharp and Anna were already there. I took the chair between them.

Napier looked up from the papers on his desk.

"I want you to be up to speed with what's going on with Dolan and so on, and I have a bit of news which might affect you," he said.

"Sir?"

"Tony Morris is taking a sabbatical, with immediate effect."

"A sab...?" I didn't know what it meant, but I didn't like the sound of it.

"Leave, Savage; a few months' leave."

The flutter of anxiety in my gut turned to panic. I was only just getting used to the idea of getting back to work, but I couldn't do it without Tony. Tony was my bedrock of security, the only person I really trusted.

"He didn't say..." I began. He would have told me if he was going off, surely?

"He's been under quite a bit of pressure recently: the crash and so on. We've advised him to take a break. Man hasn't had a holiday in three years."

I knew I was being sold a party line. "Under pressure" and "advised" sounded like euphemisms, like when they say that politicians are "spending more time with their family" or someone is "stepping aside" from their job at the BBC. Of course, I didn't believe it. Tony had said nothing to me. I glanced at Anna and Sharp, but they were looking straight ahead.

"I realize, obviously, that you work ... have worked very closely with Tony and that in many ways he's your mentor." Napier steepled his fingers and looked at me over the top of them, making me uncomfortable. "So I just wanted to reassure you that it is business as usual for you. Anna is here, and Simon is an extremely capable case officer..."

Anna smiled and Sharp nodded his extreme capability at me.

I was worried about Tony's absence, but Napier's rock-solid authority and the weight of the service behind him somehow made me mutter my agreement. There was clearly no point in further discussion.

"I'm sure I'm in safe hands, sir. I'll be fine."

"Good." Napier rubber-stamped it. "While we're here, Savage, I just wanted to say how pleased we are with your work. Your first couple of assignments have been by no means easy, but your ability to deal with difficult situations and your behaviour under pressure have been noted at the highest level." He pointed towards the ceiling. Who was he talking about? God?

"I'll make sure Savage gets everything he needs," Sharp assured him, sounding a little smug. "I'll keep an eye on him."

Sharpie smiled at me.

"Thanks," I said.

"Of course, security, protocol and so on means that you won't be able to communicate with Tony in the meantime. At least not until he's back in the fold, which I hope won't be too long," Napier continued. "So just carry on as you are, Savage ... and keep up the good work. That's all." Sandy Napier looked at me and smiled, showing his teeth. "Good man."

"Thank you, sir."

A compliment from Sandy was extremely rare, but a

smile from him was as scarce as a hairy snooker ball. I felt quite dazed as I was ushered from his room by Anna and Sharp. It was like getting a gold medal or an England cap.

He'd played me.

I found myself outside on the street. Anna lit a fag.

"Tony's 'taking leave'? Bollocks," I said.

"I know, I know," Sharp said. "It's come from above Napier."

"I don't think I've ever seen Tony look under pressure," Anna commented.

"No," Sharp agreed. "You know what it is, don't you? Paul Dolan gave us the slip. Someone has to take the flak; this time it's Tony. He's got form with the IRA, so when something goes wrong and there's an investigation from on high, the spotlight settles on him."

"Even though Tony did more than anyone to nail Dolan in the first place?" I asked.

"Probably *because* he did more than anyone," Anna said, exhaling smoke. "That's the way this firm seems to work. The better you do, the more under scrutiny you are. I'm sticking to my desk."

Sharp flagged down a black cab.

"And, Mr Savage, now you're in the picture, you will just carry on at college. We'll keep in contact. You're in safe hands." He nodded at Anna, winked at me, then waved jazz hands at us as he got in the cab.

I laughed and walked on towards Charing Cross Road, actually looking forward to getting back to college the next day and carrying on … as instructed.

THIRTEEN

A week later, at the end of a college day, I found myself walking into the tube with Hannah Connolly.

"Where you off to?" she asked.

My flat was a couple of stops away, but not wishing to give anything away, I glanced up at the tube map and said, "Willesden". I immediately regretted my subterfuge: Willesden was only a stop beyond Kilburn, which I knew was Hannah's patch.

"Just one on from me," she said. "I didn't know you lived up that way."

"I don't," I said. "I'm meeting a mate for a drink later."

"Oh," she said. "What time?"

I looked at my watch; just after six.

"Eight," I said, beginning to get caught up in my own fiction.

"That's ages," she said. "Why don't you get off at Kilburn and come for a quick pint first? I could murder one."

There was nothing flirty about Hannah Connolly – she was direct, almost blokeish.

"Why not?" I said.

Twenty minutes later we stepped off a packed tube and out into the bustle of Kilburn High Road. It was a sunny evening – one of those days that lightens your mood. Hannah stopped outside a big Victorian pub that advertised live music and comedy nights.

"Best Guinness in Kilburn," she said.

We went inside and I ordered two.

We sat in a corner where we could survey the out-of-date St Patrick's Day disco posters and general Irish paraphernalia. Stocky, red-faced men in late middle age sipped black pints at the bar and exchanged loud bursts of incomprehensible conversation. They looked and sounded as if they'd been there all day, and probably had.

I picked up my glass from the sticky brown table, noting the shamrock that had been carefully drawn in the white head.

"Cheers," I said.

I took a sip, then put down my glass. Hannah laughed and gestured for me to wipe off a blob of froth stuck to my nose. She took a gulp of hers without leaving a mark.

Hannah did not work hard at conversation; neither did she seem uncomfortable with silence. I was.

"How long have you lived in Kilburn?" I asked.

"Just over a year," she said.

"You live with flatmates?"

Hannah looked at me, fleetingly.

"No, on my own. My da owns the flat for when he's

here on business, which isn't very often."

"What does he do?" I asked.

"Building trade, mostly."

"So, what got you started in photography?"

"When I was at school in Belfast I did an art project on the graffiti around the city. There are pictures on the wall at the end of every street, not Banksy stuff or tags, but soldiers and IRA martyrs and stuff. I tried to paint my own versions of them but I wasn't very good. Then I got a camera for my sixteenth birthday, so I started taking photos instead. Then I did a foundation course, and here I am."

"Pretty political, then?"

"You can't live in Belfast and not be political," she said. "If you were born any time in the last fifty years, you would have grown up hearing about the Troubles every day."

We carried on like this for a bit, me having to squeeze conversation out of Hannah. She explained that their family was Catholic, but that her dad had got into some trouble doing business with Protestants or something, so he'd moved over here for a bit.

We had another drink and Hannah loosened up a little, telling me more about herself; no revelations, but it gave me a slightly better picture of who I was dealing with. She was guarded yet straightforward. It was as if she was hiding behind her persona of black jeans, black T-shirt and leather jacket. Even her dark hair and heavy eyeliner seemed something of a mask.

Saying that, she did not get a great deal out of me

either. I told her my dad was called Patrick Kelly, a builder; that he had lived in Spain and had also had a few business troubles. It gave us something in common.

But she seemed to detect something not quite right about me.

"I hate that jacket," she said, laughing. "It looks like it belongs to someone else."

"It did," I said, a little offended. "It's retro. I bought it from a vintage shop for college."

"Trying to fit in with the fashionistas, are you?" She was disarmingly direct, like she didn't care if she offended anyone.

"I don't really fit in," I admitted.

"That makes two of us," she said. "You want to try being yourself."

I was a bit nervous that Hannah could smell something fake about me. She was that kind of girl. I looked at my watch – it was nearing 7.30 p.m.

"Haven't you got to meet your mate?" she asked.

I had almost forgotten my lie. I took out my mobile and pressed a couple of keys, pretended to read a message. I rolled my eyes and sighed dramatically.

"I've been stood up," I said.

If Hannah saw anything phony in this, she didn't show it.

"Why don't we have another one here, then?" she asked. "You can come back to mine for something to eat if you want?"

I considered a moment. I had no real need to go back to my own place and I didn't for a second think that she

77

was coming on to me. But after all, my job was to keep tabs on Hannah Connolly.

"OK," I said. "Why not?"

FOURTEEN

Donnie's life had become more complicated since Paul Dolan's release. He'd been given another "little" job: to find out what he could about Dolan's disappearance. Word from Belmarsh was that Tommy was mad as a cut snake that the Irishman had given them the slip. Tommy wanted Dolan brought to book and given a thorough grilling about his role in his own capture and imprisonment.

Dave had given Donnie instructions to round up some of the usual suspects. The prospect made Donnie's heart sink.

He turned up to a pub near Camberwell Green looking for a man called Jimmy Gallagher. After asking the barman, he found Gallagher in the bookies several doors down. Gallagher was a scrawny man with thin, greasy hair. He was studying the racing papers and chewing the stub of a ballpoint. Donnie stood behind him watching the TV above their heads. Gallagher felt the looming presence and turned, his eyes widening as he clocked Donnie. Donnie noticed a smudge of ink in the corner of the man's mouth.

"Jimmy," Donnie said.

"Donnie!" Jimmy replied, trying – and failing – to sound cheerful.

"You winning?" Donnie asked.

Gallagher gestured at his tatty clothes and dirty trainers. "Does it look like it?"

"Let me buy you a drink," Donnie said.

Gallagher followed Donnie back to the pub. Donnie bought Jimmy a triple whisky in the hope that it might loosen his vocal cords. Gallagher was a well-known, hated grass, but more useful alive than dead. He always had his ear to the ground.

Donnie boxed him in at a corner booth, where Gallagher could barely be seen for Donnie's wide back. Donnie took a sip of lager.

"So," he said. "You heard about Paulie Dolan getting out?"

Gallagher's eyes darted about, but his field of vision was blocked by Donnie's massive frame.

"No. Yes. I mean, I heard…"

"Heard what?" Donnie asked.

"Only that he was out, Don," Gallagher said.

"Have a drink," Donnie suggested, and pushed the whisky towards Gallagher, who took a sip. "No, have more," Donnie said. "I'm buying. Fill yer boots." He sat and watched while Gallagher drank half, and continued to watch until he had drained it. "Good stuff that Jameson's, innit? Have another." Donnie pushed the table against Gallagher so he couldn't move from his chair and then ordered another triple from the bar.

"Cheers," Donnie said. Gallagher sipped from the glass again. "So what else did you hear?"

"Nothing, Donnie, honest. I don't do this any more."

Donnie sighed. "Neither do I, Jimmy. I thought I'd retired. But now I'm here, so whaddya know?"

"I told you, Don, nothing. I haven't heard nothing, I swear."

In Donnie's experience, when people began to say "honest" and "I swear" it meant they knew more than they were letting on.

"Drink up, Jimmy," Donnie instructed. He pushed the whisky closer to Gallagher, who lifted it to his lips. Donnie grabbed the bottom of the glass and roughly helped the man swallow the contents. "Have another one."

Donnie pushed the third triple whisky at Gallagher.

"So what are they saying at The Harp?" Donnie asked, referring to the private members' Irish club in New Cross, once funded by Tommy Kelly.

"I don't know, Don." Gallagher's voice was beginning to slur, nine shots doing their work on his small frame.

"Down the hatch," Donnie said again. He took the glass from the table and pushed it against Gallagher's mouth, putting his other hand behind the man's neck. Gallagher resisted, but Donnie's massive hand pressed until Gallagher's teeth parted and Donnie was able to tip the glass, raising a red weal where the rim pressed hard against Gallagher's nose. Jimmy Gallagher spluttered as another three measures of spirit sluiced down his throat.

The pub was crowded, but the barman, sensing an incident was about to happen, began to walk over.

Donnie stood up.

"You're drunk," he said to Gallagher for the barman's benefit, a note of disgust in his voice. "You need some fresh air."

"He's had enough," he said theatrically, guiding Gallagher

past the barman through the crowd.

They went outside and Donnie pushed Gallagher along the street, turning right into the darkness of Camberwell Grove. Fifty metres along, where the grand Georgian houses started, Donnie turned Gallagher down a side passage, bordered by the cast iron railings of the large house it served.

Donnie really didn't have the stomach for this; he knew a big right-hander would take the little Irishman's head off, so he would have to go easy.

"You need to sober up, Jimmy," he said. He delivered an open-handed slap, hard, across Gallagher's face. Gallagher screamed and cowered like a whipped dog. Donnie backhanded him across the other cheek, straightening him up again. "There we are, sober as a judge, now. Tell me where they think Paul Dolan is."

"I'll tell you everything I know, just don't hit me again."

"Now we're getting somewhere," Donnie said. He grabbed Gallagher by the throat and pushed him back against the railings. "What are they saying?"

"Some say America," Gallagher spluttered.

"Where?"

"Dunno. Boston, New York maybe, I dunno."

Slap.

"Don't hit me, Don. Others say Ireland."

Slap.

"Please, I'm telling you all I've heard."

"Took your time."

Slap.

"I've even heard Russia ... someone said Russia."

"Which one, who said?" Donnie growled.

"I don't know … I'm just saying what I've heard."

Donnie knew he'd made a start but wasn't going to get much more from the man today. He lifted him by the armpits and hung him from the railings by the shoulders of his faded denim jacket. Gallagher kicked and struggled as Donnie climbed up and took the chewed biro from Gallagher's pocket, noting that the blue ink stain had been joined on the other side of Gallagher's mouth by a fresh smear of blood. He took the pen and wrote a number on Gallagher's forehead.

"My phone number. You know what I want to know. Get in touch." Donnie stuffed some crumpled notes into the man's pocket.

"There's a ton, Jimmy. Get out and buy some drinks. Ask some questions. I want more details, or you're toast."

Donnie left Jimmy Gallagher dangling from the railings. He dusted himself off and was walking back into Camberwell New Road in search of a cab when his phone rang.

"Stan Dandyliver."

"Don?"

"Dave?"

"Don. What's new?"

"Not much, Dave. I've had a chat with the little Irish nark."

"And, Don, and…?"

"He reckons he's heard Ireland, America or Russia."

There was a pause as Dave Slaughter digested Donnie's new intelligence.

"That's half the fuckin' world, Don, can't you be more specific?"

"Best he could come up with, Dave. I've put him on the case."

"He'll have to do better than that. Listen, Don, I've got a fix on the kid. Fancy a trip to north London?"

Donnie looked at his watch: 10.00 p.m. already and he was only a mile or so away from his flat.

"Not really, Dave."

"Tough, Don. Go and have a butcher's. I'll give you the address, it's in Kilburn."

FIFTEEN

Hannah Connolly's flat was on the second floor, above a bank just off the High Road. It was scruffy and bohemian, with a beaten up sofa and Indian rugs on the floor. A couple of large, black-and-white prints of her work were pinned to the wall. Another photo, in a frame, showed what I assumed to be Hannah, aged about twelve, in a green Irish-dancing costume.

"Don't look at that," she said, and tipped the photo face down. "I've got some sausages, that OK? You're not veggie, are you?"

I shook my head.

"If God didn't want us to eat animals, why did he make them out of meat?" I asked, trotting out a well-worn joke. Hannah looked at me blankly and went over to the fridge.

I sat down on the sofa and flicked through *Time Out* while Hannah stood in the kitchen and snipped a string of sausages into an already used frying pan. I stood up again.

"Can I take a slash?"

"Sure," she said, pointing at the door. "You'll find it, it's not a very big flat."

I closed the living room door behind me and checked the other doors off the hall. One was Hannah's bedroom, easily identified by more prints on the wall. Next was the bathroom: grubby bath and scuzzy shower curtain.

I shut the bathroom door from outside and ducked into her room. It was untidy, but not a tip. It smelled a bit hempy. There was a full ashtray on a chest of drawers. I picked up a stub and smelled spliff. I opened a drawer and found a small bag of weed tucked in among the clothes. There was a laptop on the table and I could see by the glowing light that it was in sleep mode.

I had been taught that you needed to take opportunities when they arose, so I booted it back up. It asked for a password, so I typed in "password" and got straight in. Careless.

I typed in my code, went through the protocols and within three minutes had hacked into Hannah Connolly's computer. I cleared the history and quit and then heard a door creak behind me. I shut down the lid of the laptop and turned to find Hannah standing in the door of her room.

"What are you doing in here?" she asked.

"Oh, er... I was just wondering if there was anywhere I could check my email?"

"On my laptop?" she said.

"Sorry, I should've asked."

Hannah pushed passed me, touched the lid of her laptop.

"You need to check your mail now?"

"Sorry," I said again. "Not really … it's just habit. My phone's nearly dead. Doesn't matter, sorry." I rubbed my hand over my head. "I think I'm a bit pissed."

"Lightweight," she laughed, leaving the bedroom. "You need something to eat."

We ate sausage baguettes with ketchup off our laps in front of the TV. I sat in an armchair opposite Hannah, and while she had half an eye on the telly, I planted a bug down the back of the chair.

After we'd eaten, we sat, not talking, just letting whatever was on the TV drift by. Hannah rolled a joint and offered it to me. I refused and she smoked it by herself, relaxing back into the sofa.

"Listen, I'd better go," I said, after a while. I looked at my watch. Nearly eleven. It had been a long evening. Hannah showed no reaction to my departure; she was impossible to read. "Thanks for feeding me."

"No worries," she said. "I was having sausages anyway."

"And I'm sorry about, you know, your room, I was just…" I waggled my hand in a mime of too many drinks. "Empty stomach…"

"Don't worry about it."

"Cheers," I said, knowing that whatever she did would now be relayed straight back to Simon Sharp and Tony's department. "So … see you at college." She clearly wasn't the type for social kisses on the cheek, but it would have been weird to shake hands, so I just stood awkwardly for a second, then gave a lame wave, opened the door and let myself out.

Donnie hated public transport but he'd given Jimmy Gallagher most of his folding cash and didn't have enough for a cab to north London. He half considered going and nicking it back from the man, who he was certain was still hanging off the railings in Camberwell. Instead, he got a bus to Elephant and Castle before taking a shitty old Bakerloo line tube to Baker Street, then switching to the shinier Jubilee line heading north. The passengers were no better on this line, he thought: pasty faced late-night commuters and drunks, sweaty in the bright lights of the carriage. He caught a glimpse of his reflection in the window and thought perhaps it was better not to judge.

He got out at Kilburn and walked a block up the High Road before turning left and ducking into a shadowy doorway opposite the address he'd been given. He smoked a cigarette and waited.

After about ten minutes, a light went on in the hallway of the flat above the bank. Donnie stubbed out his fag and drew further into the shadows. A minute later the street door opened and a young bloke came out. Donnie didn't particularly recognize him. He looked pretty ordinary: medium height, medium build, wearing a tweed jacket. He was so ordinary looking that Donnie could have lost him within seconds in the dark, but he kept his eye on him and followed, hugging the walls, keeping back from the kid he took to be Eddie Savage. He followed him onto the tube at Kilburn station. Donnie got into the next carriage, keeping his distance, his face shielded by an Evening Standard. *He could only get the odd glance at the kid's face. The reddish hair and the old man's jacket were all that distinguished him from a bar of soap.*

The kid got off at Bond Street, and Donnie slipped out

onto the platform behind him, changed to the Central line and continued to follow from a carriage away. He sat down and appeared to shut his eyes for a while, giving Donnie a chance to move a gnat's closer to observe better. At Tottenham Court Road, the target opened his eyes and hurriedly stepped off the train, almost wrong-footing Donnie, who scraped between the closing doors. They left the station. Donnie ducked around the roadworks that clogged up the junction of Tottenham Court Road and Oxford Street and followed Eddie along New Oxford Street. The kid was easier to follow now that there were fewer people around, but that made Donnie's life more difficult. Years on the job had made him light on his toes despite his bulk, and he stuck to shadows and doorways. Then the kid turned left up towards the British Museum and stopped outside a red-brick mansion block. Donnie watched from the doorway of a sandwich bar while he pressed in a security code.

Donnie could have killed him there and then, he thought. He'd done it before. A few steps across the pavement and a silenced shot to the head would be quickest, or he could have done it with a knife: cut his throat or stabbed him through the ribs. Or he could have strangled him with his bare hands. Save a lot of time and energy, he thought to himself. But that wasn't the job he'd been given.

The door buzzed and the kid went inside. Donnie waited long enough to see a light go on three floors up – that narrowed down the options of where the boy lived.

Donnie walked back along New Oxford Street, looking for a night bus back to New Cross. He took out his mobile and tapped in a message to Dave Slaughter with clumsy fingers.

D. I no wear he lives. D.

SIXTEEN

I woke up late.

Sun was streaming through the blinds and it hurt my eyes. I felt groggy, and realized that I had drunk too much the night before. I pieced together my evening, remembering the pints of Guinness in Kilburn that had given me the Dutch courage to go back with Hannah, probably too soon. That had given me the bravado to go into her room and hack her computer – and nearly get caught.

I kicked myself for being sloppy; I was out of practice.

I tried to remember my return journey to the flat: a slightly fuzzy tube ride on a late-night train. I had taken none of the usual precautions coming back, none of the back alleys and side-street swerves that I usually took to disguise my destination.

Careless.

I checked around the flat, made sure all my tricks of the trade were in place. I lifted off the bath panel and checked the loose floorboard behind. There were still a couple of automatic pistols and some live rounds under there and a box full of bugging devices. I retrieved a handful of bugs and pocketed them. Then I went back into the living room and fired up my laptop. I cleared the history and changed my password, then changed the entry code on the door to the flat. I was meant to do this every two days or so, but I hadn't done it for weeks. I'd been letting things slip, and it was time to tighten up.

My mobile rang at 10. Simon Sharp.

"Good morning," he said chirpily. "So you were at Hannah's last night? Good work."

"Eh?" I said. I had almost forgotten that his computer would now be connected with Hannah Connolly's.

"*Very* good work," Sharp said. "I want you to come in."

"When?" I asked. "Where?"

"Come down to Vauxhall at 12. I'll be having a coffee with Anna in a Portuguese caff next to the bike shop opposite Vauxhall Bridge."

The mention of Anna always triggered mixed emotions. She had saved my life when I was shot, and when she became my case officer I had got way too close to her. I felt she had allowed it so that she could manipulate me.

And she had. More than once.

I ended the call and jumped in the shower. I still felt rough, so I chucked down a Coke and a couple of paracetamol and pulled on pretty much the same clothes I'd worn the day before, leaving the flats by the back entrance – a little more cautious this time.

At Vauxhall, I walked over the bridge, past the rows

of Vespas and Suzukis outside the bike shop, to the Portuguese café under the railway arch. Sharpie and Anna were sitting outside in the sun, halfway through a couple of lattes.

"Hello, handsome," Anna said.

Sharp laughed.

"Deck it, you two," I grunted. "I'm not feeling too handsome today."

"So… Hannah Connolly?' Anna raised an eyebrow. "You don't hang about, do you?"

"She's not my type," I said. I ordered an espresso. Double shot.

Sharp and Anna exchanged a glance.

"She's not," I protested. "She's deadly serious, really political. And she's a bit goth. You know, all black clothes, tats and eyeliner."

Anna rolled her eyes.

"Well, you're going to have to get pretty political too," Sharp said. "I think you'll be seeing more of her."

"Yeah?"

"Yes. Let's go to my office – I've got some stuff to show you."

I finished my coffee and caught Anna studying me. She cocked her head to one side.

"Where did you get that hideous jacket?" she asked.

We sat down in Sharp's bright office in the modern fortress-like building by the river. Anna had recently decamped here too: her "model agency" cover in Denmark Street had been shut down a few months earlier, maybe because it was becoming suspicious or, more likely, because of government cuts. We ate cheese and ham panini that Anna had ordered from the café.

Sharp took a memory stick from one of the desktop Macs that lined the room. He plugged it into another and opened some files.

"Thanks to your swift work last night, we have all Hannah Connolly's emails and a bit of conversation," Sharp smiled.

"She saw me," I confessed.

Anna stopped chewing.

"Saw you what?" Sharp asked.

"She caught me in her room," I said. "But she didn't see anything."

Sharp and Anna looked at one another.

"That explains the row," Sharp said.

He clicked on the MP3 voice recording in the file and I could hear Hannah on the phone, voice muffled by the armchair where I had planted the bug.

"He just went to the toilet," I could hear Hannah say.

There was a pause as she listened.

"Perhaps he had a shite and couldn't find any bog roll because you didn't leave me enough money."

Anna smirked at the exchange. Another pause.

"He's not my boyfriend," Hannah insisted. *"He's just a guy from college, OK?"*

"Just a guy from college," I repeated. "That'll do me."

"Anyway," Hannah went on. *"I think he's probably gay."*

For the second time that day Anna and Sharp laughed out loud.

"It's fine, we know you're a red-blooded het, don't we, Anna?"

Anna raised an eyebrow in agreement and they both laughed again. I started to get a bit huffy.

"Who do you think she's talking to, anyway?" I asked.

"That's what we hope to find out," Sharp said. "We're trying to trace the call, but no joy so far."

"Keep it up," Anna said, exchanging another smile with Sharp as I left the office.

"Piss off," I growled.

SEVENTEEN

In the absence of a real mission, I had little choice other than to "keep it up". I was missing Tony already. I missed the feeling I always had that he was behind me, even when I suspected I was being used. I knew I had been ordered not to, but I tried to call him. His number was dead – just a long, monotonous tone. A flatline. The more I couldn't get hold of him, the more I felt I needed to speak to him, just for reassurance. I tried another tack.

"Mum?"

"Hello, stranger!"

I made excuses, like everybody does, for not calling the old girl more often, and we chatted about this and that for a bit. "You seen anything of Tony, Mum?"

He often dropped in on Mum when he wasn't too busy.

"Tony? No, love. Why?"

"Nothing, really. Did you know he's been suspended?"

"No. Oh, you know Tony, he'll be fine. Nothing keeps

him down for long. Then he'll just turn up when you least expect."

"Sure," I said. This had always been the pattern of Tony popping up in our lives, but in the last couple of years I had relied on him to be there to keep me alive. "Let me know if he turns up, will you?"

"Of course, love. Nothing wrong, is there?"

"No, Mum. I'm good. Love you."

Going to college was what I had been ordered to do, and I started to enjoy it. I began to get into the photography and, after months of doing nothing, it occupied me and gave me focus, excuse the pun.

I had no friends in London, and my time in Spain had made it difficult to make any new ones. My occasional drink with Hannah turned into something of a routine. She didn't appear to have many friends either. We didn't have much in common, but what we did have was that we didn't really fit in with the fashion lot at college. Fashion was low down on Hannah's list of interests.

She was easy to be around, not because she was great company but because there was nothing tricksy about her. I asked her to join me on a photoshoot around London. We shot a few grainy, low-light pics in and around her flat, then went down to King's Cross and walked behind the station up into the cobbled back streets. It was a bleak landscape of skeletal Victorian gasworks and railway crossings, overhead cranes and wires criss-crossing the ever-changing skyline. I took some moody black-and-whites and then asked Hannah to stand in for a few of them. She refused.

"I'm a photographer, not a subject," she argued.

"Just one," I suggested. "You'll look great against this background."

She smiled. For the first time I had a sense that I was able to persuade her to do something against her will. I got a great shot: her black hair and eyes looked strong against the industrial backdrop. I showed her, and she reluctantly agreed that it was good.

I was really getting into this photography lark, and had, for a moment, one of my recurring fantasies of what a normal life might be like. I imagined myself working as a photographer, doing something adventurous like photojournalism in a war zone.

"Stand against that wall and look moody," Hannah instructed. She gestured to a flaking canal-side wall, textural and grimy with soot.

"I don't..." I began to protest.

"I did it for you," she argued.

"That's different," I said. "You looked good."

"I'm going for realism ... in all its ugliness," she grinned. I realized I had lost the argument. I had started something stupid: photos of me were never a good idea. I gave in and she fired off a few shots while I tried to keep my face turned away or in shadow, making a mental note to try and delete them from her memory card when I got the chance. Several months out of the game and I was making too many elementary mistakes.

She checked the back of her camera and nodded.

"Pretty rough," she said. "You look like a gangster. Just what I was going for."

We walked down to the canal and continued across the King's Cross basin, where brightly painted narrow boats were moored and birds dived and swooped across the water. It was picturesque and positive; far too colourful for the kind of shots Hannah and I were after.

"Pretty, isn't it?" I said. We were walking close to each other and my shoulder brushed hers.

"If you like that kind of thing." She turned and smiled at me, and our hands slipped together, almost accidentally. "What are you doing?" she asked.

"Just holding hands."

She shrugged, and we walked up to the road to a greasy spoon for a cup of tea.

Hannah was clearly at home in the run-down café. I fired off a few more shots, of old blokes and builders over steamy mugs of tea. She said places like this were "real". The last thing you would find her doing was ordering a decaf skinny latte with hazelnut syrup in Starbucks. In fact, the mere mention of a coffee chain would set her off on a rant about American commercial imperialism, their corporate bullying, how they were killing our high streets and corner shops. That would get her going about where their coffee came from and how the coffee workers were paid slave wages. Passing Primark would get a similar reaction. If you were paying a fiver for a pair of trousers, someone, somewhere was being exploited. She was right, I guess. Intelligent and well informed, but she did go on a bit. She made me realize how politically unaware I'd always been.

"So what do you think?" she'd ask, and I'd be forced to question my own ideas. Despite our growing familiarity, we were just mates. I never sensed a glimmer of interest from Hannah Connolly. I don't think I was interested in her in that way either; sometimes she looked attractive to me, other times not.

But when we left the café and I turned to head off, I felt something tug at me.

"So, see you at college next week, yeah?"

She nodded and smiled at me again, and seconds later I found myself kissing her under a bridge by the canal. We walked back to the tube, holding hands, not talking. I was slightly embarrassed that I'd made a move, and didn't mention it again. It didn't seem to make any difference to her.

We carried on like this for several weeks, knocking around at college together, comparing work – Hannah worked really hard. Once she got onto something she gave it her full attention. Sometimes I'd sit with her for lunch. She rarely sat with anyone else.

"Haven't you made friends with anyone else here?" I asked, pushing some chips and beans around my plate. She shrugged.

"Not really. I've always been a bit of a loner," she said. There was no self-pity in her voice, it was just matter-of-fact, as usual. The longer I knew Hannah, the less I seemed to know *about* her. It was like she existed in two dimensions.

Since I had nothing to report, Sharp checked in.

"Anything going on?"

"No," I said.

"Been up to Kilburn lately?"

"Not for a couple of weeks." I hadn't. After kissing Hannah I'd taken a step back. Didn't feel right. Most nights I'd gone back to my place and crashed. It was tiring, this studying.

"How's it going with Hannah?" Sharp asked. I hated the cheeky note of enquiry in his voice.

"No change," I said. "I told you, there's nothing…"

"Well, I've got a little job for you," Sharp said. "I want you to take a closer look at Hannah's place."

"How am I going to do that?"

EIGHTEEN

It was Tuesday afternoon when I went to the flat. Kilburn was quiet. Sharpie had done his homework and knew Hannah was at college, as I should have been. I'd invented a dentist's appointment.

I felt antsy, looking out for nosy neighbours and curtain twitchers. I needn't have worried: the street was dead as a doornail and no one noticed me as I walked past the flat a couple of times, climbed the three steps and put the key in the front door. At college I had taken a mould from Hannah's key when her back was turned.

The hallway smelled of damp. I sprang straight upstairs, avoiding the handrails or anywhere else I might leave fingerprints. I opened the door and went into the flat. Stale cooking. Probably more sausages. She seemed to live on sausages and pot noodles. I cooked linguine and prawns for us one night, explaining that I had worked in a restaurant for a bit. Hannah had scoffed it down, only stopping to ask if the prawns were sustainable. Otherwise it might just as well have been pot noodles; food wasn't really her main concern.

I checked each room of the flat to make sure I was completely alone. I could hear the distant hum of the traffic on the High Road. I went into Hannah's bedroom. There was a knot of clothes on the floor and the bed was unmade. I felt awkward when I saw the open top drawer of her chest, a tangle of underwear spilling out. It was not glamorous and was quite worn. I felt I was invading her privacy. I was.

Sharp had told me to be thorough.

I booted up her laptop and entered: *password*. It came up as incorrect. She must have changed it after I'd been caught in her room.

Her duvet was bunched up at the end, like a sleeping dog. Shoes and trainers were stuffed under the bed. I scrabbled about underneath and found a few carrier bags full of clothes.

I moved on and opened the drawers. I went through them methodically, carefully taking out clothes that had not been carefully put in. In the bottom drawer I hit gold. A large biscuit tin, the kind you get at Christmas. Inside were twenty or thirty bags of pills. I tipped a few out on top of the chest of drawers. They were pale green, each stamped with a shamrock. Es. It looked like Hannah had a lucrative sideline. At a tenner a pill, that was a hell of a lot of money hidden in her drawers. I was surprised. I really would never have guessed. I took a few pictures of the pills with my phone, then gently wedged the tin back into the drawer.

Out in the hall, I looked up at the small hatch that led to the loft. On a hunch, I grabbed a chair, climbed up and pushed the panel open. I levered myself up into the loft space and pulled a light cord dangling over my head. There were boxes stacked up to the left and right of the loft door. I opened the nearest one. It was full of polythene bags containing the same type of pills I had seen downstairs. Thousands of them. Multiplied by the quantity of boxes, I was looking at tens of thousands of them, possibly millions. Times ten quid a pop. My mind spun at the maths.

I closed the lid carefully and lowered myself back down onto the chair. I heard a door slam somewhere downstairs followed by feet on the stairs. Shit. I checked everything was as I had found it and tucked myself in behind the bedroom door, trying to hear above my own heavy breathing. The footsteps stopped and I heard the muffled thud of a door slamming. It was the floor below.

I had taken long enough, and the interruption made me jumpy. Music started in the flat below; I could faintly feel the beat through the floorboards. I quickly scanned the sitting room and let myself out, closing the door silently and creeping down past the door of the lower flat, the beat of house music bleeding through the door.

On the street, I breathed out my relief, checked behind me and walked in the opposite direction of the station. I called Simon Sharp.

"You knew, didn't you? There's a major stash of pills up there... Ecstasy, I think. I mean, thousands and thousands. I'll text you pics."

"OK, hold the details," Sharp said. "Tony didn't put you on to her for nothing. I want you to stick around up there for a while. Go and see Hannah later, try and work out what she's up to. It's good for you to get back in there straight away. You're going to have to stay close to this girl."

Sharp left the implication of "close" hanging in the air as he rung off. I checked my watch. It would be a good hour until she was home, so I walked down towards Queen's Park to kill time. This suddenly felt like deep water. I didn't feel like sticking around at all.

Donnie stepped out from the newsagent's. He had bought a packet of fags and pretended to read a free paper there while he kept an eye on the door opposite.

It was the same kid, he was sure. He had become more familiar the longer Donnie shadowed him. He watched him walk off down the tree-lined street and called Dave Slaughter.

"Dave?"

"Wassup, Don?"

"He's been back to the flat on his tod."

"Which flat?"

"Kilburn."

There was a pause while Dave considered.

"Tommy wonders what the fuck this has to do with finding Sophie."

"Search me, Dave, I'm just doing what I was told and sticking to the kid like shit to a blanket. I'm like his shadow."

"The guvnor thinks they're dicking us about. He thought he

had a deal with the kid's handlers to find Sophie."

"All I know is, he's hanging out in this flat in Kilburn. Perhaps Sophie's being held prisoner there?"

"Don't be a tit, Don. Kilburn? Sophie wouldn't be seen dead in Kilburn. We'd know."

"Just an idea, Dave."

"Well, don't have ideas. Go in and have a butcher's, see what's going on up there."

Donnie did as he was told. He crossed the street and, with a practised shoulder, let himself in.

NINETEEN

I wandered around Queen's Park for a while then texted Hannah.

What time you back? I'm in yr neck of the woods. Kieran

I walked around the park again and waited. She texted back.

In around 6. Drop by? Bring Guinness.

I replied that I would. I wasted another twenty minutes then walked back to the newsagent's and picked up a four-pack. Personally, I was getting sick of the stuff.

I crossed the road and was about to ring the buzzer when I noticed the street door had been forced in. I pushed it open and stepped silently into the hall. No sign of life. I crept up the stairs. The door to Hannah's flat was open. I walked into the living room and found Hannah pacing about, staring wide-eyed at the walls. The place was wrecked: cushions all over the floor, carpet ripped back, drawers pulled open and emptied on the floor.

"Hannah? What's happened?" I pulled her down on the

sofa and sat beside her. I felt sweat break out on my brow.

"I've been burgled," she said. Her voice was flat – shocked, I guess. "Someone's broken in. They've been through all my things. Look in my room."

I was confused; I'd only been gone an hour and had locked everything behind me. I went into her room. The drawers had been pulled out, clothes were all over the floor.

"Have you called the police?"

She looked blankly at me and shook her head.

"My dad wouldn't like it."

I guessed my lot wouldn't be too keen either. I was completely thrown. I had "burgled" the flat only a few hours earlier. What were the chances of another, random burglary the same afternoon? Virtually none, I guessed. Someone else was on Hannah's case.

"Are you sure it was a burglar?" I asked. I put my arm around Hannah's shaking shoulders and felt her lean into me a little. "Anything missing?"

"I don't think so," she said. "There's nothing much to nick."

"Let me just have a look around," I said. "Have a cup of tea, you'll feel better." I put the kettle on and put a teabag into a mug for her.

I did a quick inspection of the bathroom and Hannah's room. I checked the open drawer where I had found the pills. The tin wasn't there.

I went back to finish off making the tea then sat back down beside Hannah.

"Any clues?" I asked. "Why won't your dad call the

police? Is he, like, involved in anything?" I asked, innocently. "Does he owe anyone money?"

Hannah shook her head. "He doesn't trust them. He had bad experiences in Ireland. The Troubles, you know…"

"Sure," I said. "Could there be any connection? Could anyone be after him – or you – over that?"

I had heard of Irish families, both Catholic and Protestant, whose feuds from the 1970s were still running today. Tony had made me aware of that stuff.

Hannah shrugged and looked at me with panda eyes. Her tears had smudged her heavy make-up into big black patches that made her wet eyes very blue. Her cheeks were red and her lower lip trembled. It was the first time I had seen her look vulnerable.

"Can you stay?" she asked. "I don't want to be here on my own."

I agreed I would. I bodged up a bolt across the door of the flat and wedged a chair under the handle. I wanted to feel secure as well. The break-in, hot on the heels of my own, unnerved me. As did the missing pills. And the massive stash above our heads.

I looked out of the window, nervously checking the street outside. It was as quiet as usual.

Hannah cracked open the cans I'd bought earlier. They were welcome now. She opened a small tin and rolled a spliff.

"I don't much," she said. "But I'm all on edge."

"Sure," I nodded, then declined when she offered it. "Doesn't agree with me."

Hannah put some music on and we sat in near silence,

sipping Guinness while Hannah mellowed out. An hour later, her eyelids began to droop.

"I'm done in," she said. "You OK out here?"

"I'm fine, I'll crash on the sofa."

Hannah found me a hippy blanket and I threw it over the sofa. I was better off in the living room, I thought. I took my jeans and shirt off and made myself as comfortable as I could, wrapping the blanket around me. My brain was still racing with questions and possibilities, but I must have got some kip because I had disturbing dreams about fighting, Ireland, black eyes, Sophie Kelly, boxes of pills, Spain and the recurring image of an exploding car that woke me up with a start.

That, and the click of a door.

I didn't move. I could sense a person in the room, but they were behind me and concealed by the back of the sofa. I got ready to spring, then heard a voice.

"I can't sleep."

Hannah.

She padded round to where I could see her. From the streetlight outside the window, I could see her bare legs and the baggy T-shirt she was sleeping in.

"Kieran." She touched my shoulder.

I grunted as if I was just stirring, not fully awake, pretending I hadn't heard her. I rolled over to face the back of the sofa and felt the pressure as Hannah sat on the edge of the cushion, then swung her legs up to lie beside me.

I knew this wasn't a good idea.

TWENTY

Donnie felt the pill kick in.

As the rush came up on him, he realized he'd been stupid taking a whole one. Of course, he was used to narcotics in their various forms, but he'd never seen these green pills before. He should have been cautious and started with a quarter to assess their strength. Donnie knew where he was with the nose candy. Cocaine was cocaine, give or take a cut of baby laxative, but these new pills were getting stronger, and you never knew how strong till you took one. He downed a couple of lagers and a vodka chaser at the bar of a pub, trying to level off the effects of the E. He stepped out into the night air and lit a fag, feeling marginally less woozy, and his phone rang. He looked at the caller ID, not wanting to talk, but couldn't drop the call.

"Don? Dave."

"Dave," Donnie answered, his tongue feeling a bit fat. "How you doing, Dave? S'Don."

"What's new, Don?"

Donnie gathered his thoughts; at least he had something new to offer.

"She's up to something, Dave. I went up there and had a look around and..." Donnie tried to stop gabbling.

"Who? What?"

"The girl. I went in the drum like you asked. It's just a student sock, a right hole. But there was quite a few Jack and Jills in the chest of drawers."

"What sort?"

"Es I think. I've took..."

Donnie felt the bags of pills rattle in his jacket pockets.

"You took what?"

"I've secured some of the pills for testing," Donnie said, pleased with his turn of phrase.

"How many? One, two...?"

"All of 'em. About a thousand."

"You great plum, Don, you weren't meant to take nothing, you daft slab of shit! You were supposed to have a butcher's and naff off, not disturb nothing."

"Thing is, Dave, I got discombobulated during my fact-finding mission. Didn't know what to do for the best."

"Don? Have you taken one of them pills yourself?"

"No."

"Don? Troof?"

"Like I said, I'm just a bit discombobulated."

"Don, Don, Don ... what the eff is going on? I ask you to keep an eye on the Savage boy and you put your size twelves into God knows what. This is confusing, Don, very confusing. I don't like the flavour of it. Get them pills to me asap. I'll have to speak to the guvnor. He won't be happy."

Donnie wasn't happy either. He hated the thought of being dobbed in to Tommy Kelly.

"Don't tell him I done a ricket, Dave, I was just following instructions. Reacting to the situation."

Dave sighed.

"I'll tell him what I need to tell him, Don. Now don't call until you've got some good news for me. In the meantime, I've got an idea where you might deposit them pills."

Donnie rang off, deflated, his head suddenly cleared by the thought of upsetting Tommy Kelly. He'd nip up west and drop the Es. Seconds later his phone buzzed with an incoming text. He read it, felt a little better and headed back into town.

Hannah tugged at the blanket and arranged it around herself so that we were cocooned together on the sofa. She put her arms around me, and I could smell the slight musk of her hair as she tucked her face into my neck and wrapped a leg around my own.

If I'd thought Hannah getting into bed with me was a bad idea before, I *knew* it was when I felt the knife at my throat.

"What's your game, Kieran?"

I tried to struggle free, but she was surprisingly strong. Her leg was tightly wound around mine and my face was wedged into the back of the sofa, giving me no leverage. As I struggled, I felt the sharp, steel point nick the soft underside of my chin. I was powerless.

"Hannah," I wheezed. "What you doing?"

"Where are the drugs?" she hissed in my ear.

"Eh? What drugs?"

"You don't know what you've got yourself into, Kieran, you feckin' idiot, hanging around me like a bad smell. Who are you? You're never right, snooping around and using my laptop – and now you're in the shit."

She was right in a way. She'd rumbled me, but I knew nothing about the drugs. Something else was going on here.

"I didn't break in, Hannah, honest…"

I heard a key in the lock and the door to the flat open. Heavy footsteps.

"Try telling that to my da. He wants to talk to you."

I felt Hannah's grip relax as she rolled away from me, then a rough hand on the back of my neck. As I turned to look, I saw a fist coming towards my face and, too late to avoid it, I shut my eyes and felt the sickening crunch of it connecting with my cheek. Hands hauled me to my feet, then shoved me across the room; another blow to the back of my head knocked me into the door frame. I tasted blood. I was grabbed from behind and shoved out the door. A kick in the small of my back sent me tumbling down the stairs, then there were footsteps and another kick between the shoulder blades to stop me getting up. I was hauled down two more flights and, wearing no more than a T-shirt and a pair of boxers, felt the night chill and saw the glare of the street lights as I was manhandled on to the pavement. I felt something prick my arm as I was thrown into the boot of a waiting car. My head felt thick and my vision blurred as the lid slammed down on me.

Then darkness.

TWENTY-ONE

At last, Donnie had what felt like some good news.

His trip to Camberwell had borne some fruit. Gallagher had texted and agreed to meet him again on the understanding that Donnie wouldn't lay a finger on him, though when they met in the betting shop late in the evening, it was all Donnie could do to restrain himself from picking up the ratty little bloke by the scruff of the neck and slapping him about a bit. Gallagher had insisted they stay in the betting shop watching a race, while he leaked snippets of information from the corner of his mouth.

"Paul Dolan's been seen in London," Gallagher hissed.

"Where?"

"Kensal Rise."

"Who by?"

"A friend at The Harp swore he saw him in McGarrigal's, day before yesterday." Gallagher had shuffled about before adding, "It cost me, Don."

Donnie dug into his inside pocket.

"Good work, James." Gallagher's eyes widened as Donnie

peeled twenties off a roll and didn't stop. Dave had given him expenses. "Now, there's another job I want you to do. There's this kid... I'll give you an address."

Donnie stuffed five hundred into Gallagher's top pocket, wrote something on a crumpled betting slip and palmed him a bag of pills.

Donnie vaguely knew McGarrigal's, a big Victorian beer hall in Kensal Green frequented by the north London Irish. He had been there once or twice, on a minding job or to pick up money for the firm. It had been modernized by the Irish mafia into a branch of a chain of fake Irish boozers; it was generally rough, and had hot and cold running Guinness day and night and a soundtrack by the Pogues.

It made Donnie shudder. Too near Wormwood Scrubs for his liking. He hated north London.

"Good news, Dave," Donnie said into his phone, attempting cheeriness.

"Give, Don."

"Dolan. McGarrigal's. Kensal Rise. Been seen up there."

"And where are you now, Don?"

Donnie looked around him. He was sitting in his car, sipping scotch from a hip flask and smoking a fag, in the car park on Peckham Rye. He'd had a late night, and the morning – and some of the afternoon – had drifted by before he felt ready to share his new information. He knew that once he did, it would be all systems go. Again.

"Peckham, Dave."

"So why aren't you outside McGarrigal's, ready to have a reconnoitre and a verbal?"

"Loud and clear, Dave."

Donnie started up the Beemer and headed off towards the Rotherhithe Tunnel: through the pipe and on up to north London. Again.

I awoke feeling almost happy, as if I'd had the longest dreamless sleep. And then memories and images began to fast forward in my brain as I opened my eyes and focused on a single bare bulb coming out of a woodchip ceiling. I didn't know where I was, nor did I know how I got here. I was on a sofa in a strange, suburban-looking room, and I was restrained.

"He's awake, Daddy," I heard Hannah's voice say.

A man walked round the head-end of the sofa and looked at me. He had thick dark hair and a full beard. From where I was lying, his head could have been either way up.

"Kieran Kelly?" He looked at me blankly.

"Yes," I said. My mouth was dry as sand and my voice came out as a small croak.

"I'm Martin Connolly, Hannah's dad," he said, as if introducing himself to Hannah's friends while they were upside down and tied up was quite normal. "Any relation?" he asked.

"To who?" I asked.

"Tommy Kelly, of course."

The name obviously meant something to Martin Connolly. I found myself relieved that I was connected with such a powerful name. Like Tony had said, the name was my protection. I nodded.

"He your da?" he asked.

"No," I said. "He's my uncle."

"So who is your da?"

"Patsy," I said. "Patsy Kelly. His younger brother."

"Tommy Kelly doesn't have a brother."

"Not any more," I said. "He died last year."

"When did you last see him?" Martin Connolly was testing me. I stuck to the story.

"In Spain, Benalmádena at his fiftieth. I went out for a couple of weeks last summer."

"Why did you start sniffing around Hannah? I find it a wee bit suspicious that someone from the Kelly family is interested in my daughter."

"I dunno," I said. "I just met Hannah at college and we kind of became mates."

"He stalked me," Hannah put in. "Then nosed around the flat." I tried to crane my neck to look at her.

Martin Connolly took something from his pocket and held it in front of my eyes. It was the memory card from my camera. I'd been slack. I began to sweat.

"So what are these pictures?"

I strained to remember what was on my memory card. I should have been more careful to delete things. I was hoping he hadn't had time to trawl through the hundreds of images on the card that might incriminate me.

"Just photos for my project," I said. "I do documentary stuff, like Hannah."

"Snooping," Hannah said.

Connolly prodded the tattoo on my arm with a hard finger.

117

"What's this all about? You think you're Irish?"

"All the men in my family have them," I said. "It's a kind of tradition."

Connolly sniggered dryly. "Third generation pikeys, first to live in static homes in Essex, then pine for an 'old country' they don't even remember, like the Yanks. You're about as Irish as Barack Obama."

I wasn't arguing.

"What do you know about the IRA?" Connolly asked, serious again.

"Nothing," I admitted. "I've lived in England most of my life. I know a bit about the politics, but it's never really affected me. I know my uncle had some connections…"

"Like what?"

"He backed a place called The Harp, a club in south London. I don't know what they did exactly, but I think some guys there were sympathetic to the IRA cause."

Martin Connolly's interest was piqued. He prodded at the harp tattoo on my arm again.

"Anyone can get a tat. Ever go to the club?"

"I was too young," I said. "But I knew some of the people who used it, through my uncle."

"Like?"

"Um." I hesitated, genuinely trying to remember the faces. "Donnie Mulvaney, Dave Slaughter, Billy Gorman." I hoped these names would be my get-out. Connolly shook his head as if they didn't register.

I felt I was building a credible picture. I was sticking close to the truth about Kelly connections without revealing anything about myself. I hoped I was getting somewhere until Martin Connolly pulled a plastic bag of greenish pills from his pocket.

"What are these?"

"Es, I guess?"

"How do you explain them? Five grand's worth. They were found in your flat."

"*My* flat?" I croaked. My mouth went bone dry, my stomach lurched. I'd never taken Hannah there; no one knew where my flat was. Martin Connolly waved a crumpled slip of paper in front of my face. My address was written on it in biro.

"Your flat," Connolly said.

"He stole them," Hannah helped.

"These change the game, Mr Kelly," Connolly said.

"I didn't take them. I don't know where they came from. Honest! I'm telling the truth."

Martin Connolly considered the bag of pills.

"Well, I guess this puts you out of my jurisdiction, young man," he said. "There are other people who'll want to talk to you about what you're doing with these."

He took his mobile from his pocket and dialled.

TWENTY-TWO

Donnie parked up on a double yellow and put his fake disabled badge in the windscreen.

It was just after six and he galvanized himself with a smoke outside the heavy doors of McGarrigal's. He peered through the bay window and stamped out his Benson before entering; it was early, but the pub was fairly full, as it was most afternoons. He walked up to the long bar, pushing past the drinkers in his way. He found a space and, catching the barman's eye, ordered a Jameson's. As the barman handed him his drink and some change, Donnie leant forward and asked, "Paul Dolan in?"

The barman pretended to cock his ear against the music and shook his head. He had heard Donnie quite clearly. Donnie discreetly took the barman's hand from where he was leaning it on the bar, and squeezed. Knuckles crunched. "Paul Dolan," he repeated. He hardened his eyes into what he knew was his most persuasive stare and, as the barman's hand writhed inside his paw and his eyes began to water, the man said, "I don't know who he is. It's my first day."

Donnie followed the barman's glance to the far depths of the pub, illuminated by the glow above a pool table, and let go of his hand.

Four men were playing doubles and several others were watching on barstools in the shadows. It was busier than Donnie would have liked, but he took his drink and walked slowly towards the group as if watching, or waiting for a game. He shuffled into position behind two men sitting at the bar. From behind, he was sure he recognized one as Dolan. He hadn't seen him for nearly two years; Dolan had been inside and Donnie had been in Spain.

"Paul?" he asked. "Paul Dolan?" The man turned and Donnie did a double take. The man could have been Paul Dolan by his physique, the length of his wavy black hair and his typically Irish face, but he was not quite Paul Dolan. Maybe it was the heavy beard? Donnie was confused.

"Who wants to know?" the man asked, his accent thick and dark as Guinness.

"Me," Donnie said. "Donovan Mulvaney. I'm here on behalf of Tommy Kelly. I thought you were Paul Dolan – you look like him."

The other men playing pool stopped their game and watched the exchange.

"Well, I'm not," the man said.

"You know who Tommy Kelly is?"

"Sure I've heard of him," the man said. "Everyone has. He's inside; he's over. Now I'm a little tired, so if you don't mind..."

"That doesn't stop him operating," Donnie said. "Do you know Paul Dolan?"

The man shrugged. The group of pool players gathered

around as the conversation continued.

"What if I do?"

Donnie leant in closer and went to grasp the Irishman's collar to increase the pressure of the interview, but the man snatched Donnie's thumb and held it with surprising strength. Seated on his stool, he had the leverage to bend Donnie's thumb, holding him.

"Don't you touch me, you ugly fucker. No one touches me, especially not Tommy Kelly's gimp. My name is Martin Connolly. Remember it."

That was when the first pool cue crashed down on Donnie's head.

TWENTY-THREE

The men that came for me wore full-face balaclavas.

They were like black spectres as they silently blind-folded and wrestled me into the back of a car on Martin Connolly's orders.

"These gents will find out exactly what your game is, Kieran Kelly," he said. Hannah showed no compassion as I was taken away.

I felt more afraid than I ever had before. I was cold. What clothes I'd had were on the floor of Hannah's flat, along with my shoes. That meant no phone, nothing to locate me, no way of contacting Sharp – and neither he nor anyone else would think anything odd about my not being in contact for a few days. After all, I'd done a pretty good job of becoming a loner.

After driving round a few anonymous streets and out onto a main road, the man next to me pushed my head down, out of view.

"D'you bring a decent knife?" I heard one voice say.

"Aye," replied another. "It's a bit blunt but it should do the job."

Horrifying images began to run through my mind. My imagination ran riot as Irish voices bantered menacingly in the car. Tony had told me enough about IRA brutality to make me terrified.

I tried to keep my mind straight as the car sped up for a couple of miles then slowed down onto a slip road. In a way, I was hoping it might be over quickly, that they'd take me out and shoot me.

The car slowed down a few minutes later and I could feel it turning left and right over wet tarmac.

Then it stopped.

The passenger door was opened and I could just make out grey sky as my blindfold rode down, when I was pulled out of the car and on to my feet. I glimpsed the outline of an industrial building. I could smell diesel. I was shoved across the ground towards the building, heard the rattle as metal shutters rolled up.

"Put him in the box," I heard an Irish-accented voice say.

I was taken inside and thrown into a small, cold room where a thick metal door was slammed behind me. It smelled strongly of shit and disinfectant. There was no light, and when I pulled off my blindfold, I could see nothing. I felt along the walls, concrete and damp. I reached out and could feel girders on the low ceiling above and the cold, hard floor below. I was inside a blacked-out concrete cell about three metres square and, as far as I could tell, there was not a stick of furniture in it. I felt along the walls again until I came to a corner, then wedged myself in it and slid to the floor. I pulled my knees up and rested my head on them. My legs were still trembling with fear and cold. Sitting on the hard floor, I began to cry. If the aim was to terrorize and disorient me, they had done well. I couldn't tell which way I was facing; I almost had a feeling that I was spinning. My mind was racing out of control. I sat and shivered in the blackness, trying to go elsewhere in my mind, begging for sleep.

It wouldn't come, so I tried standing up and walking around in an attempt to keep warm, but the cell was too small to gather any pace and as soon as I tried, I hit a wall. I tried stamping my feet on the unforgiving concrete floor, then slapping my arms against my body, but the damp atmosphere had got to my bones and the smell had seeped into my nostrils.

I sat down again and curled into a ball, trying to keep in as much body heat as I could. In the total darkness I had no idea how much time went by, but after some hours I heard noises at the door. It swung open, and a shaft of light almost blinded me.

"Warm enough?" the figure said. Irish again, bulky and dark, silhouetted in the doorway. He threw a small object into the corner where I was still curled up. "I'll be back in a while for a wee chat." The door slammed shut again. I felt around for whatever he had thrown and found a lighter, which I used to warm my hands until my fingers burned. It also revealed the inside of my cell. I could see that the walls had been smeared with what looked like blood and shit. If the intention was to horrify and intimidate, it worked. I began to wonder who else had sat in this cell before me, and what had become of them.

After an hour or so, the door clunked open again and a smaller man in a balaclava and lumberjack shirt pulled me out. My legs had gone dead, and I shivered as I was led into what seemed to be the main room, blinking as my eyes adjusted to the daylight. The building was like a garage, with stacks of tyres and boxes around the edges. Hooks and chains hung from steel joists across the ceiling.

Another man wearing a balaclava sat on a plastic chair behind a rough wooden table. He was wearing a yellow hoodie with a mixed martial arts emblem and smoking a cigarette through the mouth hole of his balaclava. Black eyes looked at me from the eyeholes.

"Siddown," he said. He gestured to another chair opposite him. "Cuppa tea?"

He pushed a stained, chipped mug across the table. His voice was warm and unthreatening, and for a millisecond I felt ridiculously grateful for the tea and for not being shouted at. I took the mug between shaking hands and put it to my lips, scalding my mouth with hot, sweet tea. As the liquid went down my throat I could feel it restoring sensation to my empty stomach, which gurgled audibly.

"You hungry?" he asked. "Or just nervous?"

"Both," I said.

"You've good cause," he said. "But you'll get nothing to eat until you've answered a few questions."

"We wouldn't want him chucking up all over our nice clean floor," Lumberjack Shirt joined in from behind me.

The threat in his rougher voice made me want to vomit immediately.

"First things first," my interrogator said. "Let's start from the beginning. A few easy questions. Think carefully before you answer, because I'll be asking again until I know you're telling the truth, got it?"

I nodded.

"What's your name?"

"Kieran Kelly."

"Where are you from?"

"London."

"Where in London?"

"All over. Originally Deptford, New Cross area."

"So what do you know about us?"

"Nothing," I said. "I don't know who you are, or why I'm here."

"So *what* do you know about the IRA?"

"Nothing really, stuff to do with Irish politics. Wanting to be separate from the British government?"

"So you do know. How do you know? What do you know?"

"News and stuff, you know … but I hooked up with Hannah Connolly at college, she told me a bit. We were friends, I thought."

"What went on in her flat, apart from you shaggin' her and stealing drugs?"

"I didn't," I protested.

"Shag her or nick drugs?"

"Either," I said.

"I'm beginning to detect a wee lie," he said. "I think

we need a more in-depth chat. Now make sure you're telling the truth, Kieran."

He nodded at the man in the lumberjack shirt, who grabbed my arms and pulled them behind me, binding them tightly together with gaffer tape. "You didn't finish your tea," he said, picking up the mug and throwing the rest over me. "Now … let's talk properly."

TWENTY-FOUR

Donnie had no memory of being wheeled into the Homerton Hospital. He'd been here years before, when it was an old Victorian red brick, something between a loony bin and the Somme dressing station on a Saturday night.

The bright, colourful interior that greeted him as he opened his eyes was a surprise. But what had given him more of a start was the uniformed, armed copper at his bedside.

"Fuck off, plod," had been his first words on regaining consciousness. The words had strained to come out, but were clear in their intention, like a toddler mouthing its first "mama".

Dave visited on day three, by which time Donnie's battered frame was propped up on pillows arranged by a little Indonesian nurse, who was taking none of his mess.

"Lianti, get my mate a chair, will you?" Donnie wheezed.

"He's a big boy," his nurse replied. "He can get his own bladdy chair, Mr Donald Duck."

All six-foot plus of Dave Slaughter had bowed to the superior authority of five-foot-nothing Nurse Lianti. He pulled over a wing-backed chair upholstered in dusty pink plush and dumped himself in it, knees and arms overflowing the frame.

"Brought you grapes," he said, passing over a brown bag he had bought from a stall half a mile down the road. The policeman glanced over, checking out the bag.

"'Choo looking at, plod?" Dave asked. "Hungry? Missus forget to pack your truncheon meat sandwiches?"

Donnie laughed a low gurgle. The young policeman remained impassive, staring ahead, a slight red flush betraying his embarrassment and apparent powerlessness in the face of two old-school villains. He coughed, got up and left the room, closing the door behind him. Donnie watched him through the glass, talking to the second armed policeman stationed outside.

"Leave it, Dave, it hurts when I laugh," Donnie coughed.

"Don't laugh, then. How you feeling?"

"All right, apart from the lumps on me head."

Dave looked at the turban of bandages still wrapped around Donnie's skull. Apparently it had taken four of them with pool cues and a cue ball in a sock to bring him down, but Donnie had made the mistake of stabbing one of them while they were about it. The man was somewhere else in the same hospital, hanging on to his life with a punctured lung.

"You'll be all right in a minute. You're made of stern stuff."

Donnie snorted dismissively through a swollen nose. "What's new, Dave?"

"All going on, Don. The guvnor's appeal's coming through. He's got the top firm on it this time, Mishcon de Doo-Dah, the ones what done Princess Di's divorce, God rest. He's pretty confident. Lawyers reckon if Dolan got out, they can call a mistrial."

Donnie nodded his bandaged head sagely. He didn't have a clue what Dave was talking about, save the word "appeal".

"Nice one, Dave."

"He's unhappy about the Micks having a go at you, Don. Very unhappy. And he's unhappy about the Micks muscling in on business while they think he's not on the ball. I've been on the blower 24/7 having a word with all relevant parties, Don. Heads will roll."

"What about me, Dave?"

"Bit more complicated, Don. It could have been a simple GBH on you, if you hadn't shivved the other geezer. Puts you in the same boat for attempted. Can't do much for the minute with plod all over you like a nasty rash."

"I ain't doing porridge, Dave. I'll top myself before I do."

Dave Slaughter patted Donnie's leg through the cover.

"Tommy won't let you go down, Don. You're too valuable. He'll sort something. Just sit doggo here, play it up a bit so they keep you in. If you feel better, don't let on. It'll be sorted, TK's on it."

"You'll tell him I done good, won't you?"

"I have, Don. He knows ... and," Dave leant in, whispered, "he got another card from Sophie."

"Yeah?" Don said. Donnie worshipped Sophie Kelly.

"Yeah," Dave whispered back. "America."

TWENTY-FIVE

The first blow of the cable hurt like hell as it whipped across my legs.

The second of my captors had a length of heavy-duty electric cable wrapped around his fist.

I cried out but couldn't escape the next blow: my ankles were bound to the chair legs, my wrists taped behind me and I was fixed to the seat by layers of gaffer tape around my chest.

I yelled again as a third blow thrashed across my thighs.

"Feckin' smarts, doesn't it?" my interrogator asked. His voice was as even and unthreatening as it had been before. "Perhaps you'll answer my questions honestly now?"

I nodded, my face contorted with the stinging pain from my legs.

"Now, Martin's very protective about his daughter. So, I'll ask you again, did you shag her and nick drugs from her flat?"

"Nothing happened, I swear! She got into bed to put

a knife to my throat." My explanation sounded mealy mouthed.

"So you weren't telling the truth before. I was right, I can always detect a lie." He sounded pleased with himself. "And you took something as well?"

"No, I didn't."

The cable thrashed across my legs again.

"NO, I DIDN'T!" I screamed.

"Who did?"

"I don't know. I did see the drugs, but I never touched them."

"Who did, then?"

"I don't know, she was burgled."

"By you?"

Another stinging blow hit my thigh.

"No!" I screamed. "I don't know who broke in, I don't." I felt hot tears trickle down my cheeks.

"Well, who did, then? We take a very dim view of kiddies meddling with our business. Usually we put a bullet through one ankle for a first offence. With that amount of gear, we'd probably do both. You'd never play football again."

Despite the burning pain in my legs, I felt a cold chill in my gut at the thought of my ankles being smashed by bullets.

"I didn't take them!" I protested.

"What were all the photos about?"

"I'm a student, I'm doing a photography course. That's where I met Hannah."

My interrogator went quiet. Either he had hit a dead

133

end, or he was giving me time to think about my story.

I felt the tape being cut from my wrists and ankles. I panicked that I was going to be taken away.

"What are you doing?"

"I've not finished with you yet. I'm going to give you a little more time to think about what you're telling us. I have a hunch that there's more."

I was wrenched out of the chair by the second man.

"We're going for lunch," my interrogator said.

I realized that I desperately needed to relieve myself.

"I need the toilet," I said feebly.

"Well, you're in the right place," the second voice laughed. Then he bundled me back into the box and slammed the door behind me.

I scrabbled to sit upright. My legs were lifeless – tingling and burning at the same time. I picked at the scraps of tape that were still stuck to me. My bladder was bursting, and as feeling returned to my legs, I struggled to my feet and felt my way to the opposite corner. I loosened my boxers and, supporting myself with a hand against the wall, pissed on the floor, adding another layer to my misery and degradation.

I sat back down and hugged my knees.

I turned my story round in my mind. I could not begin to tell them the truth; any hint that I was working for a British intelligence organization would be certain death. I had to focus on my cover, which, if they chose, could mean certain death anyway. I tried to remember names, places, connections that would make my story credible.

I mulled it over and over in my mind, what I could and couldn't say, until I had it fixed.

It had to stack up.

TWENTY-SIX

Donnie was pleased to see Dave.

He hadn't had a visit for a couple of days. He was feeling better and bored, but trying to string out his stay by complaining of severe headaches. The nurse was having none of it, and given his status, the ward doctors on their rounds didn't seem particularly sympathetic, merely prescribing paracetamol.

They wanted rid of him, and it was making him nervous.

He wouldn't speak to his armed escort on principle. He had filled in The Sun crossword without looking at the clues, done the Sudoku without making the numbers add up. No one was going to check. A well-used Martina Cole book from the hospital library lay unread on his bedside cabinet.

"Dave."

"Don."

"Good to see you, Dave."

"You look better, Don." The turban of bandages had been removed. Dave gave a cursory glance over the stitches that held Donnie's head together.

"Apparently I'm on the mend. They're talking about moving me." Donnie signalled his unease with his eyes.

"We've applied for bail, Don."

The policeman knew better than to show a reaction to their conversation.

"Nice one, Dave. 'Preciate it."

Ten minutes after Dave's arrival, two more armed policemen arrived on the ward. One of them, a superior officer, chatted in an undertone to the duty officer, who nodded and left, pleased to be relieved of his duty.

"We're going to be moving you, Mr Mulvaney," the officer said.

"Where?" Donnie asked, suddenly anxious.

"Cool it, Don," Dave said. "It's fine."

The second officer took a pair of bolt cutters from a black bag and cut through the ankle cuff that held Donnie to the bed.

"Eh?" Donnie looked around, confused.

The two policemen helped Donnie to his feet. He stood unsteadily while Dave threw an overcoat around his shoulders.

"Can't I even get dressed?" Donnie pleaded.

"Stow it, Don, just follow the officers," Dave instructed.

Uncharacteristically meek, Donnie let himself be led barefoot from the ward by the police officers. Nurse Lianti watched him. "Where you going, Mr Donald Duck?"

Dave put his finger to his lips and winked at her.

"Police business," he said. He flicked his wallet open and showed an American Express card and membership to a gambling club.

Donnie was bundled into a service lift with Dave and the two policemen. Several floors later, they spilled out at the back of the hospital, where, among the bins and incinerators, Dave Slaughter's BMW was waiting. As soon as they were in, Dave squealed out of the loading bay and shot down Homerton high street and onto the main road out towards Hackney Wick. The police officers in the back laughed, took off their helmets and undid their uniform jackets. Job done. Donnie was confused.

"Get in!" one said.

"Nicely done, gents," Dave grinned.

"Them uniforms were the dog's," the second officer chuckled.

"Mate of mine used to work on The Bill. Half inched a dozen of them. All pukka. Apparently they burnt the rest because one or two herberts got ideas for armed robberies," Dave said.

Donnie gurgled a low chuckle, finally catching on.

"Fake plod? Fuck me, Dave. You got some big brass bollocks." Donnie turned to the two hired hands in the back. "Fake effin' plod, fuck my old boots." Donnie's laugh turned into a spasm of chesty wheezing.

"Steady on, Don," Dave said. "You'll chuck your ring in a minute."

"Or cough up a gold watch, Dave," Donnie spluttered, still laughing.

Dave doubled back onto the A13 and headed south through the Blackwall Tunnel. Donnie always felt a sense of relief once he was south of the river. Within five minutes they were outside a pub on the industrial riverfront in Woolwich. Dave and the two fake policemen sank celebratory pints and smoked, while Donnie, still in his pyjamas, stayed in the car with the door open, his bare feet on the pavement. He looked across the Thames and sipped his first beer in some time.

"Enjoying that, Don?" Dave asked.

"Taste of freedom, Dave."

"Make the most of it while it lasts."

"Where am I going to hole up, Dave?" Donnie asked.

"You can bunk at mine for a bit till we get you sorted."

Donnie continued to shake his head in disbelief at the audacity of his release. His fear of another stretch for GBH or worse had grown like a tumour while he was under police guard, and even now he had escaped, he knew his freedom would be short-lived. He wouldn't be able to hang around on the manor for long. He felt the ground shift beneath his feet all over again.

TWENTY-SEVEN

The door rattled and daylight streamed into the box again. I didn't know how long I'd been in there; I'd slept and lost track of time.

I was dragged back into the room, legs still not fully functioning, and made to stand.

There was another man with them now, this one in a dark suit. I wondered what additional torment he was there to inflict. All three continued to wear full-face, but then they blindfolded me, most likely so they could take off their masks.

"So, Kieran. How d'you feel after your morning's work?" the new man asked. "Ready to tell us a little more?" The accent was as unthreatening as that of my first interrogator, but I knew from my earlier beating that this meant nothing.

"I guess you're hungry, so we bought you a Mars bar."

A lump of chocolate was put into my hand. My mouth was completely dry. I didn't want it.

"Eat," the first man ordered.

A hand guided my own to my mouth. The warm chocolate touched my lips and the sickly smell was strong in my nostrils, making me dry heave.

"Eat."

I bit off a lump and tried to chew, but the chocolate and toffee turned to glue in my mouth.

"Have some crisps, too."

A bag of cheese and onion was opened and a fistful of crisps stuffed into my mouth after the Mars bar. Then another, and another. I gagged.

"Ready to talk now?"

I attempted to speak, but the broken crisps and molten chocolate stuck around my throat and teeth, making a sticky noise. I gagged again, spitting chocolatey drool onto the floor. A bottle of water was held to my lips. I sucked on it greedily, flushing down the chocolate and relieving my thirst. Cold water trickled down my chin and neck, making me shiver.

"My colleague here has spoken with Martin Connolly and done a bit of investigating," the new man said. "We think there's more to you than meets the eye, Mr Kelly."

"Lie down," the second voice told me. His hands pushed me by the shoulders to the floor. I felt a chain being attached to my ankles, then an electronic winch powered up and took the tension. I was hauled up by the chain until I was hanging upside down. My hands were taped behind me again and I felt dizzy as my body circled, suspended by the ankles.

"Comfortable?" my new interrogator asked. I didn't

answer. "So tell us about your family."

I tried hard to concentrate as the blood pulsed through my head.

"My dad was called Patsy Kelly. He lived in Spain. He was killed last year."

"Who killed him?"

"We don't know. Most people think it was my uncle who ordered the killing."

"Tommy Kelly?"

"Yes."

"He's doing life."

"If you know anything about him, you'll know that prison doesn't stop him killing people."

"What do *you* know about Tommy Kelly?"

I didn't know where to start.

"I didn't see much of him when I was growing up, just Christmas and that. I worked for him for a bit a couple of years ago. Just doing computer stuff, building websites for some of his businesses. The stuff he can't do."

"Are you working for him now?"

"No," I said. Was I?

I heard a cigarette being lit and then felt the heat as it was held close to the thin skin above my wrist.

"Are you working for him now?"

"No!" I shouted. "I hate him. He killed my old man!"

The heat withdrew, but the threat remained – I could still smell the smoke close to me.

"So what's your interest in him now?"

"I'd like to see him brought down, properly."

"Are there others who think like you?"

"Yes."

"Who?"

"There must be hundreds … people on the firm, everybody he's stitched up, every family who's lost someone because of him."

I heard a dry laugh from one of my torturers, took it as a cue.

"As far as I know, Tommy was supporting the IRA; he's a sympathizer. He's big on the Irish connection."

"He'd butter us up with a few grand so's he could flood Belfast with his cocaine and not get his hands dirty."

"That's his style," I said. "He's always been two steps away from the business. Or he was until Jason got involved."

"Jason?"

"His son. My cousin. He fucked up big style."

"What do you know about it?"

"I was involved. With a guy called Paul Dolan. They reckon it was Dolan who tipped off the police and got Tommy caught."

"What do you know about Paul Dolan?"

"Only that he ran The Harp, and worked for Tommy now and again."

I thought I had been doing well until I felt the cigarette burn into my skin. I bucked and yelled as the burning pain flushed through my body.

"What do you know about Paul feckin' Dolan?" The voice became more urgent.

"What I said!" I screamed. "And that he got an early release."

"Any other names? People on the firm, people you've met through Tommy Kelly?"

I thought hard.

"Terry Gadd in Spain. There's a Russian called Bashmakov who Tommy stitched up, he's a big player – drugs, arms – I met him in Croatia, helped set up a deal."

"What deal?"

"Stolen paintings. I was just Tommy's runner."

They were silent for a minute.

As I twisted in pain, my shirt had worked loose and became rucked up around my chest. I felt a finger to the left of my navel, where I had the scar from the bullet wound.

"What's this?"

"I got shot, a couple of years ago."

"Who by?"

"I think it was Donnie Mulvaney, Tommy's hitman."

"Why'd he shoot you?"

"Because I messed up."

"Did it hurt?"

"Like fuck."

"Well, it'll be over quicker this time. You're really not keen on Uncle Tommy, are you?"

"I told you. I got shot."

"So why are you still involved?"

"Only revenge," I said. "For my dad, and for me ... and I want to find my cousin, Sophie."

"Sophie Kelly?"

"Yes. She's missing."

"Why do you want to find her so much?"

"She's his weakness. He'll do anything for her."

"Well, you'll not be finding her here. You're not quite the little innocent you were making out, are you, Kieran? You're an old hand."

"I'm not innocent ... but I'm not guilty of nicking a few bags of pills."

I could hear two low voices whispering to each other, deciding, I imagined, what line of questioning to pursue next. Possibilities of increasing tortures flashed through my brain and I felt sweat run upwards from my chest, salty and stinging on my cut lips. I tried to blank out the images from my mind, but they wouldn't shift.

A bullet would be preferable.

The electric winch clicked into action again and I was lowered to the floor. This stage of my interrogation, I guessed, was over.

"Thank you for your information, Kieran Kelly," my interrogator said. "Useful. But there are a couple of things that don't get you off the hook. We'd be ... uncomfortable with you still around, poking about. So this is where we say goodbye."

I felt myself being lifted by the ankles and shoulders and taken outside. It smelled like evening. I had completely lost track of time during my ordeal. My legs smarted, and the burn on my arm stung, but the terror and disorientation were far stronger.

"I'll deal with this," the third man said.

I was loaded into the boot of a car. I could smell old petrol and fear.

Someone else's petrol, my fear.

145

The boot thudded shut and I heard a door slam and the engine start. I was bumped around as before, every jolt reminding me of the pain that had been inflicted on me. I was glad that my interrogation was over, but now I was heading towards the conclusion.

TWENTY-EIGHT

Dave's house was a neat semi in Plumstead, south London.

A pair of concrete horse heads flanked the entrance to the car port and Dave swung the BMW into the narrow space between them.

Donnie sat on the leather sofa and looked around the tidy lounge at the pictures of grandchildren arranged on the mantle above the fake log gas fire. He felt a glimmer of envy for Dave's family life.

"Thank you, Pam," he said politely as Dave's wife handed him tea in a cup and saucer. The dainty china was dwarfed in Donnie's hand and he could barely get his finger through the handle of the cup. Pam stooped to remove a bit of fluff from the carpet as she went back to the kitchen. House-proud didn't come close to describing the level of tidiness and cleanliness that Pam maintained. Dave's shirts were always ironed, his grey suits always spotless and pressed. Sitting in his pyjamas and bare feet, holding the cup by the rim, Donnie felt he made the place untidy just by being there.

"Better find you a bit of clobber, Don," Dave said.

"Thanks, Dave."

"You'll be in Tiffany's room," he told him, referring to his recently married youngest daughter.

Donnie followed Dave up the stairs and into a small, feminine room at the front of the house. The bedspread was flowery, with a frilly valance that brushed the floor. The room was scented by a plug-in air freshener that smelled of apricot and vanilla. A cushion embroidered with a heart and a soft toy poodle sat on the pillow.

"Pam likes to keep it looking nice," Dave said, as Donnie sniffed the air and looked at the girly bed. Dave handed Donnie a blue shirt on a hanger and a pair of black trousers. "These should fit," he said, patting his stomach and looking at Donnie's paunch. "I lost a bit of weight since I wore them."

"Thanks, Dave."

Silky black socks and shoes that hadn't seen the light of day since the 1980s followed. When he was suited and booted, Donnie went back downstairs, noticing instantly that the shoes pinched.

Flat feet and bunions: Donnie always had problems with shoes.

They spent what remained of the afternoon watching Deal or No Deal, shouting at the screen.

Dave had a lot of time for Noel Edmonds: "Self-made millionaire, got his own helicopter, castle in Devon. Never had to shoot anyone to get where he is. Although he did drop that bloke in a tin box from a great height and kill him."

Donnie nodded, vaguely remembering a stunt that had gone badly wrong on one of Noel Edmonds' shows.

At 6 p.m. Pam laid the table and presented them with a roast dinner. Having eaten hospital food for too long, Donnie piled in, trying to remember his manners and not lick his knife – nor the pattern off the plate – when he had polished it off.

"Very nice, Pam, thank you. Tasty."

"You was hungry, Don," Pam observed, wiping a splash of gravy from the tablecloth near Donnie's plate.

"Seconds, Don?" Dave asked.

Donnie wolfed down a second plate of roast chicken while Dave poured more red wine. Conversation mostly centred on Tiffany's wedding.

"Vintage cream Rolls, matching cream silk dress," Dave said. He was exuberant, with two pre-dinner gins and quite a lot of wine in him.

"She looked like Kate Middleton," Pam added proudly.

"Champagne reception at Charlton House – Jacobean, used by royalty. All on the guvnor. He done us proud."

"Any faces?" Donnie asked, trying to find an area he was familiar with.

"Not really, it was Tiff's day. Dave Courtney and Roy Shaw come to the reception," Dave said, name-dropping a celebrity gangster and an ex-bare knuckle champion. "Just the top end. We wanted low-key, no old lags talking about the old days."

Donnie realized that he hadn't been invited, even though he'd worked with Dave for years. Maybe he was an old lag himself. Dave seemed to realize his faux pas at the same time and there was a pause in conversation.

"How's your daughter, Don?" Pam asked, breaking the stalemate.

Donnie was stumped for a moment. He couldn't remember

when he'd last seen or heard from Donna. Last he knew, she'd dropped another kid by another bloke and her current boyfriend was doing time for dealing.

"Fine," Donnie said. "Yeah, good."

"Grandkids?"

"Yeah, think so. Good. All good."

He now felt keenly envious of Dave and Pam's domestic set-up. Although Dave was a villain, he was the kind who always managed to keep his nose clean and everything in order. Hunky Doris. Donnie couldn't remember any family weddings; neither his own, nor his daughter's. There hadn't been any.

Donnie always ended up in the shit. And he was suddenly very tired. He felt an unfamiliar lump in his throat and a tear well in his eye. Suddenly had a memory of his old man giving him a thick ear for crying when he was a kid. Pam quickly cleared the table and clattered dishes in the kitchen.

"Summink in me eye," Donnie said. He grabbed a piece of kitchen roll and rubbed hard at his eyelid.

"You're tired, Don. Have another drink and turn in early."

Donnie drained another glass of wine in silence and Pam announced she was taking Brandy, the Bichon Frise, out for a walk.

Once she had gone, Dave leant over.

"We need a quick debrief, Don."

Donnie sighed deeply. "Not now, Dave. I've had enough."

"Enough of what, Don?"

"Everythink," Donnie said.

"Don't be like that, Don," Dave said. "You're old-school. Chin up."

"I'm getting too old for this, Dave. Now I've got an eight

stretch hanging over me if I get collared."

"You're just overtired, Don. You can have a few days' R&R here, then we'll work out what to do. I'll have a word."

Donnie looked blankly at the tablecloth while Dave went across to the drinks cabinet. He came back and plonked half a bottle of Scotch in front of Donnie.

"Here you go. Turn in with a nightcap – you'll feel back up to scratch in the morning."

Like an obedient child, Donnie took the whisky up to his bedroom. He pulled the frilly duvet up under his chin and nursed the bottle until he nodded off.

TWENTY-NINE

I felt the road become smoother, and the car began to slow down. Fragments of muddled prayers flew around my brain like a swarm of flying insects colliding and battering against the inside of my skull. I had an overwhelming desire to see my mum. I'd not seen her for nearly six months. I should have been more dutiful, should have visited more often. She worried about me, with good cause.

I thought about Sophie: my quest to find her had been nothing more than a misguided wild goose chase, over before it started. And others: Juana; Tony; Anna. People I would never see again. People who might never find whatever shallow grave I would be buried in.

Disappeared without trace.

My breathing began to come in short, sharp gulps as the car drew to a halt. My whole body trembled, racked by uncontrollable spasms of fear. The boot opened, and the figure that loomed over me in the darkness cut away the tapes that were binding my wrists and ankles.

"Out you get," he said. A new voice: harsher, more Belfast. "Stand by the car, put your hands on the roof and spread your legs."

I did as he instructed, supporting my shaking body against the side of the car. I felt him come up behind me and braced myself for what was to come.

"You're lucky I got here in time," he said. "You did well, but another couple of hours with those two and God knows what they'd have done to you."

I didn't care to think what he meant, I simply willed him to get it over with. The wait was unbearable. I clenched my fists and teeth and drew a deep breath. I felt his hand touch my back. Was he steadying himself for a clean head-shot?

I flinched and felt my knees go weak.

"There's a bus stop down the road," he said. "Dawn will be breaking in an hour or so. The first bus will take you back into London. It goes along the Cromwell Road. When you get to the big junction with Earl's Court Road, get off. Go to the Premier Inn and wait there. It's just off Hogarth Road, big and anonymous. Check in as Kieran Kelly and don't leave your room or contact anyone until you get further instructions."

I couldn't believe what I was hearing.

"Now, I'm going to drive away. Don't watch me go. Just wait till I'm gone. As far as the others know you're a dead man, so keep your head down – you've had a close shave. Lucky you mentioned your connection with the Russian. His name is like a magic word in some circles. Remember that."

"Who are you?" I wanted to ask, but the words wouldn't form in my dry mouth. I guessed he didn't want me to know anyway.

He got back in the car and I stood away. The ignition started and, before he slammed the door, he said softly, "Good luck, Eddie."

Moments later, I heard a large jet screech over my head. I pulled off the blindfold and saw a wire fence in front of me. Over my head I saw the lights of an early plane coming in to land at Heathrow. It was low, I guessed I must be ten or twelve miles out of central London, somewhere on the Westway or the M4.

I looked at my feet and saw my bag.

I picked it up and pulled out clothes I hadn't seen for a few days. I pulled them on and began to walk. As I stumbled along, hot tears of relief rolled down my cheeks. It was still dark, but through the tears I could see the pale beginnings of dawn across the wide stretch of road. After a hundred metres or so, I found the solitary bus stop. I sat down on the bench and when the trembling in my legs began to subside, the pain from my beating became the dominant sensation.

As it grew lighter a mist settled across the featureless suburban landscape. A growing number of cars hissed by until finally the headlights of the bus appeared like a vision through the mist. The doors hissed open and I stepped into warmth and light. There was still money in my pocket; I offered the driver a tenner, but he waved it away.

I was the only passenger.

I slumped into the plush seat of the bus. It was the most comfortable thing I'd sat on for some time and I drifted in and out of a light sleep as passengers got on the bus and dawn broke over London.

Half an hour later, I opened an eye. The outside was more familiar; we were past Hammersmith and heading towards West Kensington.

I asked the driver where the stop was for Earl's Court.

"Next one," he said. "Look like you had a rough night."

"I did," I said.

"Wish I was young again. Good luck to you."

I got off the bus and walked through the underpass, legs smarting against my jeans. I glanced at an early morning busker, thinking how carefree and lucky he was, and wandered around in a dreamlike state, exhausted, until I turned right off Hogarth Road and found the Premier Inn, a curved, modern building that suggested everything I needed: anonymity, comfort and a safe haven.

Automatic doors whispered open and closed again behind me as I walked in to the piped music of the reception area. A pretty, dark-haired girl was behind the desk. She was wearing too much make-up and her puffy eyes suggested she had been there overnight. Her name badge said "Dawn". She looked me up and down, betraying, for a second, that she wondered what on earth I was doing in there.

"I think I have a reservation," I said. "Under Kieran Kelly?"

She tapped into a keyboard and looked at the screen, then rifled through a box of cards as if she was making absolutely sure that what she had seen on the screen was correct. It was. She placed a card in front of me.

"Name here, signature and car registration," she said.

"I don't have a car," I said, writing Kieran Kelly and signing with an unsteady hand.

"And can you leave me a credit card for any extras?"

"I don't have a card. It's all on account," I said.

She checked the screen again, and seemed to accept it.

"Room 417 on the fourth floor," she said, validating a plastic pass-key. "There's a bag here for you." She went into the left luggage room behind the desk and emerged with a soft black suitcase, which she brought to the front of the counter. "Early morning wake-up call for you?"

"No, thanks," I said.

"Is there anything else I can do for you today?"

"No, thank you."

"Enjoy your stay with us, Mr Kelly."

"I will," I said.

I put the bags on the bed and swigged down the whole of a complimentary litre of water. I checked myself in the full-length mirror by the door and realized why the receptionist had been reluctant to accommodate me. My face was dirty and battered, my shirt limp and sweaty.

I took my clothes off and stepped into the bathroom. White towels, shower.

The hot water helped clear my head and hot pinpricks massaged my tense neck but stung my legs like hell. I looked down. The red weals had settled into blue and yellow bruised stripes, the skin broken in one or two places. I switched the shower to cold and the pain eased.

Wrapped in a towelling dressing gown, I felt a little better. I opened the black suitcase on the bed. Clean clothes, a phone, money and, more worryingly, a gun. I cocked it open; it was full of live rounds. Whoever was looking after me was telling me I was still in danger. I put it under the pillow and lay back on the bed, the feathery cushions and duvet supporting my aching body. My saviour, if that's the word for him, had told me not to contact anyone; maybe using the phone would alert someone to my presence. In my paranoid state, locked in an anonymous hotel room, I did as I was told. I picked up the remote and scrolled through the channels until I found something to watch. An old episode of *Frasier*, one of those reassuring American sitcoms where you can revel in the glossiness of characters' lives, where problems are suddenly resolved by a twist of fate in the plot. I settled back into the pillows and, as the jazzy theme tune played out, drifted into a deep sleep.

THIRTY

When I woke up I had no idea where I was.

I panicked, staring up at the ceiling, taking deep breaths. Gradually I put back together the pieces of my ordeal and how, miraculously, I had got here. There were news programmes on the TV, so I guessed I must have slept through till early evening.

My next sensation was hunger, so I looked at the room service menu. The poncy descriptions made my mouth water.

Our burgers are grilled to perfection by our expert chef. Made from 100% Aberdeen Angus beef and blanketed with your favourite topping. Choose from Irish Mature Cheddar, organic smoked bacon or the chef's own secret recipe barbecue sauce.

Nothing was going to scratch my itch like a burger. I chose 8 oz, with barbecue sauce and onion rings, chips and coleslaw. Side salad. Then ice cream, plus a couple of bottles of Bud.

I pulled on a T-shirt and a pair of clean chinos from the bag. My food arrived fifteen minutes later.

"Room service." The accent was eastern European.

I opened the door a little. The tray laden with food was a welcome sight and I opened the door wider to allow the man in.

"Thank you, sir."

He put the tray on the low table in front of the TV and held out a docket for me to sign. I didn't want to sign anything, so I left a biro squiggle on his receipt. As I signed, he took a moment to glance around the room, his eyes darting here and there. I had every reason to be paranoid, but I guessed my arrival early that morning, looking like a tramp, must have stirred some interest among the staff. He looked at me, now showered and dressed, and smiled. Perhaps now I fitted into the anonymity of the commercial hotel; I really needed a shiny grey suit and a briefcase and laptop full of sales figures to disappear in this environment.

"Enjoy," he said, and left.

I did.

I hoovered down the burger and chips, simultaneously channel surfing until I found some cartoon channel. I watched SpongeBob flipping crabby patties and chuckled, probably from a sense of relief, at the optimistic way SpongeBob bumbled through life while others rang rings around him.

I wondered whether my own life was any less absurd than a sponge who lives in a pineapple under the sea. Probably not. Except I had lost that sense of optimism that carried Bob through.

I settled back, belching loudly, while a feeling of weariness crept over me again as blood rushed to my stomach and beer to my head. I inspected the red, angry cigarette burn on my forearm. Bubbles of yellow pus were forming and leaking around the edges and I began to think that I should probably find some disinfectant or a plaster, but I was too tired to do anything about it straight away and didn't want to go down to reception. I felt safe locked in my room. Maybe my eastern European mate could bring me something up.

I didn't have to wait long.

A knock at the door.

"Room service." Same voice. I looked at the debris on the tray. The melting ice cream made me feel a little sick. I wanted it gone; it was an uneaten guilty pleasure lurking in the room.

I got up from the chair and went to the door, aware of SpongeBob's banal chanting in the background: *"I'm ready, I'm ready, I'm ready-eddy-eddy-eddy-eddy!"*

I looked through the spyhole. Same man. I opened the door.

With the momentum gained by someone who is prepared, the door swung open hard and into my face. It smashed me back into the wall, the door handle stabbing me in the guts. As I half fell to the floor, my room service friend charged in, kneeing me in the nuts. I fell back and, as the door slammed shut, managed to aim my foot accurately up into his own. As he buckled, I levered myself up, smacking my head into his. He rocked back against the bathroom door and I hit him hard in the face. He grabbed hold of my arm, twisting and wrestling with it, the raw burn singing with pain. He still had a tea towel in his right hand and I could just see the tip of a short blade emerging from underneath it. I grabbed his wrist and we struggled against each other as he tried to turn the knife towards me.

Despite my tiredness, a mad, manic anger surged up inside me and I managed to bend the wrist back, smashing his knuckles against the handle of the bathroom door. I brought it crashing down again and again until his knuckles were skinned and smears of blood coloured the white gloss of the paintwork. Then I drew his wrist to me and bit, feeling tendons beneath my teeth, and drove my knee in between his legs. He yelled out and his hand finally lost its grip and the knife dropped. I drove my forehead into his face again, nutting him and feeling tooth and bone puncture my own skin.

I used my advantage to push him back into the main part of the room, across the low table, which caught him behind the knees and sent the remains of my dinner flying into the air. I leapt over the table and was on top of him, raining punch after punch into his face, my knees astride, digging into his twisting ribs.

I felt a ferocity I had never felt before. I had stabbed Gav Taylor in Spain, but that had been an accident and I had never before felt this animalistic feeling of destruction that had taken me over now.

It was as if all the brutality, pain and injustice that had been heaped upon me was being channelled into this moment. I drove two more punches into his face, then got up and knee-dropped him across the neck. I found my fingers tightening around his neck and my thumbs pressing into his throat before my anger began to subside.

He was no longer moving. He'd picked the wrong fight.

I looked around the room, found the dressing gown and tied his ankles with the cord, then rolled him over and looked for something else. I ripped down a curtain pull and tied his hands behind his back, then dragged him into the bathroom and manhandled him into the bath, gagging him with a face flannel. He groaned as I levered his legs into the bathtub and locked the door behind me.

I sat on the bed, panting, regaining my breath. I looked sideways at myself in the mirror. I didn't like what was looking back at me, bloodied and bruised with feral aggression in the eyes. I had become brutalized, a killer, no better than the rest of them.

The bedside phone rang.

"This is reception, is everything OK there?" The voice was sing-song and corporate, but wary.

"Fine," I said.

"We just had a complaint from 415."

"Sorry," I said. "I'll turn the TV down."

I replaced the handset and felt under my pillow for the gun. I wondered what to do next. Locked in the bathroom, I had a semi-conscious eastern European who for whatever reason wanted to kill me, and I couldn't leave the room.

Whoever he was, he'd got on my case pretty quickly. The eastern European link started to raise questions well

162

beyond the reach of the IRA. I tried to put building blocks together in my mind but found no easy answers. Why would the IRA have planted me here simply for someone else to kill me? Had my mentioning Bashmakov simply made me a trade-off, and for what?

I delved into the bag for the phone, then picked up my battered and muddy trainers from the floor. I levered out the insole with the dinner knife and dug in the heel until I found the compartment that concealed a SIM card. I had not contacted anyone, and that had resulted in attempted murder. It was time to change tack, so I put the SIM in the phone and texted a couple of numbers.

Help.

THIRTY-ONE

Donnie had a headache, but he gratefully accepted the full English that Pam put in front of him and Dave. He hadn't had black pudding in ages, and with two eggs, bacon, sausage, tomatoes, mushrooms and beans, it was what he called a proper breakfast.

"Thanks, Pam."

Pam was about to take the fluffy white dog that yapped at Donnie's ankles for a walk. She gathered up leads and poo bags.

"What kind of dog is he again, Dave?"

"She is a Bichon Frise," Dave emphasized.

"More like a Bichon heat," Donnie joked.

"Nice one, Don. Better mood today? Sleep all right?"

"Like a log, Dave."

In fact, Donnie hadn't slept well at all. He'd nearly fallen out of the narrow bed twice during the night, and later lost the duvet on the floor. Then, when he'd woken up at four, the smell of apricot and vanilla from the air freshener had made him feel gippy. It was only the medicinal qualities of half a bottle of *whisky that had allowed him any sleep. Once he was awake, all he could think about was his possible conviction and jail or, failing that, skulking around continuing the firm's dirty work.*

After breakfast, Donnie took a cup of tea out into the garden and smoked a fag, looked at the sky while Dave pruned his roses. A plane squealed overhead, beginning its descent into London.

"Good of you and Pam to put me up," Donnie said.

"No worries, Don. Like I said, can't be for long. We need to get you somewhere safe."

"Where?"

"I'm going to visit Tommy later, get an update."

Donnie felt safer in the back garden in Plumstead than he did in most places. He would happily have hidden in Dave's shed rather than get back to the firm or, worse, a stretch.

In Donnie's view, nowhere in London was safe any more.

THIRTY-TWO

Hold tight. Not far away.

Simon Sharp. I'd texted Anna, too, but Sharpie was quick on my case.

He was there within an hour. He rang the room from reception but I still let him in cautiously, checking the peephole. I wasn't going to be caught out again.

He was flustered. Wide-eyed and wet from the rain.

"Shit," he said. "This has been quite a couple of days."

"Tell me about it."

He grasped my shoulder and looked at me. "What a mess."

"My face or the situation?"

"Fucking all of it," Sharp said. He looked tired and drained. "I'm really sorry. I'll get us a drink."

"There's the small problem of a waiter tied up in the bathroom to be dealt with first." Sharpie looked confused. "He tried to kill me."

166

"*What?* But only me and our Irish connection knew you were here," he said.

"*Our* Irish connection?"

"You don't think you got free without a bit of horse trading, do you? We had to work fast."

"Well *this* bloke found me pretty quickly." I nodded towards the bathroom. "*Someone* must have tipped him off."

Sharp took the gun and went into the bathroom. I followed and watched from the door. He clicked the safety catch on the gun and held it to the man's head. "No, please!"

Sharp barked a couple of questions in a foreign language. The waiter nodded and began to gabble in his native tongue. Sharpie replied, asking questions in short, sharp sentences. I didn't understand a word. The waiter seemed to agree with most of what Sharp said, but he was battered, tied and had a gun at his head, why wouldn't he? Eventually, Sharp clicked the safety back on and shut the man back in the bathroom.

"Russian," Sharp said. "Someone told him you were doing a drugs deal and that you were holding plenty of cash that had been delivered for you in a black suitcase."

"Who?"

Sharp shrugged. "Anyone's guess. This lot had me tied in knots, trying to get you out. I'll tell you about it. But let's deal with Trotsky first."

Sharp made a phone call.

Forty-five minutes later, a knock at the door made me jump. Sharp opened it and two utility men in boiler suits pushed what looked like a large laundry trolley into the room. Sharp led them into the bathroom and they wrangled the trolley inside. There were voices and I heard muffled shouts of protest followed by silence as they pulled the trolley from the bathroom, heavier now.

Sharp opened two bottles of beer and some crisps from the mini bar.

"So how did you get me out?" I asked.

"We'd have found you quicker, but I had to get hold of our London guy on the inside of the IRA. We only make contact in the most extreme circumstances. You have to understand, letting you go is very high risk for him."

"So how did you persuade him to get me out?"

"We had a bargaining chip."

"What?"

Intel about Paul Dolan," he said. "The London IRA and Martin Connolly are very interested in his whereabouts for one reason or another. "

"Do you have much?" I asked. I knew I wouldn't get a straight answer.

"Probably more than you know," Sharp said. "But less than you think."

"But that way, all sorts get to know what we ... you know?"

"Collateral damage," Sharp said. "Of course we're selective, but we have to balance it out."

"I didn't know I was worth that much."

"You're important to us," Sharp said without irony. "So we offered Martin Connolly what little we have. He took the bait, and he has quite a bit of clout."

"What is he? A drug dealer?"

"Martin's old-school IRA. He's more political, tries to keep himself respectable. As far as we know, he's separated himself from the Real IRA, who are manufacturing masses of synthetic drugs, turning over millions, rearming and still bombing when the mood takes them. But we're under no illusion that the political branch is still sympathetic to the gangsters; it's all about stockpiling funds and gaining power and control. The Real IRA boys have forged big international contacts, particularly in the States, where there's a lot of sympathy for them. Meanwhile, the old guard are lining up to shake hands with the Queen to look kosher. Thirty years ago they were blowing up her family."

We sat silently for a moment. Sharpie swigged the last of his beer. I sipped mine. I was beginning to feel sleepy again.

"Well, thanks for getting me out, I guess." Inside I blamed them for getting me in. "Wish you'd been a little earlier."

I pulled my sleeve back and showed Sharp the angry cigarette burn. He winced, wrinkling his nose in sympathy.

"Your captors must have realized you were a bigger fish than they'd originally thought. Whatever you told them saved you as much as our man on the inside."

"I kept my cover straight," I said, proud of holding up under torture. "I just gave them names."

"Names?" He looked worried.

"Only ones that fit with my cover," I said. "Tommy,

obviously. Patsy Kelly, Gadd. Paul Dolan, Bashmakov."

"Bashmakov?" Sharp raised an eyebrow. Looked at his watch. "We can talk further in the morning," he said. "But I want to get you out, away from here, asap."

I had no objection.

"I'm going to bunk down in here," Sharp said. "Just in case."

"Sure," I said.

I went to the bathroom and brushed the taste of beer from my teeth. When I got back into the room, Sharpie was curled up on the sofa wrapped in a blanket. I could see the handle of a pistol sticking out from the cushion under his head.

"We'll leave early," he said. "Alarm six fifteen, breakfast starts about seven."

"OK."

"G'night," he said, and just before I switched out the light I saw an expression cross Sharpie's face that told me he was as frightened as I was.

THIRTY-THREE

Breakfast was a silent affair.

We both hunched over grapefruit juice and scrambled eggs: our nervous stomachs would struggle to digest anything else. Sharpie leafed through a complimentary *Times*.

"Not much good news," he said.

"Is there ever?"

We were the only customers in the dining room at 6.50, and the tired foreign girls who waited on us couldn't conceal their huffiness at having to start a little early. I regarded them all with suspicion, expecting any of them to pull a gun or stab me in the neck with a fork at any moment.

At reception I stood by with the bags while Sharpie checked us out. My original receptionist did the business with Sharp and cast me a glance.

"You look better than when you arrived, Mr Kelly," she said.

I did. Clean shirt, jacket and chinos. Bruises fading a little.

"You must have found your stay with us relaxing. Would you like to fill out one of our customer satisfaction forms?"

I remembered the bloodstains we had cleaned from the bathroom door an hour before.

"Very relaxing," I said. "No, thanks, I'm afraid I haven't got time."

It was a short drive through the West End to Vauxhall, but we sat in nose-to-tail London rush hour traffic. Some talk radio rattled off useless traffic updates. Sharp switched it off.

"We'll do a full debrief back at base," he said, looking at the screen, "but run me through the bullet points of what happened." I didn't answer. He looked sideways at me. "What?"

"I'd like to know what the point was first, before I have to relive it all again."

"I know you think it was all a wild goose chase putting you on to Hannah Connolly, but, believe me, there was good reason behind it."

"Yeah? Right."

"You know Tony spent a long time in Northern Ireland?"

"Yes, he's told me."

"Well, he has a strong feeling that he knows Martin Connolly, but not by that name. They are about the same age. Tony would have been there when Connolly was in his twenties too, when he would have been at the sharp end of the IRA; the bombers and the killers. So when we get a lead that an IRA suspect's daughter is in London

172

and there are a few drugs involved, Tony's mind starts to work overtime. One of his hunches. More than a hunch: you found real evidence."

I knew that Tony had a good track record with his hunches.

"And I'm the sucker sent in to sniff about since Tony's off-limits?"

"Correct. You were the man for the job anyway. We followed a lead; that's all we can do. And on the way you've picked up some very good intel on the London IRA."

"I guess there's a link," I said, grudgingly. "Tommy was financing them in a small way through The Harp, Bashmakov's hooked up with them in some way. Like Tony always says, these things have a habit of linking up."

"Sure," Sharp said. "It's a question of joining the dots. What about Bashmakov?"

"The bloke who got me out said his name was the magic word."

"Did he say why?" Sharp glanced sideways at me.

"Not really. Why does everyone jump at the mention of his name?"

"He's a new breed of villain," Sharp said. "He works on a global scale – you've seen it yourself. One minute he's floating off Croatia trading a few million in cocaine and the same again in stolen art. The next day, he's probably got a helicopter into Afghanistan to do the same again with heroin.

"Tommy Kelly's genius was to hide the skulduggery behind several business fronts. The other smart thing he did was to keep it friendly with the other factions, like the yardies and the triads … and the IRA. Tommy convinced them that working together against the law while respecting each other's territories was to all their advantages. That's how organized crime works, and that's what made him so strong, but to be honest, Tommy's operation looks like a village post office compared to Bashmakov's multinational corporation."

"But Tommy gets on with Bashi, as he calls him."

"Well, he did initially, I think. Bashmakov fluffed Tommy up when he moved in on London. Don't forget, the Russians didn't really arrive here until six or seven years ago, and Bashmakov needed Tommy as a strong London connection to do business with. Like before, Tommy thought it better to cosy up to the Russian rather than make an enemy."

"Like giving him gifts of fake pictures and stuff. So what's changed?"

"With Tommy inside, he's little use – or more importantly, little *threat* – to Bashmakov unless Tommy has something the Russian wants, in which case he just uses his muscle and cherry picks, taking over bits of Kelly business. Just takes it. There's little Tommy can do about it."

"Does Tommy know?"

"Of course he does. It's driving him nuts. He's hired the top law firm for his appeal. He'll spend his last penny if it means he can get out and back in the saddle. It's taken him all this time to realize that there are certain things he can't control from inside and it's making him mad as hell."

"Like finding Sophie?"

Sharp nodded.

"What's your hunch?"

"Anna's working on it," Sharp said. "But I think we're going to have to spread our net a little wider."

THIRTY-FOUR

Donnie was in the garden, smoking a fag and driving Brandy the Bichon Frise mental with a rubber ball on a bit of elastic. He would bounce it hard on the path so the ball would rebound well out of reach of the small dog as she leapt into the air. On its downward trajectory, the ball was given extra momentum by the elastic and would hit the dog hard on the nose as she tried to catch it, making her yelp.

Donnie chuckled and repeated the action multiple times, laughing out loud when the ball caught the dog a corker. Finally he tired of the game and offered Brandy the ball from his hand. Instead of taking it, Brandy bit her tormentor's finger and held on.

Dave returned just in time to find Donnie releasing the dog's grip by kicking her.

"What you doing, Don? Don't kick the fucking dog."

"Sorry, Dave. It bit me."

"She never bites, Don."

"She did this time, Dave, hard."

"Not as hard as my missus will bite you if she finds you've kicked Brandy."

"Sorry, Dave."

Donnie knew he had outstayed his welcome. The night before, tucked under his frilly duvet in the single bed, he had heard Dave and Pam rowing. Through the wall, Pam's voice sounded hissy and Dave's low rumble sounded conciliatory – promises to get him out as soon as, Donnie was sure.

"How's the guvnor, Dave?" Donnie asked. Dave had just been to Belmarsh to see Tommy.

"Not in the best of moods. The appeal's coming up soon. Them lawyers are shit hot, worth every penny. All Oxbridge and Cambridge, finest minds in the country, they're all over it like the pox, covering every angle: bent coppers, paid witnesses, unreliable evidence, the lot."

"So, isn't he happy about that?"

"Yes, Don. But it's taking too long. He thinks he's been had about finding Sophie, there's not been a peep. The longer he's in there, the more chancers have a go at our biz. He thinks he's being wound up so that he might give something away. When he's really down, he thinks Sophie might already be brown bread."

"No, Dave!" Donnie protested.

"Nothing from Cheryl, neither. You'd have thought, wouldn't you? Just a note. In my view he was always too good to her, yet nothing was ever good enough for her, you know?"

"Perhaps she don't want to send anything that would impli … get anyone into trouble?"

"I just think she didn't like it when the shit hit the fandango. It interfered with her lifestyle. She's been with TK nearly thirty

177

years and had it easy the last ten: lunches and shopping and that."

"D'you think so, Dave?" Donnie's experience of relationships was limited to six months maximum.

"Women don't like it when the biz goes tits-up, Don. They're frightened they'll lose the gaff, the Lexus and the tanning salon membership." Dave leant forward confidentially, patted Donnie on the knee. "That's why I always keep it sweet with Pammy. On the level."

As far as Donnie had seen, Dave was terrified of the woman. All six foot three of him flinched when he heard the front door open. "Hello darling, you home? Cuppa tea?"

It wasn't that Donnie disliked Pam, far from it. She had been very kind putting him up, feeding and watering him. She just sometimes gave Dave a look that would melt steel at fifty paces, her mouth tightening into lines like a washbag that had had its string pulled.

Donnie wondered at the power these women had over big, strong men.

"There's something I want to talk about, Don."

"I know, Dave," Donnie sighed. "You want me out."

"Well, I did promise Pam you wouldn't be here longer than a week. But there's a bit of business to do before we decide where you go, Don."

"Oh?"

"Remember that hit you done up in St John's Wood a while ago?"

"The Russian?"

"Correct. Well, it looks like the warning wasn't taken. They've snatched up a bit more of our territory. Just like that,

muscled in because they can. We've got foot soldiers out there who can take care of theirselves, but these Russkis are something else. They think we've had it our way too long. Tommy doesn't want to start effing World War III, it's not his way. He's got some good eastern European allies, but he wants to give them a dry slap, let them know he's not messing about."

"How big a slap?"

"A large one. Well aimed. There's this guy, Oleg Komorov. They call him OK."

"OK, Dave?"

"Yeah. OK. He's one of Alexei Bashmakov's chief negotiators. He works out of the Russian Embassy in London, so he looks kosher but he's as bent as a bottle of chips. A big dealer; Tommy reckons that Komorov is the one muscling in on our business."

"OK."

"Yeah, OK – Komorov. Working on Bashmakov's behalf, like his front man, picking up our contacts, buying them off."

"I thought Bashi and the guvnor were comrades-in-arms?"

"Course they was, until one sees the other one down and can pick up some action. There's a vacuum, a power shift. Like what happened with Patsy in Spain. These boys don't get on by opening doors and giving it the 'After you, Cecil', do they? They just pile in and grab it. Nature abhors a vacuum and this behaviour cannot be tolerated."

Donnie could hear the echo of Tommy's phrases in Dave's.

"S'pose not, Dave."

"Right, so here's the deal. We know Komorov is meeting a Harp contact who has worked with us in the past. So Tommy wants you to be at that meeting. We'll find out where it is…"

"You know I'm not a good negotiator, Dave – you'd be better."

"Tommy doesn't want you to negotiate, Don. He wants you to do what you're best at. He wants to send Bashmakov a clear message by shooting Komorov. And whoever he's doing business with. Make it loud and clear to Bashmakov and all concerned parties."

"OK, Dave."

"Exactly: OK, Don."

"When?"

"Tomorrow."

THIRTY-FIVE

Dave cruised round the outer circle of Regent's Park until they found a bay.

Late breakfast had been the full monty in one of the few remaining Italian greasy spoons in Camden. Where Camden had once been almost entirely peopled by Irish and Italians, now all the caffs, chippies and small businesses were run by Turks, Estonians and Poles.

Dave remarked on the fact as they walked around the park, past the giraffes and the elephant houses at London Zoo.

"It's not racialist, Don," Dave said. "It's just they all have different habits, different ways of doing things. Like the difference between them giraffes and elephants."

Donnie watched as a giraffe obligingly drifted past, several metres of neck visible above the fence.

"So which ones are we, Dave? Elephants or giraffes?"

"Neither, Don," Dave said. "We're the lions. The kings of the jungle. We have to show our teeth and claws."

"What about the Russians?"

"Big bastard ugly brown bears," Dave said. "Not proud and wily like us lions. No class. We're the bulldog breed."

"I thought we was the lions, Dave, make your mind up."

Donnie was suddenly struck by the infantile turn of the conversation when the business of the day was to shoot a Russian in the face.

They had recced the restaurant, off Regent's Park Road: The Lemon Tree, a well-established Greek, whitewashed with green blinds. It would be open in an hour or so. They walked across the bridge and sat by the canal, watching ducks drift by in the morning sun. Donnie smoked while Dave checked his BlackBerry. He read an email a couple of times and smiled to himself.

"Bit of good news, Don."

"Dave?"

"The Savage kid's back. I thought we'd lost him while you was indisposed – he went off piste."

Donnie wasn't overjoyed to hear this. Just meant another job he didn't want to do.

"I'm too hot to keep an eye on him," Donnie said. "Get Jimmy Gallagher back on it. I'm a wanted man. Bit risky."

"I'll be the judge of that, Don. I look after you, don't I? No beat copper is going to feel your collar. Listen, let's concentrate on the job in hand and tool you up."

They got back in the car and slowly drove out of the park and across to Primrose Hill. Donnie admired the pretty, ice-cream-coloured houses that he guessed were worth a couple of million each.

Dave turned into a narrow mews off Regent's Park Road that ended in a row of garages. He took two pistols, wrapped in a cloth, from the glove compartment. Donnie unfolded the cloth and examined them; they were sleek with freshly applied oil.

"Smith & Wesson 9 mm?" Donnie asked.

"Correct, Don."

"Big boy for the job, innit? Silencer?"

"No silencer, Tommy doesn't want a quiet job. He wants everyone to know about it. The 9 mm will make sure of a messy kill, Don."

"Two guns?"

"Just in case one of them's armed. I want a gun pointing at both heads at the same time. Bang, Don. Bang. We don't want crossfire, we want a clean kill. There will be people in there, and we want them to see a good show; it'll rattle everyone's fucking bars. Bang, Don. Bang." Dave held out two fingers of each hand to demonstrate.

"Yes, Dave."

"No one will be looking at you because their eyes will be on those two chicken-faces crapping theirselves while you shoot them off, and the punters will all be too traumatized to check you on the way out. Livener?"

Dave offered Donnie a small poly bag of cocaine and a rolled tenner. Donnie didn't tap any out, simply opened the bag, sniffed half of it through the note and tucked the package into his top pocket for ron. Later ron.

"Cheers, Dave," Donnie sniffed.

Donnie knew what Dave was doing: geeing him up so that when he went into The Lemon Tree he would be feverish to kill someone and wild horses wouldn't stop him. Like a corner man, psyching him up before a fight. Donnie checked the guns over and stepped out of the car, placing a pistol in each of his jacket pockets. Dave got out and took an oversized, stone-coloured raincoat from the boot.

"Burberry, Don, nothing but the best for you." He flashed the checked lining and the label, showing that the pockets had been cut away inside to allow Donnie access to his guns.

"Thanks, Dave," Donnie said, putting it on over the grey suit Dave had dressed him in that morning.

"It's a high-tone area, Don, don't want you standing out like a spare prick. There, you look like an American business-man, one of them big, fat blokes that looks like a quarterback but controls an oil company."

"Thanks, Dave," Donnie said, ignoring the sideways compliment.

Dave took some glasses from a case: pale-tinted, wire-framed Ray-Bans. Donnie put them on.

"Rosy-tinted spectacles," Dave grinned. "Now, I'll drop you off at the end of the road, you go in, straight to the waiter and tell him you're meeting Mr Komorov. He'll point him out and you will head for the toilets, just to get your bearings. When you come out, head for the table. Bang, Don. Bang. Walk straight out, a burgundy Merc will be waiting. Johnny Reggae will be driving. He'll drop you back in Regent's Park, where Stav Georgiou will pick you up on the south side in a blue Beemer. Bosh. Got it?"

"Yup." Donnie nodded. Dave checked his watch.

"Let's go."

Donnie felt his heart pump and his breathing become heavy as Dave drove back to the end of Regent's Park Road. He could feel his blood rising, as the combination of adrenaline and cocaine did their work. He held out his hands: they were steady.

Dave let Donnie out of the car.

"Good luck, Don."

"What's the geezer's name again, Dave?"

"Komorov."

"Komorov, Komorov, Komorov…" Donnie repeated to himself as Dave pulled away. He walked back up the street until he was outside The Lemon Tree.

There was a young couple outside, smoking, drinking coffee in the sun. They didn't acknowledge Donnie's presence, too posh to even look at him, Donnie thought. Good. Fine.

He pushed through the door, and a smiling waiter greeted him immediately. The restaurant was like a big conservatory, half full with a lot of glass and straw chairs, sun streaming in through a skylight.

"Hi. I'm having lunch with Mr K … Koromov … Russian," Donnie said, in an accent that he thought was mid-Atlantic but which sounded more like something west of the Welsh border.

The waiter nodded and gestured to the far corner. Komorov was seated in the back of the restaurant so he could see who was coming in. Another man had his back to Donnie. "Thank you. I just need the bathroom first."

The waiter pointed to the back of the restaurant, to the right of Komorov's table. Donnie walked straight towards the gents', catching a glimpse of Komorov from the corner of his eye. The Russian was talking animatedly and didn't look round. For a big hulk, Donnie had a strange knack of being inconspicuous if need be. Donnie pushed open the toilet door, went in, checked himself in the mirror, took three deep breaths, turned around and went back out. He put his hands in his pockets, grasping the handle of each pistol. Now he could see the identity of Komorov's companion.

Nothing would give him more pleasure, he thought.

Donnie walked over to the table. It was covered with mezze plates of prawns, hummus, taramasalata, green chillies, feta cheese.

"Mr Komorov?"

The man looked up; navy business suit, bouffant grey hair. It was him. The other man was dark, bearded, familiar. Donnie slid the guns from either side of his coat and drew them up to face level for each man. Eyes widened.

"You told me to remember your name," Donnie said to the second man. "I just did."

Donnie pulled the triggers simultaneously and watched, as if in slow motion, as the bullets entered their heads. The rounds had been doctored, Donnie thought – filed or dum-dummed – because rather than leaving a neat entry wound they splintered on impact, blasting flesh, bone and teeth from each man's face and becoming messier on exit, leaving brain and blood across the cracked glass conservatory and creating astronomical dry cleaning bills for the other diners.

Certain that the job had been done, Donnie turned on his heel and walked out between the curtain of screams from other tables.

Oleg Komorov, late of the Russian Embassy and Bashmakov's man in London, died instantly.

Martin Connolly, aka Michael Dolan, gave his final death spasms in a spreading pond of blood on the tiled restaurant floor and died a few seconds later.

THIRTY-SIX

I was called into the office. I was in fairly good spirits after a few days' chilling out in a safe house and a good night's sleep.

I took the lift up to the fourth floor and walked through the glass doors.

Anna was sitting in a leather swivel chair, her eyes glued to the screen.

"Hiya," I said.

Anna swung round. She was looking businesslike in a dark tailored suit nipped in at the waist, the skirt tight across her legs. I always forget how hot she is until I see her again.

"Here comes trouble," she said.

"That's rich coming from you," I laughed. "What are you dressed up for? Job interview? Moving over to HSBC?"

"She looks more like she's moonlighting as Miss Whiplash in those heels," Sharpie said archly, walking in after me.

"Thank you, children," she said. "I've actually just come from lunch with Sandy Napier. You haven't heard, have you?"

"What?" Sharp nearly shouted.

"Martin Connolly's been murdered."

"*What?*"

"You heard me."

"Where?"

"North London, Primrose Hill, in a Greek restaurant. Sandy was trying to get an injunction on it until we could find out what was behind the killing, but it was in broad daylight, lunchtime. Shot dead. Primrose Hill is crawling with media wonks who were on their iPhones to news-rooms within five minutes. They even got photos – which can't be published, they're just too much."

Anna clicked on her screen and brought up some images. I looked and looked away, sickened, and then looked back again. I wouldn't have known it was Martin Connolly save for a tuft of black, wavy hair and beard, either side of a gaping red hole of flesh and gore. The slideshow continued from other angles.

"Who's the other man?" Sharp asked.

"That's where it gets really interesting," Anna said. "He's called – was called – Oleg Komorov. Worked at the Russian Embassy."

"Komorov?" Sharp said.

"We think he was Alexei Bashmakov's front man in London." Sharp leant in and peered closer at the image, as if he might recognize one bag of mince from another. He shook his head.

"Fuck," he said. "Who did it?"

"Professional hit," Anna said.

"Anyone see him?"

"The waiter said he was a big man, sunglasses and raincoat, spoke with a Welsh accent."

"Great," Sharp said. "Let's comb Cardiff and all the rugby teams between here and there."

"So, no clues?" I asked.

"We know Komorov had connections with Bashmakov. And that Connolly was part of The Harp, and senior IRA. That's enough to put them together."

"So who does Sandy think shot them?"

"Guess who?" Anna said. "Since Tommy Kelly's been inside, Bashmakov's muscled in on plenty of areas of his business. We imagine Tommy's got the real pip because the Russians have cut him out of the Irish deals. They've dispensed with the middle man. Compared to Bashmakov, Tommy's funding suddenly looks like small beer, and you know what Tommy's like about his Irish roots."

"So he's taking it personally?" I asked.

"We think so," Anna said. "This shooting has all the hallmarks of a Kelly assassination, showing his reach from inside Belmarsh. It was showy and messy, a loud, clear and bloody message that he's still a player."

"What it shows," Sharp added, looking at me, "is that we were on the right track putting you on to the Connollys. It's beginning to stack up. But I think we should rest you for a bit, Eddie. It's a bit hot for you out there at the moment."

Sharp's phone rang. He looked at the caller ID and

signalled that he had to answer it. As he left the room to take the call, Anna nodded to me to follow her. We went into the canteen area and I got us both coffee while she sat down. I joined her at a table overlooking the river.

"Why does Sharpie want to rest me?"

"He thinks you might still be a target," Anna said.

"Have you spoken to Tony about this?" I asked. "You must have *some* contact with him?"

Anna looked as if she might be about to say something, then changed her mind.

"No, I haven't," she said. "Rules is rules, Eddie. You know walls have ears." She rolled her eyes for my benefit. "And I'm sure you understand that any contact with Tony would compromise your work?"

"Right," I said. "So what's new?"

She hesitated a moment, then took an iPad from her bag and flipped it open. "This is," she said. "Let me show you something." She put her finger to her lips, then called up some images that looked as if they had been taken on CCTV in a department store somewhere. They were lined and grainy.

Anna pressed play and they came to life. Two girls, shopping. Both good-looking, one dark, one blonde, like rich kids from an American soap. They were just walking and chatting, checking out clothes. Another angle, cosmetics counter, trying out lipsticks on the backs of their hands.

"Very nice," I said. "Who are they?"

"We think the blonde is Petrina, Bashmakov's daughter," Anna said.

"Whose surveillance is this? Yours?"

"No, this is stuff we've been sent from a contact."

"Who's the other girl?" I asked. Anna froze the picture and zoomed in to the blurred face surrounded by a sharp, dark bob and long fringe. It was a strong look that drew attention away from pretty features.

"Look closer," Anna said. I did.

"Nope," I said, shaking my head.

"I think it's Sophie Kelly."

The hair prickled on the back of my neck. I looked again.

"Can you sharpen it at all?" Anna took a frame of the still and opened it in Photoshop. Then she added contrast and sharpening filters, artificially focusing the face.

I had been thrown by the hair. It could have been Sophie. It was Sophie.

"Where was this taken?" I asked. "When?"

"Last week," Anna said. "In New York."

THIRTY-SEVEN

The car picked me up outside the British Museum.

Anna was already sitting in the back and I breathed in her fresh, lemony fragrance. It was a sunny morning and London looked like a heritage film set on one side, with the Tower of London behind us, and a futuristic metropolis on the other, with the Gherkin and other tower blocks dwarfed by the Shard, which stabbed violently into the clouds above London Bridge.

We didn't say much until we were almost at Bermondsey, an area that brought back memories of my first encounters with Tommy Kelly nearly two years earlier.

"Sharpie got over his mood?" I asked. Simon had kicked off when Anna told him our plan, but she had pulled rank and told him it was a done deal.

"I think so," Anna said. "He only got the blouse on because he wants to run the show. He's smart and ambitious and wants his name all over this one."

"Promotion?" I asked.

"Well, yes," Anna admitted. "But this is turning into a bigger, more complex affair than we imagined when you first went to see Tommy."

"You're telling me," I said. "I thought it was a missing persons thing, but until now the last thing on anyone's mind seems to have been finding Sophie Kelly."

"I'm sure Tony told you it was never simply about finding Sophie. The promise of finding her is the only thing that gives us leverage with Tommy. In the meantime, we get on with the job of finding who he's dealing with ... or who's trying to turn him over while he's inside."

The lack of importance placed on Sophie's whereabouts rankled me; as well as being Tommy's motivation, it was my own. I wanted her back.

"A visitor. How lovely," Tommy Kelly said, chirpy. "Hello, stranger. What do I call you these days? Kieran?"

I stood up and we shook hands, his grasp dry and warm as I had remembered, the visiting room at Belmarsh as stark and institutional as ever.

"You look well," I said. He did. He had a light tan and his hair had been recently cut.

"I am," he smiled. "I've been outside, doing a bit of gardening. Privileges for my immaculate behaviour." He laughed. "Grown some tomatoes."

"You've had a haircut."

"One of the nonces used to work for Vidal Sassoon," he said, brushing a palm across his hair. "Before he chopped up a fifteen-year-old rent boy." He laughed again. "I wouldn't buy a pie off him." He appeared in good spirits. "So what's new, old son?"

"Not much," I said. "Or not much I can tell you."

"I shouldn't worry on that score," he said. "I tend to keep abreast of current affairs."

"I brought you a present," I said. I lifted a heavy art book: *Contemporary Art, 2000–2015*. It had already been heavily vetted by prison security and was found not to contain a file, gun or length of rope.

"Thank you," he said. "I've been doing a lot of reading, and a bit of painting myself. I'm big on Lucian Freud at the minute. I can knock out a fair copy. Maybe you can sell them to some Russians for me?" He smiled at his own joke. "I didn't think much of him when he was alive, but in here I've had time to have a proper look. Fantastic flesh tones. He doesn't do likenesses as such, but really gets at the soul of his sitters, like he's looking under their skin." I nodded my agreement. "Apart from the one he did of the Queen. Made her look like a blind cobbler's thumb."

"I haven't had much time for culture," I said. "But this is a great book. I've been getting into Gerhard Richter a bit."

"Photo-derived stuff." He curled his lip.

"Yes, like surveillance photos, video-based work … there's an interesting one on page 236."

He flicked through the book, stopping to look at things that held appeal until he arrived at the designated page. I leant over.

"This is one of his New York pieces."

I pointed at the picture on the page. It was the photo

of Sophie in New York, which had been carefully Photoshopped and printed onto a false page, the typography and paper quality identical to the rest of the book.

"Nice work," he said.

"Yes, it was part of a series taken in New York department stores, using surveillance cameras. Read the bumf, it's interesting."

Tommy ran his finger over the small print buried within the art-speak: *Miss S Kelly, Barneys Department Store, New York.*

It was dated a week before. Failed to mention the name of the second girl, who had been cropped from the picture.

"You sure?" he said. He looked up at me, eyes locked on mine.

"Sure as we can be," I said. "It's from a good source."

"Hair's confusing," he said. He looked closely at the photo. "But I think it's right."

He used the language he would use to describe a real painting over a fake, and could not conceal a smile at the thought that his daughter was alive and apparently free in New York.

"I think it's right," I said.

"Good work," Tommy said. "So what are you waiting for?"

THIRTY-EIGHT

Sharpie's objection to me going to New York was stronger than his objection to me visiting Tommy. Although he was my case officer, Anna seemed to have engineered my visit to Tommy and was encouraging the possibility of my going to the States. I couldn't work out why she was apparently working against Sharp's wishes. Did I detect the guiding hand of Tony Morris somewhere in the background? Whatever the case, Sharp was having none of it.

"You're diving in too quickly," he said crossly. "You don't know what sort of hot water you might be jumping into."

"It's never stopped anyone throwing me in at the deep end before," I protested.

"Yes, well, I wasn't your case officer then."

"You have been recently," I said sniffily, "and I've been in some pretty deep water in the last week or so."

"New York is a different kettle of fish," he said. "It's a

big place, we have few leads. I'm not sending you off on a blind Sophie-hunt."

"I thought you had CIA links," I said, getting smart.

"We do," Sharp snapped. "And that information is a bit above your pay grade."

It was a phrase I'd heard from Ian Baylis, Sharpie's and my former superior. It stung to hear Sharpie use it – I considered him a mate. He could see I was hurt, and softened a little.

"Listen, Eddie, as your case officer I do also have your safety in mind. You've done great work digging up links here, stuff that has already had repercussions. We have to digest some of that before we even think of making a transatlantic link. My feeling is that it does join up, but we don't know how, exactly; Anna's still working on it. You've just been roughed up pretty thoroughly and I think you could do with a rest. When we're exhausted we make rash decisions, our focus isn't as clear and neither are our judgements. That's why we all need someone above us making sure we're taking the right steps."

I began to concede defeat. Maybe he was right. After my ordeal, my adrenaline was running on reserve, but it had also given me a manic energy to continue. My meeting with Tommy Kelly had geed me up too. I had left Belmarsh fired up to go looking for Sophie. Maybe Tommy had cranked me up a bit.

"OK," I said. "But don't treat me like some wet-behind-the-ears kid."

"That's the last thing I'd do, Eddie. For your age, you are one of the most experienced operatives we have. I've

197

been doing this a few years longer than you, with some good results, but I have never been in some of the tight spots that you have. I respect that."

I was surprisingly buoyed up by the compliment.

"It's just that I have a broad overview of this situation that's taken me months, or longer, to assemble. I don't want to wreck things by jumping the gun."

"OK, Sharpie," I said. "I'll hang fire."

"Don't take it personally," he said.

"I won't," I said. But I did.

I had a drink in the bar with Anna after work.

We stood on the balcony overlooking the Thames so she could smoke while she drank a large glass of white. I watched a couple of Thames luggers making their slow progress up the river. I was a bit moody.

"He might be right," Anna said. "You could be wallowing around in New York looking for a needle in a haystack. It's a big place."

"So's London," I argued, sulkily waving at the city-scape. "But you lot still managed to wheedle Hannah Connolly out and involve me in that mess."

"But we're on the ground here, Eddie. Our intel is instant. Over there we're relying on second-hand information. There's no one more secretive than American intelligence agencies. We're lucky to get a man on the ground over there at all. We often don't let the Yanks know what we're up to, because if we asked permission they'd say no. We're stupidly grateful if they pass on a phone number, let alone surveillance pictures."

"So how did you get the pics of Sophie?"

"I have a friend in the NYPD."

"There you go," I said. "You could put me in touch with your friend."

Anna took a sip of wine and gave me a sideways glance.

"I don't think it's the kind of friendship you would be able to maintain," she said. Unconsciously, she smoothed her skirt and I got the message.

"Do you sleep with everyone to get them to do what you want?" I asked. My voice sounded cold and dry in my mouth, and my tone was petulant.

"Harsh," she said, cool. "And I think you've over-stepped the mark."

"Sorry."

"I know what you think," she said. "But I'm also fucking good at my job – and whatever else, I've looked after you and got you out of quite a few difficult situations."

It was true. She'd come and found me when I was out of my depth with Tommy Kelly and Bashmakov in Croatia. She'd got to me first when I'd been shot by Donnie Mulvaney, and saved my life. She'd flown me out of Spain when my cock was on the block.

"Look, I'm sorry…"

She hadn't finished. "So don't give me your petty moralizing, Eddie. Of course I have associates, colleagues, people I get close to; people I *have* to get close to. You know the score. It goes with the territory."

I was beginning to feel ashamed of myself. I remembered staying in her flat when I was down and insecure, how she had looked after me.

199

"I'm sorry, Anna, I'm out of line."

"Bang out of order." She stared out across the river, avoiding my eyes. I felt awful now. She was as tired of it all as I was.

"Anna, can I get you another drink, and then maybe we can go and eat?"

"Sure," she said, finally. As I left for the bar I thought I saw her wipe a tear from her eye before lighting another cigarette.

THIRTY-NINE

I woke up to sun streaming through the window. I could smell freshly laundered sheets, and my head sank deep into a feathery pillow. I turned to see Anna's chestnut hair spread across the next pillow. I looked at her face, beautiful, thick-lashed and relaxed in sleep, as the night before came back to me.

It had been a release of tension for both of us, and Anna wasn't one to hold a grudge. We'd drunk some more wine and eaten in an intimate Japanese restaurant near Hyde Park, then piled into a cab, laughing and tipsy, recounting old times. I'd felt the pressure of Anna's leg against mine in the cab and remembered what I'd been missing, then we'd kissed until the cabbie muttered something about getting a room.

We'd tumbled out into the square in Stockwell. There was no question of my taking the cab back to my flat.

There were more drinks, and some music. I had the

feeling that Anna hadn't let her hair down like this for a long time. Neither had I, and I barely remembered jumping into bed in the early hours with a night's booze on our breath and Anna's smooth, warm body against mine.

Well, I remembered a bit.

"Morning." She opened an eye as I brought her tea and put it by the bed. "What time is it?"

"Seven-fifteen," I said.

Anna picked up her phone.

"Working from home this morning. In after lunch," she dictated to herself.

I slipped back into bed beside her, sipping my tea, then felt Anna's arm stray across the bed, lazily stroking my stomach. I put down my tea and rolled towards her again, inhaling a baby powder and slightly sweaty bed smell as I put my face into her neck.

We sat drinking coffee at eleven, a couple more hours' sleep making us feel more human.

"I'm sorry, Anna," I said suddenly.

"What for? Never explain, never complain."

"I just feel…"

"What?"

"That maybe we use each other."

"Hmm," she considered. "Nice, isn't it?"

"Well, yes."

"So what's there to be sorry for? We're not cheating on anyone, are we? We're grown-ups. Sometimes we need simple human contact with someone familiar."

"I guess so," I said. "We always have a good time."

"And we're a long time dead."

We kissed again, but within the hour Anna was back into work mode, firing off emails and texts, checking her phone, showering and drying her hair with brisk efficiency. Fun over.

"I'd better be going," I said.

"No hurry." But it was clear from Anna's tone that our respite was finished and she had to be back on the case.

"I was thinking," she said, looking up for a moment. "Instead of knocking around here, why don't you go back to your mum's for a couple of days?"

"You think?" A few days of R&R, kip and square meals wasn't a bad idea. "Just until you and Sharpie decide on the next move?"

In truth, I felt secure up at my mum's. In the depths of the Midlands, I felt like no one could get at me.

"Do it," she said. "You're only a phone call away, and a couple of hours on the train. I think it's a good idea."

"When will I see you again?" I found myself asking.

"Don't be a sap, Eddie," Anna said. "You know where I am. You know what we have. You know the score. Don't go applying terms and conditions."

I considered myself told and got dressed.

Anna went off to the office and kissed me on the mouth as we left.

"Keep it cool, Eddie," she said. "I'll let you know if there are any developments. I'll tell Sharpie where you are. I think he'll be glad that you've decided to take a few days off. He's very uptight at the moment, but you've got to let him have his head. This is a big case for him, and these things tend to drive their own pace."

"Understood," I said and kissed her again.

I got the tube back to the flat, threw a few things into a bag and left. Euston was a short walk away; if I got an afternoon train, I'd be in Stoke by early evening.

"Dave?"

"Don?"

"Yeah. How'd you know?"

"What is it, Don?"

"He's gone on the train."

"Who?"

"The kid, Savage, Kelly, whatever."

"Where?"

"Euston."

"No, I mean to where?"

"Dunno. Manchester train."

"Why didn't you get on it and follow him, Don?"

"I was tired, Dave. You know I'm tired. I'd only just woken up when I got the nod from Jimmy Gallagher about where he was. It was all I could do to catch up with him, and he was on the train by three."

Donnie was exasperated. He'd subcontracted Jimmy Gallagher to do some of the watching and waiting. He'd thought he'd be off-duty after the hit, and then the kid turned up at Belmarsh again. What was going on?

"I don't want to go up 'effing north, Dave. You don't know who you're going to bump into. All them Scouse gits,

204

Manchester Tony and Billy Whizz. I don't want to get mixed up in all that toffee. It's complicated enough already."

"Don't be a wanker all your life, Don," Dave said crossly. "Take a day off. He's gone to Stoke-on-Trent, where his old tit lives. I'll text you her address. Get on the train and keep an eye. Treat it as a holiday. Plenty of old boozers and curry houses up there to keep you happy for a day or two. TK said five grand bonus. On top of what you're owed."

The money clicked a synapse in Donnie's brain.

"Someone said they do a naan bread the size of a table up there in the Balti houses?"

"Land of milk and honey, Don," Dave assured him.

"Do I need tools? I might just take a shiv and a five mil?"

"No action, mate, it's easy. Just watching and waiting. Take a flat cap and a whippet and you'll fit right in, you plum."

"When, Dave?"

"Toot dee sweet," Dave said. "That's French for yesterday."

"I'm tired, Dave. That time in hospital took—"

"Have a kip on the train, Don. Plenty of time for sleep when you're dead."

FORTY

As the train pulled in to Stoke I began to regret my decision.

I had left London in sunshine, and as soon as I stepped onto the platform I felt the drizzle of a dull Midlands day on the back of my neck. It brought it all back to me like a conditioned reflex: the months I had spent here, recovering from the bullet wound and post-traumatic stress after I was shot.

I got into a cab and gave the driver my mum's address. We headed out around endless ring roads before turning off and crawling in among the red brick terraces.

I had decided to arrive unannounced: a nice surprise, I thought. I knocked on the door and waited. No answer. Knocked again.

She was probably out. Stupid not to have just sent a text to say I was coming. Still no answer, and I didn't have keys. I walked across to the other side of the street to check the house for signs of life. An upstairs curtain twitched, so I knew someone was in.

Being in this line of work, I always suspect the worst. I walked back across the road and banged harder on the door. Footsteps on the stairs followed, and my mum opened the door.

"I didn't hear you," she said, flustered. "I had the radio on. What a surprise." She hugged and kissed me, held my face between her hands and cried a bit, then we went in.

"Cuppa?"

I looked around as she put the kettle on. An unfamiliar laptop was open on the kitchen table.

"Got yourself a laptop?" I asked. That was unlike Mum. She managed to order stuff online, but beyond that, computers were not really of any interest to her.

"No," she said. "I've got a guest staying."

"Kath?" I asked. Her sister often stayed when she was not travelling around India or Thailand.

"No," she said, offering no further information.

"Hello, mate," a voice came from behind me.

I spun round to see Tony Morris standing in the doorway.

"Tony! What are you doing here?"

"Probably same as you," he said, shaking my hand vigorously and clasping me in a bear hug. "Keeping my gourd out of the firing line. Getting a bit of P&Q."

I returned the hug. I was really pleased to see him.

"Cuppa, Tony?" Mum asked.

Tony had always been a regular visitor when I was growing up, but there was something else here, an ease between him and Mum in this domestic situation that made them seem like an old married couple.

"Ta, yes," Tony said. "Coming outside?"

He winked at me and we went out through the kitchen into the small patch of garden. Tony began to make himself a roll-up.

"Smoking?"

"Just the odd twister. I gave it up for five years," he said. "But, as you probably know, I've been having a bit of a stressy time. Stupid, really, fags aren't going to solve it."

"So what's new, apart from taking up smoking again?"

"Bit of a deadlock, really. Napier's working to get me off the hook. I don't know how much you've been told – they know it's a load of bollocks, but they have to follow the necessary protocols to keep the Met and the Awkward Squad happy until I'm cleared. Of course, they all know I'm working away in the background, they can't stop me … but I can't be seen to be making contact with you or anyone else on our firm. But what about you, more to the point. You OK?"

Whatever had happened to me, he knew. He always did.

"I'm over it, but I've been having a bit of a prickly time since with Sharpie," I said. "Without you there, he seems to have taken it upon himself to run things."

Tony nodded. "Sharpie's ambitious. Likes to know the ins and outs of the cat's arsehole. I sometimes limit what I tell him."

"And then he limits the information he gives me."

"Nature of it," Tony said. "Too much information can be more dangerous than too little. It's all on a need-to-know basis. So is he getting in your way?"

"I went to see Tommy Kelly."

"Good move." He didn't seem surprised.

"Anna thought so, Sharpie didn't. He thought it was too soon." Tony shook his head. "Anna supported me, so he got outvoted."

"Good girl," Tony said approvingly. "She thinks the world of you. So how was Uncle Tommy?"

"Not bad," I said. "He more or less admitted responsibility for the Martin Connolly hit."

Tony agreed. "Sure he did. He's pleased with himself. From our point of view it would have been good to have Connolly alive a bit longer. Once you'd drawn him out, he was a good lead."

"Why?" I asked.

"Because he is – was – Paul Dolan's brother. Michael Dolan was his real name. He was a player."

"Shit." Suddenly the familiarity of Martin Connolly's face and build made sense. The reason I had been sent to spy on Hannah suddenly joined up. "Shit."

"We're sure it was Connolly – Michael Dolan – who spirited Paul Dolan away on that video we saw. He made sure he disappeared before Tommy could get to him. So Tommy got to the brother instead, and Bashmakov's bitch into the bargain."

"Deliberately?" I asked. Tony shrugged.

"Seems too good to be a coincidence. Whichever way, it'll have put a smile on Tommy's face."

"I managed to sneak in a picture we got of Sophie," I said. "That really cheered him up."

"Good," Tony said. "He's still showing his soft

underbelly. If we can bring Sophie in, we have a strong bargaining tool. What did Tommy think?"

"He wanted me to go straight to New York and try to track her down. I was all enthusiastic and geed myself up, ready to go."

"And?"

"Sharpie blocked it. Said it was too early again – but he really dug in this time. So I said I'd wait for his instructions and came up here."

Tony flicked out the roll-up. Thought for a moment.

"What's he waiting for?"

"I don't know," I said.

"I'm generally of the strike-while-the-iron's-hot school. Maybe Sharpie's playing a longer game. I'll have a think about it."

"This tea's going cold," Mum called from the kitchen.

"Sorry," Tony called back. "We've been chatting."

We went inside.

"What do you boys fancy for your tea tonight?" Mum asked.

Tony and I looked at each other.

"Curry," we grinned.

FORTY-ONE

Donnie checked into the Stoke Travelodge.

He didn't like "up north" and he didn't like Travelodges, either.

They never had a proper bar. Or nosh.

As soon as he'd dumped his grip, containing socks, pants and a worn toothbrush, he went back to reception and ordered a cab.

He gave the driver an address and they drove a mile or so through the rows of terraced streets in an area that Donnie couldn't pronounce. He asked the driver to drive past the address he had given, clocked the house, then asked to be taken to the nearest pub.

"You sure, pal?" the cabbie asked. "The nearest one's a bit rough. You're better off going to The Greyhound."

Donnie wasn't bothered by the idea of a rough pub; he had spent plenty of time in them over the years, and his presence usually added to their reputation. However, he took the cabbie's advice and was dropped off outside The Greyhound. It wasn't bad at all, a good old-fashioned boozer with areas divided by wooden panelling.

It was busy, and Donnie waited patiently while several locals were served before him. He found himself a seat in a corner booth and sipped his first pint. He didn't spot the kid at first. An older, nondescript bloke was buying the beer. It might have been his dad, and as they chatted and joshed while their drinks were being poured, Donnie envied their easy father-son bond.

For a second he was sorry that he was going to have to kill the kid.

They were on the other side of the pub, a good distance away, the other side of a wooden divide, but Donnie couldn't afford to be seen. He couldn't spend an hour with a copy of the local paper in front of his face, they'd spot that a mile off, but to leave he would have to walk past them. The only available door on his side of the pub was the gents'. With his back to the bar, as subtly as he could manage, Donnie slipped across to the toilets – on second thoughts, stopping to take his beer with him – and locked himself in the cubicle.

As custom dictated, Tony and I had a pint in The Greyhound before picking up the takeaway. The pub was pretty full, so we stood at the bar. Tony was affable off-duty.

"How long you been up here, Tony?"

"Just a few days. Your mum's been very good to me. We've had a nice time. Went out yesterday for a spot of lunch and a walk round Trentham Gardens. It's relaxing. I feel safe up here, out of the way."

"I know what you mean," I said. "But lying low gets a bit boring after a few days. That's why I ran off to Spain last time I was stuck up here."

Tony laughed.

"And look where that got you."

"Told you I get bored easily," I joked.

"You're a young bloke, though, plenty of energy. I'm tired of it, mate. Years of stress have worn me down. A quiet life up here looks quite appealing sometimes."

"You're not retiring, are you?"

Tony shrugged.

"Might have to. Sharpie and Anna would look after you if I did."

The idea unsettled me. They hadn't done a great job since Tony had been out of commission. Tony wasn't without his faults, but I trusted him.

"Don't abandon me, Tony!"

"Never, old son. I know I haven't been much help recently, but we'll see what happens when I've done my purdah."

"If you're not on the firm, neither am I," I said.

"Not sure you have a choice, mate," he said. "Now let's stop talking shop and go and get the curry in."

Donnie realized he was trapped. He had finished his beer accompanied by the stench of bleach and urine. The door to the cubicle had been tried twice; someone desperate for a tom-tit would be getting very impatient.

He would have to make a break for it. He flicked the bolt.

213

A man was washing his hands. Looked at Donnie.

"I'd give it ten minutes," Donnie said, gesturing at the cubicle.

The door opened straight back into the bar, so he nudged it open a sliver and peeked out. Someone yanked the handle from the other side and pulled the door wide open, exposing Donnie to the bar. He glanced around rapidly. He couldn't see the kid and the older bloke any more. The other side had emptied out. They had gone. Donnie left the pub; it was getting dark outside. He looked up and down the street, then made his way back towards the terraces.

He found the number again, walked straight past, then ducked into an alley that led behind the houses.

"Sag Prawn, Rogan Josh, Aloo Gobi, Chicken Balti, Tandoori Chicken, Keema Naan..." Tony reeled off the usual selection of Indian dishes as he undid the foil takeaway containers and the steamy, spicy smells filled the kitchen.

My stomach gurgled and I munched a poppadom with lime pickle, my appetite sharpened by a pint in the pub. I was starving.

"You two look like you haven't eaten for a month," Mum said.

Tony and I looked up from our plates. We had wolfed down a tub of onion bhajis and were well into a pile of assorted curries and rice and had not exchanged a word.

"Sorry, very antisocial," Tony said. "What shall we talk about?"

"Don't let me get between a man and his stomach,"

Mum laughed, picking at a tandoori chicken leg, and we carried on in silence until we heard a crash outside the back door.

Tony's head bobbed up like a chubby meerkat. He was never off-duty.

"Those cats again," Mum said.

"Bloody big cat," Tony said, standing.

He went out through the kitchen, picking up the torch that hung by the back door. I followed him into the garden. The steel dustbin that stood by the back window had been knocked over, its contents strewn across the path. Tony shone the torch around, and then up the short garden path to where the back gate swung open. He traced the torch to the unplanted bed that ran across the back of the garden by the gate.

"Bloody big cat," he repeated, pointing the torch at the bed.

It took me a moment to focus, and then I saw, clearly outlined, the print of a very large foot.

Donnie limped along the alley, his ankle burning where he'd twisted it slipping off the wet dustbin on leather soles. He turned left, then right, checking behind to make sure he hadn't been followed, then turned on to the next street in search of the Balti house near the pub.

That curry had looked good, and he was starving.

FORTY-TWO

Tony was bothered by the idea that someone was spying on us.

Stoke-on-Trent had been chosen as a safe place for my mum to be once I'd first got into trouble in London. In case someone came for me. She'd lived there as a kid and liked it, and we all felt secure hidden away there, but this intrusion had rattled Tony's bars.

"You never told anyone about being up here, did you?" he asked me the next morning.

"No way," I said. "It's the last thing I'd do. It would be mad. Only Anna knew I was coming up here."

"And Sharpie?"

"Sure," I said. "But couldn't it have just been some random intruder...?"

"No such thing," Tony said. "There's always a reason. You should know that better than anyone."

Tony tapped away at his laptop all morning.

"We might have to move you again, love," he said to

my mum later, putting a protective arm around her.

"Oh, Tony, I've just about got used to it here," Mum sighed. "I've made a few friends. Got settled."

"I'm worried about your safety," Tony said. "Leave it with me. I'll make a few calls and see what's best."

"You're not doing very well at being off-duty, Tony," I said. I was kind of glad he was here and on the case. If I'd been here by myself, I think it would have made me very jumpy.

"You know me, mate." Tony picked up his laptop and headed upstairs to the spare room. "I'm going to shut myself away for a couple of hours, try and sort things out."

I felt agitated and couldn't settle. I tried reading for a bit, then sat and watched an old film on the TV with Mum. As keen as I was to lie low and relax, my body still seemed to crave adrenaline and excitement. It didn't take long for things to change again.

Tony came back downstairs. He looked pale and shell-shocked.

"You all right?" I asked.

"I've just had a call from Sandy Napier," he said. "I got the tin-tack. I've been sacked."

"*What?*"

"Immediate effect." Tony dumped himself on the sofa and put his head in his hands.

"They can't just sack you like that, Tony," I said. "What about the inquiry?"

"Found against. Someone's got it in for me, dobbed me in with a load of confidential stuff about IRA links."

217

"But there's nothing on you, is there?"

"Everyone's got *something* on them," he said. "Grey areas, areas of doubt, things done not quite by the rulebook. You know what it's like, mistakes are made."

"Like Paul Dolan giving us the slip?"

"Sure. The Met wouldn't let it drop. It was on my watch. Napier told me I'd have to fall on my sword." He shook his head in disbelief. "After twenty-five years."

I didn't know what to say. My first thoughts, I'm ashamed to admit, were for myself.

"What am I going to do?"

He looked up me, surprised.

"You? You're going to dig in, mate; pick up the pieces and carry on. The first thing you're going to do is copy all my stuff onto an external hard drive – sharpish, before they cut me loose and take everything away. If they want to find me, it won't take long. I'll give you what I can, what I know, stuff that even Anna and Sharpie don't know."

I plugged three terabytes of external hard drive into Tony's computer and he dragged and dropped files marked "secret", "confidential" and "high security". Names I'd heard, or half-heard, appeared on the files that were now transferred to me. There were dossiers of information on individuals and surveillance photos that went back a few years.

"Guard this stuff with your life, Eddie," Tony said. "It's taken years to accumulate, and as soon as I pass it back to the firm it will disappear. My life is on there, and some of yours. You have to stay a step ahead of the game. Put it in a safe deposit box at Manchester Airport.

218

Somewhere only you know. Even I mustn't know where it is."

"So what now?" I asked.

"As far as I'm concerned, I haven't seen you and you haven't seen me. Got it?"

I nodded. "Safer that way. So where are you going?"

"Well, I'm going to get your mum fixed up elsewhere for a while, then I'll have to go to London, hand in my badge and face the music."

"Can you appeal?" I asked.

"Sure. Could take a year, though."

"What do you want me to do next?"

"I thought that was obvious," he said. He fished in his briefcase and pulled out a printout of an airline booking. "Go to New York and finish the job."

FORTY-THREE

I checked into Bewley's Hotel: modern, slick, a shuttle ride from the airport. My flight was in the early hours, so I wanted to be on the spot and somewhere nobody knew about.

"Do you have safe deposit boxes?"

"We do," the head receptionist said. Crisp, camp, courteous.

"Can I see them? I'm going to the States for a couple of weeks…"

"It's not usual, sir. I can assure you that we are a hundred per cent secure."

"I know," I pleaded. "I'm just a bit OCD about this stuff, all my work's in there." I patted the leather laptop case I wanted to deposit.

The head receptionist raised an eyebrow and lifted the hatch in the front desk, allowing me through. I followed him down a strip-lit corridor, past staff changing rooms, distinctly scruffier than front of house. He unlocked the door to a bare, concrete-walled room. A row of silver-fronted boxes faced me.

"Our vault is Grade 8, tested in accordance with European Standard EN11-43. The strong room has passed the demanding explosives and core drill tests and therefore certified EX and CD. You see, you're not the only one who's OCD," he said.

"That'll do nicely," I said. "Thank you."

He unlocked and slid out a deposit box and I laid the laptop bag inside. It contained a few things that might have given me problems at airport security: some bugs, a knife, a small pistol. And an external hard drive that contained Tony Morris's whole life and career.

"That will be secure with us, Mr Kelly. Enjoy your stay and we look forward to your safe return. Have a good trip."

I had bad memories of Manchester Airport. The last time I was there, I had been stung at customs with half a kilo of cocaine, planted on me by a so-called mate. The memory made me sweat, but once the plane climbed and banked over the Irish Sea I felt better, and glad I was in the air rather than on the ground.

I woke up from a nap somewhere over the middle of the Atlantic, feeling a weird mixture of excitement and foreboding. I had always wanted to go to New York, and the idea that I might find Sophie there filled me with optimism. I started fantasizing about her running into my open arms, finding somewhere to live together; romantic visions of us walking along a beach. I conveniently ignored the idea that there might be a few obstacles in the way before I found her.

Seeing Tony had made me realize the truth of what I had suspected – that the organization always knew more than I did.

I half watched one of the Bourne films for the rest of the flight. Ridiculous, I thought, but the chase sequences were fantastic.

When I arrived at JFK, my excitement diminished as I stood in a queue waiting for a yellow cab. My phone buzzed with incoming texts from Sharpie.

Where are you? SS

Report in ASAP. SS

Call me. Now. SS

Can't get fix on yr phone. Where U? Are u OK?? SS

I decided to ignore them.

I was acting against everything I'd ever been trained to do, but Tony had been in no doubt that I was to go. Then again, Tony was not now officially on the firm, nor was he my case officer. I really should have checked in with Sharpie, and now, thousands of miles away, I began to panic that I'd done entirely the wrong thing.

Tony had not always been right in the past.

I sweated the problem as the cab I'd hired dodged along the expressway towards Manhattan.

I texted Tony.

Arr NY. SS mad & worried. Pls advise. KK

I sat back in the cab and waited for an answer as the towers and skyscrapers of New York City came closer and closer. I had never been to America, but the panorama was as familiar to me as the title sequence of *Friends*, as if I'd known it all my life.

During the flight, Tony had emailed me the address of a hotel, tucked away in Greenwich Village, which I was to make my temporary base until I found my feet. As we drove into the city, I felt dwarfed by the wide avenues, four lanes of cars flanked by towering blocks of buildings on either side. The idea of finding Sophie in all this began to feel even more remote.

We stopped in Waverley Place outside the Washington Square Hotel, a large brownstone built like a fortress, and I paid the cab. I felt relieved: it looked safe, and the reception staff were super-friendly and welcoming in the way only Americans can muster. Once I shut the heavy door of my second-floor room, I felt I could breathe again.

I sat on the bed and breathed deeply, then my phone buzzed with Tony's text.

Sit tight. Don't panic. Will talk to SS. Await instructions.

I read the text a few times and realized that once again I had bitten off more than I could chew, and once again my fate was in the lap of the gods. Or, at least, the lap of the people who controlled my life. I tried to overcome the feeling that the best thing I could do was get a cab back to JFK, get on a plane somewhere – anywhere – and disappear without a trace.

FORTY-FOUR

"New York, Dave," Donnie said. "New Bleeding York."

"What?"

"'Merica."

"I know it's in America, Don."

"I got up at the crack of a sparrow's fart to follow him to Manchester."

"Well done, Don, but if you hadn't, you wouldn't know where he was, would you? So you got a ticket?"

"Ticket for what?"

"New York, Don. New York."

"No, Dave. You're having a laugh. I never been to America."

"First time for everything, Don. It's only a few hours away. It's a bit like the Isle of Dogs, but bigger. Get a ticket and I'll dig about and ask a few questions. We know he's travelling as Kieran Kelly. I've got a bent official at Gatwick who does some bits for us. Shouldn't take long to find out where he is. They get the full SP at US immigration: where they're staying, how long, name of their mum's cat, the lot."

"No, Dave."

"Here's the deal, Don. You go, and I'll have a word with the guvnor and make sure you get a long holiday after. He's got a bit of evidence that Her Ladyship is alive and over there. You pull this off and it's early retirement for Donovan Mulvaney."

"I've heard that before, Dave," Donnie whined. But he chewed it over; the kid would do the work, he'd just have to follow. Once he'd found Sophie: bang. Job done. Deliver the girl into the safe hands of her father. A wave of chivalry rose in Donnie's chest as he thought about Sophie Kelly. The girl could do no wrong in his eyes. He remembered her beautiful face and old-fashioned, curvy figure. Nothing improper in his interest, he reminded himself, he just felt protective. Loved her, in his way.

"OK, Dave," he said finally.

"OK what, Don?"

"I'll do it, but here's the deal…"

"What are you thinking?"

"100 k and off the firm."

Dave laughed.

"I'll ask, Don. I'll put some money on your card. Just get that 'effing ticket and get out there."

Donnie had everything he needed with him: a platinum credit card and a fake passport. He was the type of bloke who could get tooled up anywhere in the world. People would just look at him and offer him weapons or nose candy. He realized that Dave had organized him with a bag so that he could hop on a plane anywhere. He had been manipulated, as before: nothing but a killer puppet for the firm, kept alive on booze and empty promises. He didn't feel at home in London any more; it had changed. He couldn't go back to Spain – every villain on the Costa had him marked – and he certainly wasn't happy here, "up north". He looked at the fake passport, the false name, fully stamped up US visa, valid for three years. He envisioned a bank account with 500 k stashed. One more job, and a picture of a life by the pool began to materialize. Donnie had heard Florida was nice...

He went to the American Airlines desk, where he had seen the kid check in.

Two hours later, after a Burger King and a couple of large vodkas to settle his pre-flight nerves, Donnie was in the departure lounge.

Donnie hated flying. Even when he'd done the two hours to Malaga he'd never wanted to set foot on a plane again. It was unnatural. He didn't like the take-off or the landing. He didn't like the bit in between, either, especially when it got turbulent and bumped along like an old holiday coach with shot springs.

Despite the drinks, Donnie had the jitters by the time he settled into his seat. Dave had said no to business class, and he found himself next to a plump, middle-aged American lady who smelled strongly of perfume. An airline seat was barely wide enough for Donnie at the best of times, but given a neighbour who looked fond of the Dunkin' Donuts diet, he found himself cramped.

"They never make these seats big enough," the lady said conversationally.

"No," Donnie said. She bustled up her handbag, newspaper and stack of novels in an effort to make room for Donnie, but in fact leaving less space than before.

"You English?" she asked.

Donnie grunted and shuffled meaty legs into the small area, trying to kick off his shoes.

"I love your country," the lady said.

"Stow it," Donnie huffed. He was in no mood for seven-odd hours of chat.

"Pardon me?"

"Put a sock in it," Donnie said, attempting to make the message clear. The lady looked absently for what needed stowing, and then at Donnie's feet.

"Your feet swell when you fly," she commented.

"Shut up," Donnie clarified.

The woman looked blankly at Donnie.

"You're just nervous," she said. "Don't worry, I'm a frequent flyer. You sit tight and relax. You'll be fine. I'm Marcie."

She patted Donnie's hand, and he was relieved when she opened a novel that looked like it would take six weeks to read.

Marcie kept her headphones on through dinner. Donnie ate microwaved sausage and mash, and after racking up a few miniature bottles of wine managed to nod off during a Bourne film, the headphones protecting him from any unwelcome intrusion.

Somewhere into the flight, Donnie was awakened by a chime as the cabin lights came on and an announcement came over his headphones.

"The captain has switched on the seatbelt sign. We are entering an area of turbulence. Please return to your seats and fasten your seatbelts."

Donnie blinked and looked around nervously, remembering where he was. Marcie, next to him, was already awake and belted. She helped Donnie wrestle his unhooked belt from under his legs. Donnie grunted his thanks and looked at the seat back *in front of him. He took deep breaths and tried to focus, suddenly feeling, as the plane hit the first bumps of turbulence, the watery-gut sensation that he never felt when confronted by a baseball-bat-wielding thug. As the bumps levelled he let out a long breath, but then he saw the flight attendants lock the trolleys into place and belt themselves into folding seats. He was sure he could see panic in their faces. If they were panicking, he thought, he should be shitting his whack. As the plane hit the next, deeper troughs of turbulence, he thought he would. His breathing quickened and his fists tightened on the arms of the seat, his knuckles whitening.*

"Don't worry," Marcie said. "These bad boys are designed to take this. I used to be a fearful flyer, I went on a course…"

His companion chattered on about air pressure and lift and resistance, stuff that Donnie didn't understand, but her soft American voice, which came deep from an abundance of chest and chin, strangely comforted him.

Then the plane dropped suddenly. It felt like free-fall on a fairground ride, hundreds of metres.

Donnie gasped and found himself clutching Marcie's hand.

"It's OK. It's OK," she said. "It's a pressure drop."

Donnie squeezed Marcie's hand tight, engulfing it in his massive paw. As the crockery rattled in the galleys and other flyers gasped, Donnie heard himself emit a whimper.

"We're experiencing an electrical storm," the voice came over the speakers. "No need to panic. We'll just be switching off the intercom for the moment and will come back to you as soon as it passes."

The communication cut-off had exactly the effect on Donnie that the air crew were attempting to avoid. His legs shook, trembling against those of his plump neighbour.

"It's OK," Marcie repeated like a mantra. "When things like this happen, we put our faith in the Lord Jesus Christ. What's your name?"

"Donnie," he told her.

"Well, Donnie," Marcie said. "If we believe in Jesus Christ, he will see us through times like these."

Donnie couldn't remember the last time he'd thought about God or Jesus or anything else beyond where the next feed, drink or job came from. He looked out of the cabin window into the darkness and saw lightning flashes momentarily illuminate the wing. He suddenly saw himself as small as an ant, powerless, being tossed around in a storm, trapped in a steel tube in the middle of the sky. He began to say his prayers.

FORTY-FIVE

"What the fuck do you think you're doing?" Sharpie's voice was crystal clear despite the distance between us. I didn't really have a good answer for him.

"Tony told me to come. Didn't he speak to you?" I asked. I was on the back foot.

"Maybe he did, for what it's worth. But Tony is not your case officer, Tony is not running this case. Tony's not even on the firm at the moment. Anyway, he told me quite categorically that he'd told you *not* to go."

"*What?*" I was thrown. Why would Tony give Sharpie a different version of the story? I decided not to pursue it for fear of getting in even deeper.

"Someone was on to me, up in Stoke," I said. "I'm sure of it. Thought it best to get away."

"So you should have come back to me while I decided what's best. You didn't tell me about anyone being on to you up there. Who do you think it was? Or are you just making up more lies to cover your tracks? Why aren't you keeping me in the loop? What are you up to? Where are you staying?"

"Tony told me not to…"

"Don't give me that!" Sharp shouted. "Where?"

I had been getting on OK with Sharpie, and I was grateful to him for coming to rescue me when he had. Now I felt that all his goodwill had evaporated. I had broken every rule in the book, and I felt bad about it. He had a point: I wasn't reporting back to him as much as I should. I felt cross that Tony had made a bad decision and landed me in it.

I told him the address of the hotel.

"Shall I come back?" I asked.

"You're there now," Sharp said. "Stay put while I decide. I may have to come over myself."

"What shall I do?"

"Nothing, until I tell you. Take in the sights for a couple of days."

"OK, I said. "Look, Sharpie, I'm really sorry, I know I'm out of order. I'll do what I can to make amends."

"That may be a disciplinary matter above my head," Sharp said. "You're a good agent, but you're a hot-headed little fucker."

"I'm sorry," I repeated, but he had rung off.

I felt chastised, but I had been trained to work on my own initiative. They didn't seem to mind me making my own decisions when I was out in the field, getting in up to my nuts with Irish gangsters. Then, when it suited them, they reined me in.

I sat on the hotel bed reviewing my case notes, licking

my wounds, looking for something to emerge to make sense of it all. Nothing did. It was about three o'clock. I had eaten a massive all-day American breakfast of crispy bacon, scrambled eggs, hash browns and endless refills of coffee several hours earlier and my stomach was still bloated. I was jumpy and agitated. I had been cooped up ever since I'd got here and was getting a little stir crazy. At least Sharpie's suggestion to go and see the sights gave me licence to stray outside, and a short walk around the park or the shops would be a welcome diversion.

I put on a clean shirt – a Ralph Lauren Oxford – and sailing shoes. I wouldn't stick out. I wasn't armed and had nothing to defend myself with, but I made sure I had money and my phone.

I was about to leave when I noticed a letter under my door. A hotel envelope, probably containing details of that night's menu or cleaning services, I thought. I opened it and found a handwritten note. The writing was poor, in looping capitals:

KIERAN – Fancy hooking up with an old friend while you're in town? You need one. Meet me for a beer at Kelly's bar, 12 Avenue A, East Village. 6 pm. You'll know me as Michael.

What the…?! I sat down again, my heart in my mouth. Read and reread the note. The tone was not threatening, but neither was it over-friendly. I didn't have any friends in New York, old or otherwise. "Old friend" was the kind of thing they said in *Doctor Who* or Sherlock Holmes stories.

Had Sharpie put someone on my case already? Fast work if he had.

I looked at the map. The East Village and Avenue A would only be about fifteen minutes' walk from the hotel.

Kelly's Bar. There had to be something in that.

I didn't want to go. Also, Simon Sharp had told me to wait for his word, so I decided I would follow his instructions.

Five minutes later I changed my mind, the old phrase "curiosity killed the cat" running through my mind.

I turned the corner into West 8th Street, magnetically drawn towards the East Village. I decided that I would check out Kelly's Bar. It would still be a good couple of hours before the suggested meeting.

I crossed Broadway, checked the map and walked across Astor Place and on to St Mark's Place, where the street became narrower and tree-lined. It felt a little safer, more like London in scale, and I continued until the junction with Avenue A.

There was a park opposite Tompkins Square. I walked in and strolled along the path under the trees, parallel to the street, until, across the road, I could see the arched door of Kelly's, complete with the green, white and orange Irish flag.

I decided to sit and wait.

By 5 p.m. I was bored stupid. I had seen few people come and go from the bar. I walked around the park, watched kids playing basketball and toyed with the idea of going back to the hotel, the butterflies in my stomach building. I was getting cold feet.

At 5.30 p.m. a few more punters started to go into Kelly's. I didn't recognize any of them. Then it occurred to me that if I was to arrive early and find myself a quiet corner, I might steal a march on my "old friend", whoever he might be. I could always work out an escape route if it went wrong.

I went across the road and, after checking the windows, pushed the central door open.

A large TV screen at the end of the bar played a silent baseball game. It was dark. Good. Squeezing between a couple of big men wearing baseball caps, I ordered a Bud.

I found a booth hidden in the shade of the bar and watched the door. Like someone in an old movie, I picked up a sports paper and pretended to read it, bringing it up to eye level when any new customer entered.

Ten minutes later, the door opened and I raised the paper again. I peeped over as the man scanned the bar and went to order a drink. Lit by the overhead lights, I recognized him. I now knew who my "old friend" was.

And I didn't like it one bit.

FORTY-SIX

The plane began its descent into New York.

Donnie had finally relinquished his grip on Marcie's hand, but she continued to pat his, resting on the seat arm, as the captain apologized for the turbulent flight and thanked them for flying with American Airlines. The sense of relief in the whole cabin was palpable. A bonhomie born of fear had struck up and engendered conversations and connections that would never otherwise have taken place. People chatted and exchanged phone numbers, all the while praising cabin staff for their calmness. Free drinks were circulated once the storm had passed, and Donnie had swallowed a large brandy with shaking hands and then drunk Marcie's, too.

The cabin staff had been attentive, helping Marcie calm Donnie, bringing him water as his body shook and sweated with fear and he struggled for breath. He seemed to have had some kind of crisis or panic attack. The biggest, scariest looking man on the flight had also been the most scared of dying.

"There we go," Marcie said. "Nearly there. I told you we would be fine."

"Thank you," was the best Donnie could muster.

"But Donnie, I get a strong feeling from you. A strong sense of sadness. I think you are a good man, but there have been many bad things in your life."

Donnie looked sideways at Marcie.

"Yeah?"

"I sense a loneliness, and I don't know why you're coming to New York, but I think you will be lonely here, and sad, too, unless you make some changes. You were so scared back there, so alone. I'm glad I was here for you. You need to make your peace with God and he will always be by your side."

Donnie considered.

"Will he?"

"He will." She grasped Donnie's hand again and looked at him. "I see a beautiful girl, maybe your daughter?"

"Donna?" Donnie never really considered his daughter beautiful. He couldn't see beyond the nose piercing and dyed black hair.

"Blonde."

Not Donna.

"And a young man, lonely, like you. Look after the girl, Donnie. Look after them both."

Donnie began to sweat again as he digested Marcie's words and felt the bump of the undercarriage lowering.

"Nearly over," she said, and seconds later they were on the runway.

Donnie helped Marcie down with her bags from the overhead locker. She took a card from her purse and handed it to him. It had pink edges.

Marcie Kahan
Life Coach

Donnie struggled to read the kooky font on the card. He tucked it into his top pocket.

"Don't you go losing that, Donnie," Marcie said, patting his chest. "My number's on the back, so if you're ever stuck in New York, or just need to talk, you know where I am."

Donnie muttered shame-faced thanks, then walked slowly along the walkway to passport control. He had barely been able to squeeze his shoes back on at the end of the flight; his feet had swollen, and they hurt. He heard a rumble behind him and quickened his pace, paranoid on foreign ground. The rumble came closer and he realized that it was the wheels of a case being pulled along. Another few seconds and Marcie Kahan was back at his side.

"Whoa, Donnie. Where did you get to?" she puffed. "I musta lost you back there."

She wittered on about dos and don'ts in New York, how much Donnie should tip a cab and the best place for a salt beef sandwich, until they reached immigration.

"I guess this is where we say our goodbyes," she said finally, joining the queue of US citizens and pointing Donnie at the sign that read Aliens. "I'd offer you a ride into the City, but my sister's collecting me and she only has a tiny Yaris."

"I'll be fine," Donnie assured her. "Thank you."

Marcie reached up on tip-toes and planted a lipsticky kiss on Donnie's cheek.

"Remember, Donnie, put your faith in the Lord." She patted his chest.

Donnie watched as his travelling companion waddled off to US passport control, dragging her wide load and her trolley case behind her. His shakiness was beginning to lessen, but, as he disappeared into the queue, he felt the unfamiliar catch in his throat again.

FORTY-SEVEN

The man at the bar was one of the last people I expected or wanted to see in New York, or anywhere else. He was dressed like a construction worker in a sweatshirt, worn jeans, boots and a Dodgers baseball cap. Dark-haired, black stubble. Looked hard as nails.

I slid back in my seat while he ordered, worked out my escape route. I was not going to hang around.

His back was still to me as I stood, and I decided that a straightforward walk to the door would attract the least attention.

Then he turned.

"Kieran?" he said, putting an arm out to stop me. "I'm Michael. It's been a while. I'll get you a drink, but I warn you, the Guinness is shite here."

He presented two bottles of Rolling Rock and pointed me back to where I had been sitting. We sat down.

"Cheers for coming," he said. "I thought the name of this bar would raise your curiosity."

"Curiosity killed the cat," I said. He smiled.

And I found myself clinking bottles with Paul Dolan.

"So how long have you been here?" He sounded exactly like his brother, Martin.

"Not long," I said, cagey as a schoolboy caught shoplifting.

"Anything interesting?"

"No," I said. "I've been cooped up in a hotel. Jet lag."

"Who knows you're there?"

"You do." I wasn't going to give a thing away.

"Tony Morris? What about your case officer?"

"How did *you* know?" I asked.

"I didn't get to where I am today by dishing up everything I know straight off the bat, did I?" He grinned and winked at me, just as he had on the marshes a couple of years back, the night he and Tommy got pulled in.

"Tony Morris? Sure," I said. "He sent me here."

Dolan clearly knew plenty. Pointless denying it. At least it would let him know I was protected. All the time I was talking my mind was racing, trying to work out whether it had been Tony or Sharp who had told Dolan where I was, and why. And, more importantly, whether or not I could trust him.

Dolan chuckled.

"If you take my advice, you'll move as soon as possible. If I can find you, then other people can. You know what it's like in this work, you stay still too long and you're a sitting duck."

"I don't know where else to go."

"I know a few places," he said. "Bet your case officer

told you to stay put as long as possible?"

I shrugged but didn't deny it.

"'Course he did," Dolan said. "They always want you where they can keep an eye on you. It's all about control. They want you in your place until they pull your strings and then you dance off into the next sticky situation. You're a puppet."

I had to agree. This man was nothing like the Irish thug I had seen working for the Kelly firm in London a couple of years before, the thug who was known for his expertise in kneecapping and extreme violence. This Dolan was affable, as warm as his brother Martin had been steely cold.

"You need to be your own man in this game, Kieran," Dolan said. "The feckers you're working for mess you about just as much as the ones you're working against."

His view chimed with my own and, against my better instincts, I felt myself warm to Paul Dolan.

"Listen, there's plenty of stuff I want to talk to you about," he said. "But not here. Let's finish our drinks and then we can go somewhere else. Somewhere quiet."

I checked myself. I was being suckered in by blarney charm. Somewhere quiet would probably mean a bullet in the back of the head in the park opposite; another statistic on New York's daily list of shootings.

"I'm OK here," I told him.

"Sure." He wasn't pushing it. "So how did you find your way to New York?"

"I got on the plane in Manchester and seven hours later, there it was."

"Didn't know you were a wise guy," he said.

"I'm not," I said.

"Listen, Kieran, there's not much I don't know about you. I know what you've been up to. I keep in touch. You were on a college course with my niece, Hannah. I know you managed to lure my brother out of hiding, which is a miracle St Anthony would have been proud of."

I wondered if he knew his brother's fate.

"I don't think I lured him," I said. "They just let me hang around Hannah long enough until her dad got funny about it…"

Dolan gave a humourless chuckle.

"Unfortunately the same guys who are after me got to Martin first."

"I'm sorry about that," I said. I'd seen the pictures.

"Well, that gives us something in common. We've both had brothers murdered by the same firm," he said flatly. "Probably by the same killer."

I looked at him, taken aback. He knew about my brother?

"Who do you think?"

"You know the big fecker? Tommy's hitman?"

"Donnie Mulvaney? Yes, I know him."

"He had a go at shooting you as well, didn't he, Eddie Savage?"

I walked around Tompkins Park with Paul Dolan.

I started to feel a little more sure he wasn't going to kill me. Just a little. We probably had similar motivation in terms of getting even with the Kelly firm.

"How did you know I was Eddie Savage?" I asked. "Did you recognize me?"

"You don't look that different," he said. "Your hair's different, or something."

I rolled up the sleeve of my polo shirt and showed him my harp tat. He laughed.

"Who made you get that?" He shook his head. "Every little wannabe Paddy gangster has one now, along with a Celtic band and a Claddagh ring. There was a time when that tat would have opened any door and put the fear of God up people. It means nothing any more."

"So how *did* you find me? How did you even know about me?"

"Tony," he said. "Tony Morris told me you needed someone to look after you."

"Now you're messing with my mind," I said. We sat down on a bench and Dolan tipped a Marlboro from a soft pack. "Tony didn't know where you were. They had you under surveillance when you got out of prison and you gave them the slip."

Dolan looked at me and raised an eyebrow.

"Tony's colleagues might not have known where I was, but Tony knows everything. He contacted me when he thought you'd had your chips."

"So *you* got me out?"

"I did. Tony pulled a big, fat favour on me and I contacted Martin and our IRA colleagues when they were holding you. It was a feckin' high-risk activity stepping in and getting you out."

Dolan took a long drag on his cigarette.

243

"So Martin didn't know you were working on Tony's behalf?"

"No way. I'd have been dead by now if he had. Now he can't know. Weird that my bro's death makes me a little safer."

He exhaled the last of his Marlboro and stamped it out.

"So you were in London all the time, when they thought you'd done a runner?"

"Sure I was. But the net was closing in. I had to get over here for one reason or another."

"My lot didn't want to bring you in, anyway," I said.

"I guess they didn't, but they didn't want Kelly to wipe me out on the mainland, either. That wouldn't have been useful to them. I was hiding from the Kelly firm more than anyone else."

"So what were you doing?"

"Gathering a bit of information. And counter-intelligence stuff, like sending Tommy Kelly postcards from here and there from his daughter to crank him up."

"That was you? Why would you do that?"

"Because Tony Morris told me to."

I started to feel uncomfortable, my vision of Tony altering as he spoke. Suspicions rose in my mind: wrong leads that Tony had given me; information slipping into the wrong hands; Tony turning up at my mum's. Coincidences.

Tony being suspended.

"Why do you do what Tony tells you to?" I asked, knowing full well that when Tony said jump, I jumped.

"Because I work for him," Dolan said.

FORTY-EIGHT

"Tony Morris is one of the most manipulative, conniving, cold-hearted bastards to walk this planet," Dolan told me.

As it got dark, we had walked back into the East Village and found a small, quiet Italian for a plate of pasta and meatballs.

"He twists, he turns, he lies, he slips under the wire. He deals with killers and pitches killers against killers, and doesn't mind too much who gets caught in the crossfire. Yet if he walked in here now, you'd never even notice him; he's like a shadow."

Some of Dolan's description rang true, but this hinted at hidden depths that put Tony in a different league. If what Dolan said was right.

I had to keep reminding myself that I was eating meatballs with a proven IRA killer and not just a sociable Irishman who knew a worrying amount about me.

"But you *work* for him? Like I do?"

"I owe him my life. And Martin's ... until just now."

"How?"

Paul Dolan looked around. There were only a couple of tables eating, out of earshot from us.

"Imagine two young men, not unlike yourself, full of fight and energy, and put them into what they see as an unfair political situation. Me and Martin were very active in the nineties."

"IRA?"

"Sure. It's in our blood. Even my great-granddad fought in the twenties. He was there with Michael Collins in 1916, so we'd hear all the tales growing up. It came natural to us."

I could hear the start of a long, Irish story about to unfold. I cut in.

"So where does Tony fit into this? I know he was in Ireland in the army, then intelligence."

"Well, Martin and me were involved in a plot to blow up King's Cross Station in London, mid-nineties. It was to be our big showdown: we didn't care how many would be killed. I would have been about your age, a wild kid, fucking and fighting. Martin was twenty-two, more serious. We were passionate, wanted to earn our stripes. We wanted to bring London down to show them how serious we were, that they couldn't just gloss over the Troubles with a few feckin' mealy-mouthed politician's words.

"There was this guy who'd been drafted in to help us, Michael O'Neill, from London. He was an expert bombmaker, been in the army, had worked for London Transport and knew London and the Underground system inside out. We didn't; we were in Belfast making plenty noise

246

and not much action. O'Neill's bona fides were good: Irish family living in Kilburn, he'd been sanctioned by Martin McGuinness and Gerry Adams themselves. God knows how. Well-placed British intelligence, I guess.

"Mikey O'Neill came up with a fantastic plan that four well-placed bombs would fuck up every single underground line. Feckin' genius. The ones who weren't killed at King's Cross would have been suffocated in tunnels or crushed as tube trains tried to evacuate hundreds of metres below the streets. Then there would have been gridlock on the roads, and other, smaller bombs at key points from Covent Garden to the City would have killed more and brought all of London's transport system to a standstill. It would have been Armageddon, IRA-style."

"So, Michael O'Neill," I vaguely remembered the name, "was Tony?"

"Right, Sherlock. He was good; really good. We were all a few years younger than him and he spoke like a leader. It was an amazing plan and he blindsided us with it. He got us excited – so excited we got whipped up by the size of the enterprise. We chatted about it to one another when he wasn't there, got drunk, spoke to too many people, impassioned that this was going to be our war to end all wars and that after that, the British government would roll over once and for all."

"What went wrong?"

"Like I say, as our enthusiasm took hold, too many people knew. We played into his hands. As you'll know, when too many people know something, there will be a leak. A couple of things started to filter through to

London. All the Paddies from Lewisham to Cricklewood wanted in. So Mikey O'Neill, Tony, calls a meeting in the back room of a great big beer hall way out in the country in Omagh and reads us the riot act. Stands there with the IRA beret on and all. Tells us that if we're blabbing, this is never going to come off and we're to shut the feck up and report only to him. And anyone found talking will be severely punished. So we did. Reported every movement, via him, straight to anti-terrorism intelligence in London. Or what he chose to tell them."

"So he gathered all the information to himself."

"Sure he did. Like I said, he's a manipulative bastard. What information he kept to himself gave him leverage over us and his bosses. Hundreds of names and addresses. Some would even admit to previous bombs, murders and punishments to show him they were man enough for the job."

"Took some balls," I said. "A lone Brit, making the IRA report back to him."

"I never said Tony Morris doesn't have bollix," Dolan said. "Nuts like bastard watermelons. But cold, like I said."

"Tony?"

Dolan laughed. "He worked like a feckin' Nazi. He'd raise suspicion among us that so-and-so was talking, so they'd be taken out and given a hiding as an example to the rest of us."

Tony had hinted as much to me.

"Punishment squads?"

"Yeah. Trouble was, my old man was in charge of punishments."

"What was his name?"

"Padraigh Lynch. That's the family name. I've changed it once or twice. Da was a very instinctive guy, he'd been on the front line for most of his life. He began to have his suspicions about this London Irish bloke calling all the shots. We were kneecapping guys I'd known all my life, played football with as a kid."

"So what happened?"

Dolan took a sip of beer, looked upwards as if recalling a bad memory. Breathed out.

"My old man goes to Michael O'Neill, Tony, and tells him we can't keep beating up our own or there'll be none of us left. O'Neill tells him we have to weed out the blabbermouths if we want this thing to come off."

"And?"

"So, Mikey O'Neill calls my da a couple of days later, says he has an informer and to make sure me and Martin are there to see the job's done properly.

"We turn up at the farm, just outside Newry. There's a couple of cars there outside the abattoir where they kill the pigs and cattle. Mikey O'Neill's driven up outside and he's got this eejit kid, Christie McCarthy, bound and gagged in the boot."

The scene was familiar to me. I could picture it, just as I had been dragged from a car to a warehouse, and it made my neck prickle.

"Da's standing there, looking none too pleased. 'This isn't right, lads,' he says. 'The kid's a feckin tool.'

"'A tool who can scupper this whole operation,' your man Mikey says. 'Take him inside and hang him up.'

"So Mikey instructs me and Martin to get the kid out of the boot. He's about nineteen, but simple, acts like twelve, and we drag him in. I can still see his eyes begging me to let him free, let him know what's going on. But Mikey's having none of it. He bullies it through, showing my old man the charge sheet; that Christie's been talking about how he's going to blow up London and the Queen.

"So we hang Christie up with chains around his ankles and he's crying, and Mikey says to me, 'What are you waiting for?', and I say no. Then Mikey gets cross and says he thought we were men with a cause, and if we can't deal with an informer, how are we going to blow up feckin' London? And Christie's squealin' like a pig, he sounds pathetic, crying like a baby.

"Then Martin loses it; starts whacking Christie on the legs with a lump of wood, shouting, 'Christie, admit it, get it over with,' and Christie's screaming, not knowing what he's admitting to…"

Dolan was silent for a moment.

"I don't know if it's some kind of bloodlust, or whether I'm trying to get it over for the kid, who's screaming the place down, but suddenly I'm whacking his shins and body with an iron bar."

He looked down at his plate, continuing quietly.

"Eventually, we run out of steam and his body's there, twitching, tortured and we see his shattered legs, teeth gone from his mouth, burns on his body. And your man, Mikey – Tony – says, 'This will be a lesson to all of them.' Like he didn't want to lose any proper men, but it was OK to sacrifice Christie. Then he says to my da, 'Finish him

Kent Libraries,
Registration and Archives
www.kent.gov.uk/libraries
Tel: 03000 41 31 31

Borrowed Items 13/02/2020 14:40
XXXXXXX7217

Item Title	Due Date
* Shadow box	05/03/2020
City of bones	22/02/2020

* Indicates items borrowed today

Thank you for using self service

off, Padraigh.' And my da's crying now, holding a gun to the back of Christie's head, and he puts him to rest with two shots."

I shook my head and drank a glass of water. It was hard to hear. Things I could not bear to believe about Tony.

"So we bury the body in the country, and Mikey goes back to Belfast. Then at three in the morning, me and Martin are dragged from our beds, blindfolded and beaten, and at seven we find ourselves in an interview room somewhere in Belfast with Mikey – Tony Morris – sitting the other side of the desk with some plainclothes men."

"What did he do?"

"Acts like he's never seen us before. Tells us there's been a simultaneous round-up of all bomb suspects in London and Northern Ireland, names and addresses we'd all given him. Tells me and Martin that as we're the ring-leaders we'll get the worst of it, spreads in front of us evidence of bomb plans, secret camera pictures of Christie being killed, and asks us what we want to do. Stitches us right up and has us by the bollix."

"What were the options?"

"He had enough for four life sentences each. And another for circumstantial evidence of killing Christie, the eejit kid. It didn't look good. It still haunts me. We'd have never seen the light of day again. Or we could do a deal: continue as we were, as fully signed up members of the IRA who'd slipped off the hook, but at his mercy. He could get us shot or pull us in at any moment to do the time unless we fed him information. He guaranteed he'd keep his sources secret; he didn't want every clerk in intelligence knowing where he got his information. I chose to have a life, if not exactly freedom, and so did Martin, until recently. Our secret was safe with each other."

"So you became informers?"

"Up to a point. Like I say, you have to play your own game, but we had to be careful or he could have handed us back to the IRA as informers working with him, which would have been worse than the peelers. We were stuffed. Then, a couple of years ago, Martin couldn't take it any more. He cut ties with Tony and went off the radar."

"So he went AWOL and Tony put you inside the Kelly organization?"

Dolan nodded. "Same deal, making the Irish link with Tommy through The Harp. And we fucked Kelly over, with a little help from you."

"You still had to do time after that, though," I said.

"It was welcome, to be honest. It had to look good. I only got the conspiracy to pervert justice charge, so I took the rap. In fact, I'd never felt more relaxed – fifteen months in an open prison, reading books and playing pool. Most of my prison mates were pretty civilized, City fraudsters and the like. I learned a lot. And Tommy Kelly wasn't going to get to me in that kind of jail."

Dolan had finished his food. Mine remained uneaten, my stomach churning with horror and uncertainty.

"So that's your Tony Morris for you. He's the hardest, coldest bastard alive, but, I have to say, true to his word. That's why I'm here, and that's why Martin's dead. You don't need to see me again and I don't need to see you, but if you do need me, I'm duty bound to help, if you see what I mean."

He called for the bill and wrote a number on a napkin.

"Don't put this in your phone, for Jesus' sake. Keep it safe. I have a few other things to do for Tony, and if any of it affects you, I'll let you know. But take my advice and change hotels until your case officer arrives. There's one on the other side of Waverley Place where you can keep a lookout for him, and he can call you when he gets here."

Dolan wrote the name of the hotel on the napkin and handed it to me.

"Be safe," he said. "But be your own man, or they'll yank your bollix in all directions."

We shook hands as we parted, and I walked back through the East Village, my mind working overtime about what exactly Tony's game was. Neither Napier nor anyone else knew anything about his off-record dealings, as far as I knew. He always acted the innocent in front of Napier. After all, he had been suspended for letting Dolan give him the slip, but now it looked like he had done so deliberately.

I got back to the Washington Square Hotel and told them I'd be checking out in the morning.

FORTY-NINE

"Welcome to New York, Mr Maloney."

The information on the screen obviously added up.

"There are some papers here, which you will have to fill in when you get to your hotel." The official looked at Donnie without a trace of intrigue or suspicion; they spent their days stonewalling immigrants, making even tourists feel paranoid about entering America. Donnie found that the wheels for his entry into New York had clearly been oiled somewhere back down the line.

"Have a good day."

Donnie nodded and took the brown envelope, stepped outside and hailed a yellow taxi into the city. He wasn't interested in landscapes or the stunning displays of modernist architecture as Manhattan came into view. Dave was right, it looked pretty much like the Isle of Dogs and Canary Wharf. He studied the contents of the envelope, reading slowly, following with his finger: the address of a hotel; the place on Canal Street where he could pick up a weapon; some dollars in cash. He always *admired Dave's neat ability to organize things from afar. Made him feel secure.*

According to Dave's information from his contacts in immigration, the Washington Square Hotel was where the kid was staying, so Donnie had been booked into one across Waverley Place so he could keep an eye open without being too close for comfort.

I checked in across the road at ten.

The Waverley Hotel wasn't as good as the Washington Square, but I took Dolan's advice, for better or worse. Too many people already knew I was at the Washington Square, so better to keep on my toes, even on Dolan's recommendation. I couldn't see a reason for him to turn me over. He was, after all, doing a favour for Tony.

I had hardly slept through the night, turning over the new information Dolan had told me about him. Going through it detail by detail. Dolan's story horrified me, but it stacked up; it began to help me fill in some of the gaps about Tony. I had become more and more aware that he kept plenty of information to himself and let it out as and when it was an advantage to him. I thought back to the cases where he had thrown me in at the deep end, being economical with the truth about what exactly I was up against. It had happened again recently, sending me after Hannah, knowing where it would lead, and now I knew he'd had one – if not two – senior IRA men on his payroll all that time.

Now Tony had been suspended and sacked for not

255

keeping tabs on Dolan, who as it turned out was in his pocket all the time. I tried to work out Tony's agenda. Maybe someone was on to him? Perhaps his time was up. I wanted to call him, to hear his calm voice gloss things over, but with the image of a broken Irish boy in chains fresh in my mind, the last thing I would do was ring Tony. He was always close to my mum, but I didn't even know when they'd met – never questioned it. He'd been part of the family, but then had been my brother Steve's case officer – and look where Steve ended up.

I wanted reassurance and back-up, and I wasn't going to get it from Tony Morris.

I texted Sharpie.

Are you coming over to NY?

I waited half an hour for a reply, chewing things over again and again. I was in a bit of a deadlock until Sharpie told me what to do. I had seriously disobeyed him once and couldn't do it again. With my growing doubts about Tony, I knew I should have listened to Sharpie in the first place; he clearly knew more about what was going on with Tony than I did.

Be there tomorrow eve. New intel. Sit tight at Washington Sq until I arrive. SS

His text calmed me a little. I would wait, and change back to the Washington Square Hotel when he got here. I might have a bit of time to look for Sophie.

I decided to take a walk uptown. The Museum of Modern Art was not too far away and would be somewhere to kill a bit of time. I took the lift down to reception and walked across the hall. I didn't register the big man sitting with a beer at first – he was turned three-quarters away from me – but a sixth sense kicked in and I looked back and clocked Donnie Mulvaney. He glanced up, but I was sure he hadn't seen me; I looked like just another American college kid. I pushed through the revolving doors as quickly as I could, showing him only the back of my head.

I walked briskly up the street, turned a corner and stopped dead, letting out a breath I realized I had been holding since I left the hotel. My heart was thumping. What on earth was Mulvaney doing in New York? In the same hotel!

First Paul Dolan, now this. No coincidence.

I couldn't go back while he was sitting there. That gorilla had dogged my life for two years now. Everywhere I turned, Donnie Mulvaney was there, like a massive black shadow looming over me. What if he found my room and broke in? All my stuff was there: laptop, memory sticks, passport. A theft would scupper me.

Only Dolan knew I was there; he could easily have set me up and then sent Donnie Mulvaney round.

I panicked again, thinking that I should just have followed Sharpie's orders, stayed in the UK till he was ready.

Donnie Mulvaney in my hotel! Help! KK

He texted straight back.

Keep your head down. Keep calm. Will contact on my arrival. SS

I paced about a while longer, my plans for the day taking a back seat, and decided that somehow I had to go back to Waverley Place and get my stuff before anyone else got to it. I walked round the block and approached the hotel from the opposite direction, glancing in through the distortion of the revolving doors to see Donnie Mulvaney still sitting there, reading a paper.

I went round the back and climbed up the fire escape to the floor my room was on. From there I stepped out onto a window sill and, balancing on one foot, one hand holding the fire escape, smashed a window pane with my other heel. It made little noise above the whir of the air conditioning units that stuck out from the rear of the building. I picked out the remaining shards of glass from the window frame and squeezed myself through the gap. Dropping down into a laundry room, I found that a stray sliver of glass had sliced through my shirt into my forearm. Hot drips of bright blood fell onto the pile of dirty sheets at my feet, staining like rotten windfall cherries. I was creating a forensic nightmare for myself. I ripped up a pillowcase and bound my arm as tightly as I could, eager not to leave a bloodstain trail to my room. I pushed open the laundry room door gently and checked the corridor. No one. I slipped out and, holding my arm close to my body, found my room, swiped the room key silently and crept in.

The room was undisturbed, as I'd left it an hour before. I went to the bathroom and pulled off my shirt. The cut was quite deep and the sink filled red as I washed it under the tap. I looked at the cigarette burn scar – combined with my latest injury, I was beginning to look like a self-harmer. I dried my arm and covered it with a wad of toilet roll before binding it tightly again with a strip of pillowcase. I couldn't hang around. I put on another shirt and a jacket and bundled the bloodstained one into a carrier bag. I didn't want to leave more DNA around than I already had. I packed my bag and laptop and went to the door.

There was an envelope that must have been pushed into the corner as I'd come in through the door. I opened it and found a message like before:

> KIERAN – *this will interest you. Le Bernardin restaurant, 155 West 51st Street, 8.30 p.m.*
> *Proceed with extreme caution,*
> *Michael*

I folded it and put it in my pocket. No time to think about it now.

FIFTY

I made my exit back through the laundry room and cut around the block away from the hotel, taking the long way round Waverley Place. My arm was beginning to throb; God knows what New York grime and germs had entered the gash. I might morph into a cockroach. I felt pretty much like one of New York's ever-present roaches, scuttling through back alleys and windows. Even in the smarter places there were always one or two of the indestructible insects scuttling around the toilets.

No wonder I identified with them.

I found a drugstore, bought antiseptic, bandages, Band Aids and superglue, and headed to the Washington Square Hotel.

I went up to the reception desk.

"Mr Kelly," the receptionist said, surprised. "Good to see you back. Did you forget something?"

"No, I'd like to check back in, please. The new place didn't suit me."

He tapped the keyboard, raising his eyebrows and pulling his gilt-buttoned blazer cuffs as if he knew nothing else was going to match up to this hotel.

"Same room?"

"No, a different one, please. Something quiet. I haven't been sleeping well."

"We have a double on the sixth floor, tucked right away at the end of the corridor, no elevator or doors near by."

"Sounds good," I said. "I'll take it." I was eager to get a room as soon as I could. I could feel my arm pulsing and checked my jacket for seeping blood.

"We still have your credit card on record. OK if we use that?"

I nodded.

"Oh, a gentleman was looking for you earlier."

"Who?" I asked.

He spoke to the woman next to him. She leant over.

"English guy, very big." She made herself look large by pulling her shoulders up and widening her arms. "Half an hour ago. Said he was an old friend. I told him you'd checked out."

"Thanks," I said, gulping down fear. Another "old friend". I think I knew who this one was. "If he comes back, I'm still not here," I said. I winked as if I was simply being cheeky about someone I wished to avoid. Actually, I was shitting hot conkers at the idea that Donnie had come to pay me a visit. My temporary hotel switch had been lucky. I hoped it might temporarily put him off my scent.

"Sure." She winked back.

I went up to the room on the sixth, threw my bags down and headed straight for the bathroom. The blood was beginning to seep through my makeshift bandage. I untied it and peeled the toilet roll off. The cut was becoming sticky and dark. I dabbed at it with antiseptic; it stung like hell, but I had to do something to fix it. I couldn't risk hospital. I patted it as dry as possible, undid the superglue with my teeth, and applied spots of adhesive along the edges of the gash.

The sting of the disinfectant was nettle rash compared to the burning of glue on raw flesh. I held my breath and squeezed the edges of the cut together. The glue bonded the skin instantly, like chemical stitches. Once it had fixed, I taped it over with a layer of Band Aid, then wound the bandage over the length of the wound.

It hurt like shit, but I was getting used to pain.

I lay down on the bed. It had been quite a morning.

Dave, hes checked out. What necks? D.

Don, sit tight. Will advise.

Wen Dave? Im 6s and 7s. D.

Have u sorted shooter?

No. Necks job on list.

Get on it. Could need soon.

Wil sort it. Hows the dog Pam.

Don. Assume you mean dog and Pam.

All good, but Brandy at vets for worms yesterday.

Tool up and keep em peeled. D.

Wil do. Going down Canal Street now. Arthur Ritus.

Donnie left the hotel and got a cab to an address on Canal Street. It was time to arm himself.

I woke up at 6 p.m. My arm was throbbing, but the bleeding had stopped. I got up and swallowed some paracetamol with a Coke, switched the telly on and looked again at the note from Dolan. It was a trap, whichever way I looked at it. Either I was going to walk into the barrel of a gun or, if the intel was well meant, I would be getting deeper into some form of trouble.

None of this was helping me find Sophie.

On the other hand, I considered, while Sharpie wasn't here, I might gather useful intel that would get me back in the good books. I could make use of my pre-emptive arrival in New York.

I cracked open a beer, ate a bag of complimentary pretzels and watched the early evening news. It was only about New York, as if the rest of the world didn't matter. I hummed and hahed about what to do. I looked at my watch: 7.30 p.m. I couldn't stay in all evening. I showered, put on a smart jacket and was outside on the street by 8.00 p.m.

At 8.10 p.m. I was in a cab heading towards 51st Street, wondering what the hell I was doing.

FIFTY-ONE

Le Bernardin was uber-swanky. No two ways. Red rope, doormen who looked like extras from a Batman movie. The cab driver had told me it was one of New York's top five restaurants and he hoped my credit card would stand it. Did I work on Wall Street or something?

I told him I wouldn't be eating there. I would probably have a burger in a nearby diner and watch.

I jumped out of the cab behind a queue of fat-cat limos that idled outside the modern glass and steel canopy of the restaurant. I kept a distance as the limousines deposited their rich contents onto the sidewalk. I didn't recognize anyone; they were a mixed clientele in terms of age, but the thing they had in common was that they all looked like they could afford dinner there. I watched for a couple of minutes until a doorman noticed me, so I crossed the road and looked on from the other side.

I waited until just after 8.30 p.m. and saw nothing out of the ordinary. I didn't want to hang around too long for fear of being conspicuous, so I wandered further up 51st Street and found a Belgian bar. I ordered a Leffe and sat at the bar flipping the beer mat, wondering what to do next. I was still curious as to why I had been tipped off to go to Le Bernardin – nothing dramatic seemed to be going on there.

Three-quarters through my beer, I got antsy again. I was just wasting my time. I resolved to go back downtown and get something to eat. But once I was back on the street, I couldn't resist another look at Le Bernardin and approached it from the other side. As I began to walk past, I caught the eye of the doorman who had seen me earlier.

"Hi," I said.

"Good evening, sir."

"I'm waiting for a date. She's half an hour late – can I wait inside?"

I peeled a twenty from my back pocket and he opened the door for me. In New York, money talks. For all he knew I might have been Justin Timberlake.

"Do you have a reservation?" The waitress's accent was French, she was very good-looking and a little snotty.

"I don't. I was waiting for a friend, who's late. Will you have something free in half an hour or so?"

She ran a long finger down the bookings sheet.

"Your name?"

"Kelly," I said, sounding very English. She looked at me and back at the sheet. Cracked a half-smile.

"I think so," she said. "Just for two?"

I nodded.

"In about twenty minutes. Perhaps you would like a drink at the bar?"

"Sure," I said. "Thanks."

I ordered a Bloody Mary, hot and spicy, almost a meal in itself. The price tag would have bought dinner in most other places. From the bar, I could get glimpses into the dining area. It was incredibly sleek, with sculptured walls, crisp white linen on the tables, leather-and-chrome chairs. It reminded me of an ocean liner from the 1930s. The lighting was subtle and golden, and the waiters drifted silently in starched, Chairman Mao jackets. My eyes followed them as they carried dishes of precise-looking food to tables. Quantity clearly wasn't their selling point. Everything filled about a quarter of each plate.

From my vantage point I could see between two pillars while keeping myself well concealed. I followed the journey of another waiter to a table and saw him deliver a dish to a glamorous-looking blonde woman, middle-aged and well preserved. I recognized her instantly and realized the reason for the tip-off.

It was Cheryl Kelly.

Tommy's wife had been missing for as long as her daughter, Sophie. I hadn't seen Cheryl since I'd been Sophie's boyfriend in London almost two years before. She hadn't changed. Her hair looked good, and she was always well dressed in subtle, expensive colours. I looked again, to make sure.

I was absolutely certain when Alexei Bashmakov joined her. The Russian businessman was bald and tanned. He kissed her on the cheek, hugged her and snapped his fingers for drinks; he looked as if he'd had a few already.

Cheryl accepted champagne and drank, raising her glass to the person sitting opposite. With my gaze fixed on Cheryl and Bashmakov, I had barely noticed another presence at the table.

The third person leant over as the Russian filled his glass. The back of his head seemed familiar as he leant into the light, but it wasn't until he raised his glass in turn to the other two that I thought I recognized him, too. I took out my phone, as if texting, and took as good a picture as I could without drawing attention to myself.

Then I left, sharpish.

FIFTY-TWO

"Anna, it's me."

"I know it's you." Her voice sounded sleepy and husky on the other end of the line. Sexy. "It's three in the morning. This'd better be good."

"I'm sorry. It is. There's been a bit of a development. When's Sharpie coming over?"

"Er, I think he's leaving today. Should be with you by the evening."

"Do you know where he is now? I've been trying to get hold of him."

"As far as I know he's up in Beaconsfield. He's been there for a couple of days, he'll be coming straight from there to New York via Heathrow."

"OK," I said.

"So what developments?" she asked.

"I guess I should report straight to Sharpie," I said.

"Really? Get back in his good books?"

268

"But," I couldn't resist, "I think I've tracked down Cheryl Kelly."

I had raced back to Washington Square after making my excuses at Le Bernardin. I couldn't speak on the street, and waited for the security of my room before making my call.

I was both excited and anxious about my discovery. To find Cheryl and Bashmakov together was quite something. I was sure Tommy Kelly knew nothing about it, especially if Bashmakov, ugly as he was, was muscling in on Tommy's wife as well as his business.

The third person at the table confused me – if it was who I thought it was. And it would need some careful thought and delicate handling. I would have to wait till tomorrow to work out what to do.

Donnie had got lucky.

He'd arrived back from Canal Street at around six with the 9 mm: a calibre big enough to make a nasty mess and ensure a kill. He felt happier with a firearm on his hip. He had showered and gone out for a steak and a couple of beers and was beginning to like New York a little better. The portions were massive. For lunch he'd had a sandwich, something called a sub, with enough cheese and ham to feed a family for a week. His steak and chips that evening had brought him to a near standstill, but he'd ploughed on through to the end.

He'd walked back from Greenwich Village about ten and stopped in the square for a fag before going back to the hotel. Then he'd spotted the kid.

He texted Dave.

Found kid. Hes gon back to Washinton Sq mate

He momentarily forgot that his incoming text might wake Pam and set Brandy off. Dave would get his ear chewed. Donnie chuckled to himself, then went back into the square for another fag before finding himself a large Jack Daniel's to celebrate.

FIFTY-THREE

Arr NY 5pm your time. Meet Wash Sq hotel 6.30. SS

Sharpie's text woke me up the following morning. I
stared at it. I really couldn't begin to act on what I'd seen
until he arrived. My arm was still sore, but I changed
the dressing and it didn't look too angry. My superglue
stitches had held up. I was eager to get on with looking
for Sophie, but thought it wiser for various reasons to
wait for Sharp's nod – and besides, I was worried about
running into Donnie Mulvaney.

I had a big breakfast in a diner, then found my way
up to the Museum of Modern Art. I found myself drawn
to the American abstract expressionists Rothko and de
Kooning, whose massive, savage portraits of women
were brutally splayed on the white walls. I remembered that my mentor in discovering this work had been
Tommy Kelly himself. His connoisseur's eye had shown
me a way of looking at things that revealed meaning: art
that expressed the darkness and savagery of the human

271

soul, thinly concealed by a layer of civilization.

Afterwards, I drifted back to Central Park, walking, sitting, people-watching. In the back of my mind I kept thinking I might coincidentally bump into Sophie. Of course, I didn't.

I had a late lunch at McDonald's then went back to the hotel to wait for Sharp. My story was that I'd stayed here and kept my head down until his arrival, which, of course, I hadn't. It was easier to be economical with the information I had gathered. Should I even tell him about Paul Dolan? Given that Dolan was Tony's contact, probably not.

I went down to the bar at 6.30 p.m. and ordered a drink. Sharp turned up at 6.45 with his suitcase and checked in.

I got him a beer and he joined me at the table.

"Good flight?" I asked.

"Not bad. Got a bit of kip." He looked fresh as a daisy. He glanced at his watch. "Not bad for time."

I sat quietly. I wanted him to give. Sometimes a silence can force a gush of information to fill the gaps.

"So," he said, breaking it. "Mulvaney, eh? Where did you see him?"

"He was in a hotel just across the square."

"Big coincidence." Sharp laughed dryly. "Of all the hotels in all the towns in all the world…"

"On the same *square*?" I said. "I don't believe in coincidences. Why might he be here? On Tommy Kelly's say-so?"

Knowing what I knew about Cheryl being in town, I decided to push a bit.

"I have some good news on that front," Sharpie said.

"Tommy Kelly's appeal has fallen through. It's almost general knowledge that he was behind the shooting of the Russian diplomat Komorov and Martin Connolly. He overplayed his hand. The Russian Embassy has kicked up one hell of a stink that's going to keep Tommy behind bars for quite a bit longer."

"He'll be pleased."

"He's livid. He moved too fast, got cocky. A bit like you. That's when people come unstuck."

Sharp took a sip of his drink, looking at me over the rim of his glass. I took the criticism.

"We get on OK, don't we?" he said.

"Sure," I said. We did; it was only when I disobeyed his orders that we didn't.

"There's nothing we can do out here, but when you get back, there will be some kind of disciplinary proceedings. I wanted to let it go, but Napier said these things have to be observed. After the trouble he's had over Tony, he's doing everything by the book. I think we're going to send you back home. With Tommy safely inside a bit longer, finding his daughter is not such a priority."

The idea made me nervous. I didn't love being in NY, but I felt I was on to something big. It had become more than a job for me, and finding Sophie was a personal mission but one that seemed to be frustrated at every turn.

"Don't send me back now I'm here, Sharpie. You said you've got new leads."

"Not to be discussed here," Sharp said. "Let's have something to eat and then I'm going to have an early night. I have to get busy tomorrow."

273

We ate sushi in a Japanese in the village. After tempura and some warm sake, Sharp went into his more relaxed, chatty mode.

The one where he tries to pry a bit.

"So anything else you've noticed over here?"

"No," I lied. I was sulky. "You told me to stay put, so I did. I've been bored shitless."

"Maybe best you go back, then. There's nothing I can't handle here."

"I don't really know what you *are* doing here, Sharpie. I was just here to look for Sophie, with Tommy Kelly and Tony's encouragement."

"The less we say about Tony at the moment, the better. He's given you some bum steers which have landed you in the shit and mucked up my operation. I can't give you details, but there is a big arms deal going on between the Russians and the IRA."

"Why am I not surprised?"

"This is major: it's not just arms, it's drugs, prostitution, people-trafficking, the lot. And Tommy getting Connolly *and* Komorov shot has really upset the applecart. If I were him I wouldn't want to be out of prison. Now the Russians and the Irish are blaming each other for security leaks, like how Tommy Kelly knew where Connolly and Komorov were meeting. They were on the brink of pulling it all together when the deal brokers got blown away. So now the big bosses are getting shirty, things will move fast."

"Bashmakov?" I suggested.

"Probably," he said. "Bashmakov may be involved; in

fact it's very likely. But we don't even know where he is."

I took a sip of my drink to cover the look on my face.

I imagined that Sharpie knew *exactly* where Bashma-kov was.

FIFTY-FOUR

"I've spoken to Sandy Napier," Sharpie said. We were eating breakfast in the hotel the next morning: crispy bacon and maple syrup on waffles. "He's agreed to send you home."

"No!" I said.

"Afraid so. If Mulvaney's sniffing about here, he *could* be looking for you. If we can slip you out tonight, you'll be out of danger. I shouldn't worry too much about the disciplinary stuff – your track record is pretty good."

"Which is why I need to be here," I said.

Sharp shook his head.

"Take today off. I have things to do uptown and then I'm out this evening. There's a seat for you on the red-eye tonight."

"So that's it?" I asked.

"Yep," Sharp said. "I'm sorry. It's out of my hands now. It's just business."

"Sure," I said submissively. "I'm sorry it didn't work out."

"Well, maybe next time we can work together again. You listen to Tony Morris too much. He's too old-school, acts before he knows the facts. And what he does know, he keeps to himself. A lot of our new intel comes from stuff Tony was sitting on, things we've found on his computer. Intel he should have shared."

From what Dolan had told me, this rang true.

"OK," I said, admitting defeat. "Maybe we could go for a drink before I leave this evening?"

"That would be good; quick one," Sharp said. "Maybe I'll come and see you off safely." He waved away an offer of more coffee from a nice-looking waitress whose tight uniform passed him by. He flicked his suit with a napkin and picked up his briefcase. "Meet back here around six?"

"Sure thing," I said.

I watched Sharpie order a cab at reception, then leave the building a couple of minutes later. I gave a little wave.

I left the hotel seconds after him and watched him get into a limo. I took the next yellow cab and, like they do in the old films, asked the driver to follow the limo. It headed north, driving steadily through morning traffic. The sun was bright and the day was heating up.

"You a private dick?" the cabbie asked.

"No. My boss forgot his phone."

"You English? From London?"

"Yep," I said, eyes on the car ahead. The conversation ground to a halt. We drove past Central Park. Several blocks later the limo stopped in front of a huge, impenetrable-looking building.

"What is this building?" I asked, but the driver had ceased to be conversational after the first attempt.

"Businesses, some apartments, I guess." I paid him, thanked him for the information and got out. Sharpie had disappeared inside, but the flow of people on the street concealed his entry. Brass plates advertised names of corporations and anonymous numbers.

I'd drawn a blank.

I cursed inwardly. I knew I would get into further shit if I was caught trying to spy on my case officer. Sharpie knew what he was doing and didn't need me. He'd cut me out of the loop. I decided it was probably time to go, and started to walk through Central Park in the sunshine. I had yet another day to kill, so I headed to Madison Avenue and found Barneys, the department store where Sophie had been spotted weeks ago. Again, I wandered around in some foolish hope that I might bump into her.

But, like I said, I don't believe in coincidences.

There were well-maintained girls everywhere: rich Madison Avenue princesses out with their girlfriends, admiring clothes in honking, nasal voices that sounded as if they had been brought up on *Sex and the City*.

I browsed around the men's department. I hadn't been in a shop for a long time, let alone considered what I would like to wear. I was still working from a small wardrobe of clothes given to me as Kieran Kelly. I caught sight of myself in a mirror and thought I looked a total mess. My hair had grown and the reddish colour was growing out, showing lighter at the roots. I was fed up with Kieran Kelly: he was a waste of time. Going under the Kelly name hadn't done me many favours so far. I bought myself some narrow navy trousers and a pair of oxblood preppy brogues. I was pissed off and felt like I needed a treat. I picked up a white linen Brooks Brothers shirt and a sharp Ralph Lauren blazer. The bill came in just under $900 and I didn't care. I had money. A pair of horn-rimmed sunglasses like Johnny Depp's pushed it just over a grand.

I felt exhilarated as I continued down sunny Madison, my Barneys shopping bags swinging along, suddenly glad I was being sent home. I walked over to Astor Place and got a haircut. A finger-length crop that made me feel more like myself.

I did some more shopping, bits for my mum and stuff, then got back to Washington Square around four. I was hot, so I had a bath and tried out my new clobber. I looked better, sharper.

I looked like me.

FIFTY-FIVE

At 6 p.m. I put on my regular clothes and went down to meet Sharpie in the bar.

"Good day?" I asked.

"Not bad," he said. He looked agitated. "You look different."

"Just had a bit of a trim, ready to go back home."

We ordered drinks and Sharpie looked at his watch.

"Can't be long," he said. "I need a shower. It's been a sticky one."

"Off anywhere nice?" I asked.

"No, strictly business," he said. He looked around; no one was listening. "I'm hooking up with a CIA contact," he whispered, touching his nose almost subliminally. "We've been working a long time gaining their confidence, sharing our intel. This is turning into a big international deal. Some of our lines of enquiry are beginning to come together."

He took a sip of vodka and tonic and smacked his lips shut; he'd said enough.

"I'm sorry I can't be more involved," I said. "I've come this far."

"Believe me, you're best out of it. Listen, I'm not going to have time to see you off. I've got to get ready. You'll be OK?"

"I'm a big boy now," I replied. I was pleased he wasn't coming. I had no intention of going to the airport.

"Cool. Have a good trip and we'll debrief when I'm back."

"Cheers," I said. We shook hands. "See you back in Blighty."

I let Sharpie go upstairs, finished my drink and went up in the elevator to my room. I changed into my new clothes and came back down well before Sharpie would be ready. Out on the street I crossed the road, watching the front of the hotel. Twenty minutes later, the limo that had picked Sharpie up that morning cruised up and idled outside the front entrance. I walked up to the corner and flagged down a yellow cab and asked him to wait for me. Another five minutes and Sharpie came down the hotel steps. I ducked into my cab.

"Can you follow that limo up there?"

"Sure, man." The driver turned and grinned at me. He was black, with a strong New York accent. "You some kind of spy, or you stalking a rich lady?"

"Bit of both," I joked. "I'm a spy, following a man who's about to broker a big arms deal between the Russians and the IRA and a rich lady."

"Heavy stuff, man." He laughed again. "You ain't gonna get me into some kind of shoot-out? Don't expect that this end of town."

"No," I said. "But keep your head down just in case."

He laughed again, and pulled out as the limo drew away from the kerb.

Donnie had done as Dave had told him and had kept an eye on the front of the hotel since 6 p.m. He had smoked half a dozen cigarettes and was gasping for a drink by the time he saw his target come out of the hotel.

He looked different: smartly dressed, haircut, like he was going on a date. Donnie thought that was promising. When he saw the kid hail a cab, he stepped out of the shadows and flagged one down himself.

"Follow that cab, mate," he said.

"Sure. You a private dick or something?"

"Yeah," Donnie said. End of conversation.

The cab took the same route as I had the evening before, following the limo to 51st. I asked the driver to stop some way further down the street.

"Shit, man, that wasn't very exciting," he said.

"Yeah, spying's not quite as dramatic as you'd think." I gave him a twenty for a fifteen fare. "It's mostly hanging around, getting shafted and waiting to get paid."

"Just like driving a New York cab," he said. "Hope you crack the case, Columbo." He wrote a receipt and put out his

282

hand for me to shake in a homeboy grasp. "Name's André."

"You haven't seen me, right, André?" I tapped my nose, gave him another ten.

"Thanks. I ain't seen no one, man." He laughed again and drove away.

Sharp had gone into Le Bernardin.

It was obviously a favourite; discreet and expensive. I would leave it twenty minutes for him to settle in. I walked back and had a beer in the Belgian bar, then, stomach churning and nervously belching hops, I headed back across the road to the restaurant.

The same French girl was on the door. She smiled.

"Welcome back, Monsieur. I hope you meet your date tonight."

"I got the day wrong," I said. I rolled my eyes in mock-stupidity. "I'm joining some friends over there." I gestured vaguely into the room. She ushered me through and I crossed the floor amid the clink of cutlery and restrained chatter.

As I approached the table, Cheryl Kelly looked up first, glanced at me, then did a cartoon double-take that would have made Walt Disney proud.

She blanched as if she had seen a ghost.

She had.

I decided to make her the focus of my approach.

"Cheryl?" I said. "Hi. How amazing!"

She recovered herself quickly and went into a fixed grin, but nothing could disguise the confusion in her eyes. I leant down and kissed her on both cheeks, giving it the international playboy treatment. She was flustered.

Bashmakov looked at me curiously.

"Have you met Alexei?" Cheryl said, in an attempt to sound social and unruffled.

"We met once before," I said. "In Croatia, on your yacht."

He looked blank. There had been plenty of liggers on his yacht.

"With Tommy," I said. He gave a flicker of recognition.

"Your son?" he asked Cheryl.

"No, an old friend," she said. I turned to Simon Sharp. He also looked as if he had seen a ghost. "And Peter Pasternak," Cheryl said, introducing Sharpie.

"Hi," I said. "Eddie Savage." I shook his limp hand. He looked furious but said nothing.

"Have a glass of champagne," Bashmakov offered, not unfriendly. He gestured to the empty chair next to Cheryl.

"Thank you," I said, taking the seat. "I won't stay long, though, I'm meeting someone."

"So what are you doing in New York?" Cheryl asked, still keeping composure and a fixed smile.

"A bit of picture research at MoMA," I said. "I'm flying back tomorrow. How's Sophie?"

While Cheryl looked nervously at Bashmakov and searched for an answer, a waiter stepped between us to fill our glasses. I slipped my hand into the handbag that dangled from the back of her chair and palmed her mobile phone, dropping it into my pocket as my hand returned to the table and champagne glass.

"She's fine," Cheryl said.

"She here?" I asked casually.

"No," Cheryl replied quickly. "She's in Spain." She tucked a strand of stray highlighted blonde hair behind her ear. "Peter here designed the interior of her apartment," she added, deepening the lie.

Sharpie, looking defeated, nodded.

I smiled at him and nodded back.

I looked up as Paul Dolan, shaven and sharp-suited, walked across the restaurant towards the table. He looked hard; impassive and unsmiling. He raised his eyebrows when he saw me sitting there.

"Our other guest has arrived," Cheryl said, relieved.

"I must get going," I said. "Lovely to bump into you. Give my love to Sophie when you see her." I nodded to Bashmakov, thanked him for the drink. "Good to meet you, Peter," I said to Sharp. I stood up and offered my seat to Dolan. "Kept it warm for you," I said, and he winked at me.

I turned on my heel and walked straight out of Le Bernardin. It was only once I was outside that I felt my legs shaking and the sweat cold on my back. I had put on a good show, but now I was a jibbering bag of frayed nerves.

FIFTY-SIX

I scrolled through the numbers on Cheryl's phone, texting them to mine, then picked up my own phone and speed dialled.

"Anna? You still in the office?"

"No," she said wearily. "I'm in bed. Sharpie arrive OK? Is he with you?"

"No," I said. "That's why I'm calling. He came here a day earlier than he told you. When you thought he was in Beaconsfield he was already here."

"What?"

I took a deep breath.

"Having dinner with Alexei Bashmakov … and Cheryl Kelly."

She was silent for a minute.

"Are you absolutely sure?"

"I saw them last night – I'll text you a picture. I've just come back from having a glass of champagne with them."

"Now I'm really confused."

"He said he was meeting a CIA contact. I followed him, and he was with Bashmakov and Cheryl. I crashed the party."

"Oh, fuck," I heard Anna curse under her breath.

"Have I done the wrong thing?"

"Yes … no. I'm not sure."

"What?"

"It's just that … I really don't know if I should tell you."

"Come on, Anna, something's going on here."

"OK. It's just I think I've found out that Sharpie planted some evidence that stitched Tony up."

"Does the name Peter Pasternak mean anything to you?" I asked her.

"No," she said.

I finished the call. I decided I wasn't going to do as I was told and leave tonight.

"Be very careful," Anna had said when she rang off.

A text came in minutes later.

**Be there when I get back 11.45. Meet my room. Urgent.
SS**

I went down to the bar and sat in a dark corner with a drink, awaiting Sharpie's return. He came in at 11.45 on the dot, rushed straight past, not seeing me, and got into the lift.

I gave him a minute, then took the elevator to the fourth. I knocked lightly on the door, ready to face the music.

The door opened and I was greeted by a punch on the

nose. I reeled and he pulled me into the room, kicking me in the back towards an armchair. I didn't defend myself.

"You stupid fucking idiot," he hissed. "You complete and utter twat." He examined his hand and shook his knuckles out. He'd hurt himself on my nose. I could feel it, too. "What do you think you were doing? You were under strict instructions. You were to leave tonight. You have disobeyed every single order I have given you. What's your game? I will have you drummed right out – you'll never work again."

"Like you did to Tony?" I snuffled, holding my nose. This angered him and he aimed another kick, catching me hard on the shin.

"What do you mean, you…" More violent expletives followed. "Tony's over. He fucked up. I have been working on this for two years," he hissed. "I have tiptoed around, grooming Cheryl and Sophie in Spain, softly, softly, creating a cover as an interior designer, half-Russian. I've even managed to get the contract to refurbish Bashmakov's yacht, getting right into the belly of the beast. I can fly anywhere in the world and be put up by Bashmakov in hotels, dachas, boats. I have inside access to the way he works and the way he has levered Cheryl away from Kelly. She likes the high life, she wasn't ever going to be a villain's ex in bloody Kent. She follows the money."

"What about the arms deal?" I sniffed.

"Of *course* there's an arms deal, a big one, and plenty more, and where I'm positioned I can keep tabs on all of it. I am on the verge of bringing down one of the world's biggest crime syndicates and then Eddie effing Size Tens comes in like he thinks he's James Bond, and puts us on the spot."

"What about the other guy?"

"Who? Bashmakov?"

"No, the IRA man."

"Lynch?"

"He might have been called that once," I said. "But that was Paul Dolan."

The anger drained from Sharpie. And the colour from his face.

"Paul Dolan? How d'you know?"

"He was on the Kelly firm, remember?"

"So Cheryl would know him?"

"He was an outsider, but possibly, yes."

"Fuck," Sharpie said. He thought for a moment. "Does he know who I am?"

"Not sure," I said. "Don't think so."

"Did he recognize you?"

"Maybe," I lied. "If he did, he didn't show it."

Sharp was mollified. He sat down. He chewed a nail, eyes darting around the room.

"Sorry I hit you," he said. "That's a useful bit of information, really useful, but I just have to keep a watertight grip on all of this. I can't afford a slip-up. I still want you to go, but you've missed your flight now. We'll book another and get you gone in the morning. I'm coming too, we've sat still for too long."

I thought that was rich coming from Sharpie – he always wanted to keep me in one place where he could keep an eye on me. Now he looked edgy, thinking things over.

"What about Sophie?" I asked. He turned on me.

"You still don't get it, do you? Sophie doesn't matter. Sophie was only ever Tommy-bait. She is no longer important to us."

"She's important to me," I said.

"And that's where you've always fucked up, you idiot. You get involved, you let your emotions rule you. Why do you think so many poofs have made the best spies? I'll tell you – because we *don't* get involved. We keep our eye on the bigger game, keep relationships light and don't get bogged down in personal details. You, boy, are led by your dick."

"Bit harsh," I said. "Of course I get involved with people. I have emotions, I *do* get involved; these are lives we are dealing with."

"Harsh, maybe, but true. You're a slave to your feelings. You're too young. Immature. You're over. I think you should turn in. I'll book the 10 a.m. Check out of here early, at six."

"OK," I said, slapped down. "Sorry if I put my foot in it tonight. I won't be in your hair much longer."

He looked at me, about to say something, stopped himself, but then couldn't resist. He was scared.

"You *sure* that was Dolan?"

"Sure as I can be," I said.

I left Sharpie thinking in his room and went up to the sixth. I had no intention of sleeping in my bed that night.

FIFTY-SEVEN

I was right to be suspicious.

I went to my room and padded the bed with pillows and blankets as if I was asleep in there. Then I packed a light bag with the essentials and found myself a large broom cupboard on the corridor, where, propped up by a cushion from a corridor sofa, I sat and waited. I kept a chink of the door open. It was past midnight and the lift was no longer busy. Nearer 1 a.m. I must have dozed a little, then I woke up as I heard the rumble of the lift coming up to the sixth floor. I shook myself awake and watched as the door chimed open and clanked shut.

A man stepped out, suited, someone who would look perfectly in place walking across reception. He checked numbers, then knocked lightly on my door. Waited. I held my breath. Through the gap by the hinges I could see a sliver of him and my room door as he pulled a balaclava from his pocket. He put it on, then gently worked the passkey on my locked door. I saw the silenced pistol at his side as he entered my darkened room. I stayed still and waited, keeping my breathing light and even as I heard the dull report of four silenced shots going in, I imagined, to my dummy body.

I watched him leave and close the door silently.

I was "dead" again.

Twice I had been approached by an assassin in a hotel room in which Simon Sharp had told me to stay put.

I decided to wait it out till six o'clock to test my theory. To see how surprised Sharpie would be that I was still alive at breakfast.

I was in reception by 5 a.m., dozing on a sofa as the new day's staff arrived. At 5.40 a.m. I was able to get some coffee, the weak American stuff that only gets you going after five cups. I was wary, having been "assassinated" during the night, but people were still thin on the ground and I was safer in a public place.

At 6 a.m. I started to get twitchy. Sharpie was always on the dot. At 6.15 a.m. a new anxiety came over me; he'd fled, or done a runner, thinking me dead. By 6.45 a.m. I was asking the desk if Mr Sharp had checked out. They had no one of that name.

"Try Mr Pasternak?"

"No, Mr Pasternak hasn't checked out."

I waited five more minutes, then decided to walk up to the fourth floor. I listened outside Sharpie's room. Quiet. I knocked gently. Nothing.

Louder. Nothing.

I waited.

An old cleaner trundled along the corridor pushing a

trolley of towels. She looked Mexican or Puerto Rican.

"*Buenos días,*" I said.

She stopped and looked at me.

With a mixture of signs and rusty Spanish, I told her I'd left my key inside. She looked impassive, but a ten-dollar bill released her passkey.

"*Muchas gracias, señora,*" I said as she pushed Sharpie's door open for me.

It was dark. I crossed the room and opened the curtains. The bed had not been slept in. I started to feel like a fool. I switched on the lights and opened the closet, but Sharpie's bags were still there. Hanging up were a couple of shirts, and inside a Gucci bag was a new pair of shoes. Expensive taste, Sharpie had.

I went to the bathroom and switched on the light. The door was heavy as I opened it. The bath was full, so I dipped my fingers in the water, which was cold. I felt the door move behind me and turned to see the weight of Sharpie's body swinging it shut.

I shouted something out loud. I don't know what.

He was hanging by the dressing-gown hook attached to the back of the door. His leather belt was tight around his neck, the skin red and blue where the rough edge cut in. His mouth was open in a wide "O" that seemed to shape a silent scream, fat tongue lolling out obscenely. His eyes bulged, ready to pop from his purple face, staring down at me accusingly.

I felt paralysed, but forced myself to take out my iPhone and take a picture. I closed my eyes and pressed the button.

Then I grabbed the door handle to exit, trying to avoid the corpse, but made it no further than the toilet bowl, where I vomited out my shock and horror convulsively. I went back into the room, wiping my mouth, tears streaming from my eyes, and searched frantically through his bags for anything incriminating or confidential. There was nothing, not even a phone or passport. Either Sharpie was super-cautious about where he kept his things or someone else had been in. Shaking, I went through the drawers: nothing there, either.

I could hear the sounds of the hotel coming to life in the corridor; doors being slammed, papers being delivered. I realized I needed to get out. Being found in here with Sharpie's body would have taken some explaining. Only the little Mexican woman had seen me come in. I put a tag on the door and, checking the corridor, closed it behind me. "Do Not Disturb."

FIFTY-EIGHT

I checked out.

The hotel staff would have seen me with Sharpie in the bar, so I would probably be number one on the list of people they would want to talk to when he was found.

I swerved my favourite diner and walked a few blocks away to another, where I ordered food that I couldn't eat and sipped weak, sweet coffee while I considered my next move. I had my exit plan: I could change my air ticket to that evening.

I texted Anna.

SS dead. For real. I'm coming back. Dets to follow.

It was still early. I was terrified and traumatized. I had a day to look for Sophie Kelly. And I had Cheryl Kelly's phone.

I looked through the names, many of them Russian-sounding, ending in -ov and -ev. I was sure there would be a number for Sophie somewhere on there.

I tried *Sofia*.

It rang. New York ring tone.

"Hi."

"Hi, is Sophie there?"

"This is *Sofia*, who's this?" The accent was American, the voice unfamiliar.

"I was looking for Sophie Kelly?"

"No, I'm Sofia Greenberg, you have a wrong number."

"Sorry. I'm looking for Sophie Kelly, Cheryl Kelly's daughter?"

The phone went down.

I tried several others, *S*s and anything that might be cryptically linked to Sophie or Kelly. I got a series of wrong numbers and voicemails. Dead ends. I stared at the phone's contact list.

Petrina. It rang a bell, so I called it.

"Hi, is Sophie there?"

The voice on the other end was weary, foreign-accented. Tired and vulnerable.

"No, this is Petrina. Sophie's asleep."

My pulse began to race.

"I have a message from her mother, Cheryl."

"We had a party last night. What time is it?"

"Sorry, eight-thirty, a bit early ... it's just Cheryl asked me to deliver some flowers. She's sorry she didn't make the party."

"Oh, sure, who is this?"

I was thinking fast.

"Kieran, I'm a colleague of Peter Pasternak."

"Well, I have to go out at ten o'clock. I'll leave Sophie a note that you're swinging by."

296

"Thanks. Oh, Petrina, can you just remind me of the address? I can't read Cheryl's writing…"

She paused momentarily, then reeled off an address uptown: 3F, The Ormonde, West 70th and Broadway.

"Thanks," I said. "Her writing makes it look like 8E – I would never have found it."

"No problem," she said.

It had only taken an off-guard, sleepy and hungover Russian princess to lead me straight to Sophie Kelly.

I gulped my coffee and took a cab to the Upper West Side, where I could disappear into well-heeled Manhattan, trying to shake off the nightmarish vision of Simon Sharp's dead body.

I bought flowers that cost me an arm and a leg and walked up Broadway to kill a little time.

I found the block on the corner of West 70th. It looked French, turn of the century, old by New York standards, but the balconies and red blinds that decorated the frontage looked more attractive and welcoming than most New York brownstones.

I waited on the street, and at ten-fifteen, a fashionable fifteen minutes late, I saw a dyed-blonde, leggy girl in Lady Gaga heels teeter out and allow the doorman to hail her a cab. Petrina, I was sure.

I was still well dressed and, waving the flowers, slipped by the concierge with a nod and a wink. I fitted in, as I had at Le Bernardin. I went up to the third floor. I rehearsed over and over again what I was going to say once I saw her. I imagined the door opening, imagined the passionate embrace that would surely follow.

I pressed the buzzer and waited.

"Hello?" London voice.

"Flowers for Sophie Kelly," I said. American.

"OK," she said. "Coming."

Stupidly, I held the flowers in front of my face as I waited outside the door.

I heard double locks being opened. The door opened and Sophie Kelly stood there, looking at the flowers. I dropped them away from my face.

"Hi, Soph," I said. "Surprise."

FIFTY-NINE

She was wearing a dressing gown, still towelling shower-wet hair. She'd lost a lot of weight. Too thin, I thought. I waited while she stared at me for a couple of beats, then she dropped the towel and screamed.

I held my hands up trying to silence her; dropped the flowers, grabbed her forearms and edged her back into the room. I closed the door for fear of other residents hearing her screams and coming to her aid.

"Please, Sophie," I said, soothing, "I know it's a bit of shock."

"You're dead! You're *dead*, you bastard," she screamed, shaking my hands off her. "How could you do this to me?"

I realized that my approach might have been wrong.

I should have tried to contact her first, but I was running out of time. If I was honest with myself, for months, despite telling Sharpie otherwise, I had secretly felt like a knight in armour on a quest to find and rescue the princess. It had kept me going.

As Sophie slapped me in the face, I realized it had never occurred to me for a millisecond that the princess might not actually want rescuing. That she might never want to see the knight in shining armour again.

"How are you here? Why? You ruined my life, you complete arsehole!" She reached for a cigarette from the glass table. There were empty bottles all over it and a mirror and a razor blade that betrayed evidence of dusty white lines of cocaine. Her hand shook as she lit and inhaled deeply on a Marlboro. She had never smoked much when I knew her.

"I survived being shot," I said. "Your dad asked me to come and find you."

"*Dad* asked you?"

"He knew I was the only one he could trust."

"After what you did to him?"

"It wasn't just me," I said. "It was an inside job. The Irish and the Russians are closing in on him. Since he's been inside, they've all been eating away at his businesses in the UK and Spain. I've been over there as well. I've been looking for you for months."

"Well, you shouldn't have bothered," she said. She was calming a little but still shaking, glancing at me warily as if making sure that I was really me and not someone from a dream – or a nightmare. "I have a new life here." She waved her arms at the vast, high-ceilinged apartment flooded with morning light. An impressive collection of modern American art hung on its white walls.

"Courtesy of Mr Bashmakov, I imagine?"

She nodded.

"Alexei's looked after me," she said defensively.

"Of course he has. He's been keeping you safe and out of the way while he muscles in on your old man's business."

"He hasn't! He looks after Dad's stuff while he's ... away."

"You *sure*?" I asked.

Sophie had always been very good at turning a blind eye to Tommy's business affairs, seeing only what she wanted to, but I could see doubt creeping over her – or perhaps what knowledge she did have was becoming crystal clear.

"All I know is that he's been very good to us."

"Us?"

"Mum's here too," she said.

"I know," I said. "I've seen her."

"Did she see you?"

"Yes, I had a drink with her last night. And a man called Peter Pasternak. Do you know him?"

"Of course I do," she said. "Peter's our interior designer. He did this flat. He works for Alexei. He's a friend."

"You met him in Spain, right?"

"How did you know?" she asked, surprised.

"He told me."

"Peter told *you*?"

I nodded.

"So, how come you know Peter?" she asked.

I took a deep breath, the memory of Sharp's strangled body fresh in my mind.

"I've worked with him for a while."

Now she looked really confused.

"Worked? What? Interior design, art?"

"No," I said. "Peter Pasternak is actually a British intelligence agent called Simon Sharp."

"You're mad!" she said. "Is this some kind of joke?"

"No, I'm afraid not. And I'm also not joking when I tell you that he's dead."

"No, he's not. I only saw him…"

"Last night."

"How do you know?" Her face was white; she reached for another cigarette with a shaky hand.

"I saw his body this morning. Someone tried to kill me, too."

"Who?"

"I don't know. But I guess your sugar daddy might have had something to do with it."

"Alexei? No. He loved Peter. I need a drink."

"Bashmakov doesn't love anyone he suspects is double-crossing him," I said.

She went to the fridge. I watched her go. She returned with a bottle of cold vodka and poured some into a used wine glass. She didn't offer me anything, but I didn't mind. Then she picked up a small ivory box from the table and took out a plastic sachet of white powder, tipped a little onto the mirror on the table and began to chop at it with the razor blade. Her hands were trembling.

"Cocaine? *You*, Sophie? Smoking and drinking neat vodka in the morning?"

She shrugged. "It's been a stressful time. I've changed,

Eddie, and so have you. You should go. Forget about me. Go, and carry on doing whatever it is you do."

"This is what I do."

She ordered the powder into two neat lines and took a twenty-dollar bill from the box and rolled it into a tube. She leant over and sniffed one of the lines into her nostril, then pushed the mirror over to me.

"No, thanks. I don't." She snorted the other line and began to relax.

"Listen," I said. "I promised Tommy I would find you and bring you back, and I intend to do exactly that."

"I'm not going anywhere, Eddie. Especially with you. I live here now. I'll see Dad when he gets out. He'll sort it. It won't be long."

"His appeal's been turned down. He won't be out for a long time. Tommy got Bashmakov's main man in London shot and I don't think Alexei's very happy about it. He has ways of making things difficult."

She looked at me.

"How do you know all this stuff?"

"There's a lot you don't know, Sophie. I'll try to explain if you come with me. You're not safe here now that people know where you are. With Peter Pasternak dead, others will follow. Maybe even you."

"How do I even know he's dead? You're a liar. You were dead too, as far as I knew." Her confidence seemed to be returning as the cocaine entered her bloodstream.

"I can prove it."

"How?"

I took the phone from my pocket and scrolled through

my photos, the only proof I had. Handed her the iPhone. She looked at the image, horrified.

"Oh. My. God."

"I think you're in real danger here."

"I'm protected," she said. She sat back in the sofa and lit another cigarette. She looked at me with her blue eyes and I could see the Sophie Kelly I remembered. I wanted to kiss her – but suspected she'd hit me again if I tried.

I can't pretend I wasn't disappointed. After all this time I expected to be welcomed with open arms, but she continued to stare at me as if she was trying to work out what exactly I was.

Her phone rang and she checked the number.

"Hi, Pet." Her face scrunched up. She listened for a moment. "Who is this? Where is she?" She looked at me. "Why? No. Where … hello? *Hello?*" She put the phone down and looked at me as if whatever had happened was my fault.

"It's Petrina," she said. "She's been taken."

SIXTY

It did not take me much longer to convince Sophie that she was now high-risk. But she was still reluctant to go. Stuck in her ivory tower, she had become confident that no one could get to her, protected as she was by Bashmakov – who, in my view, was keeping her as some kind of five-star hostage anyway.

Now I'd found my way here and someone else had found Petrina.

"How can I trust you, Eddie? You fucked up my family. Fucked me up."

"Your family fucked itself up," I said. "Thought it was untouchable. Then Tommy slipped up. You're like your dad, you can't trust anyone. But like he said, of all the people you can't trust, maybe I'm the best of a bad lot."

"Why?"

"Try and remember what we had, Soph. We loved each other. You know it's true. I looked after you."

"You used me," she said.

"Whatever's changed, I won't stand by and see you used as a pawn to get to your old man. You could be held hostage too, or worse. If I can get you back to London, I can make sure you're safe. But we need to go today."

"I can't," she said.

Her phone rang. Petrina Bashmakov's number again. I urged her to answer it. She took the call.

"Hello? Yes. Who...?" She held the phone out to me.

"He wants to talk to you."

I took it from her.

"Who's this?" A man's voice. Irish. Dolan?

"Kieran," I said.

"You're with the Kelly girl?"

"Yes."

"I've got the other one. Get her out of there, double quick. It's not safe."

"Who is this?"

"Michael," he said, and hung up.

"The IRA have got her," I said, only partly bluffing. "We need to go. Now."

I frisked the apartment while Sophie, now panicked, packed a bag. I found a few bugs and a surveillance camera, planted, I suspected, by Bashmakov to keep an eye on the comings and goings of his charges. I disabled whatever I could. Above all, I didn't want there to be evidence of me having been there. But I couldn't be certain that I had everything.

Minutes later, Sophie emerged from her bedroom with two large bags stuffed with clothing. She wore a tight

306

T-shirt and pale jeans. I couldn't help but notice she still looked pretty good.

"You're going to have to travel lighter than that, Soph," I said. She stood smoking, chewing her lip, wired, as I emptied her bag and repacked what could be managed in one hand. She reached for the box on the table.

"No, Soph. We've got to stay alert. Leave that stuff behind."

A shift had taken place; the news of Petrina had shaken her and she seemed willing to follow my instructions.

"Passport?" I asked. She went and fetched it from a drawer.

Five minutes later we were ready.

"Where are we going?" she asked blankly.

"I don't know," I said honestly. The flight I had booked wasn't till later that night. I would have to call and try to book another ticket. Get in touch with Anna, tell her I had Sophie. Put the wheels in motion. "We should probably get on the subway and go somewhere obscure where we can hole up for a few hours while I sort things out."

"I've never been on the subway," she said.

"You'll have to slum it," I grinned. "We can be followed too easily in a taxi."

I grabbed her bag and opened the apartment door. And found myself shoved back into the room.

Standing in the doorway, sweating and holding a gun at waist level, was Donnie Mulvaney.

SIXTY-ONE

Donnie felt terrible.

He'd had a rough couple of days. He seemed to have hung around outside a posh restaurant for half a lifetime, unable to see in, being made unwelcome by high-tone doormen who clearly viewed him as a thug.

Couldn't blame them.

He *was* a thug.

He felt subhuman, and now his initial impressions of New York had worn off, he felt diminished by the scale of the city. The antlike feeling that he had experienced in the plane became greater. A big fish on his old manor, he was nothing here, and once he'd trailed the kid back to his hotel for yet another night in yet another yellow cab, he felt even smaller and more isolated.

The kid looked at home to Donnie, confident and in control. Made Donnie feel way out of his depth.

He'd taken to trawling the bars late at night, a big, lonely man who downed drink after drink with little or no conversation

*for the barmen or the night owls who would sit near him hoping
for another free shot.*

*Old habits dying hard, he'd scored a couple of grams of nose
candy and used them over the course of a day and a night, trying to blot out this feeling overwhelming him. Instead of filling
him with false energy and bravado, the drug had the opposite
effect, making him jumpy and paranoid out in the street, and he
had taken to his room, emerging only to watch the kid's move-
ments from the hotel opposite.*

*One afternoon he'd even found himself wandering into the
Catholic church a few blocks away. It was cool and smelled of
incense in contrast to the hot, dusty street. He found himself
staring at the stained glass crucifix that glowed at one end. It
brought back childhood memories and feelings long since buried.*

*The words of his travelling companion, Marcie, echoed
through his head, as they had during his sleepless nights.*

*A white-haired priest had touched his arm and asked if he
was here for confession. Donnie hadn't choked to anything since
he was six, and felt there was just too much to confess to now to
know where to start.*

*The priest had blessed him and Donnie had gone back out-
side for a fag, wondering what was wrong with him. He didn't
feel right. He went back in, put fifty dollars in the collection box
and lit a candle.*

*Perhaps he had come to fear for his mortal soul, or perhaps
he was simply lonely, tired and depressed.*

*He had gone back to his room and snorted the rest of the
cocaine with a bottle of vodka and had a couple of hours' rest-
less sleep before returning to his post outside the Washington
Square Hotel.*

His timing had been good. The kid had emerged and got straight into a cab. Donnie had tailed him to the Upper West Side and shadowed him as he went into a florist. When he emerged with the flowers, Donnie thought that – at last – he might be on to something.

SIXTY-TWO

"Sit down," Donnie ordered. I did.

"Hello, Sophie," he said. "Sorry 'bout this."

Sophie looked bewildered. She would. Her father's nemesis and his hitman had turned up at her New York apartment within an hour of each other.

"What are you doing here, Donnie?" she asked.

"I've come to take you home, princess. Dad wants you back. You're not safe here."

"So it seems," Sophie said. "Especially with you waving that gun around."

"Just protection, Sophie." He swung the gun round to point at me.

"You're not safe here either, Donnie," I said.

"Stow it. You've given me the run-around long enough."

"No, I mean it. The IRA have just taken Sophie's flatmate hostage. They'll be back."

"Don't try it on."

"Suit yourself. I'm just warning you."

Donnie was sweating heavily. He took a handkerchief from his pocket and wiped perspiration from the top of his head. The pistol was shaky in his hand. "Looks like you're getting your bits together already, Sophie. When you're ready, we'll get going."

"I'm not going anywhere with you, you stupid lump," Sophie hissed. She seemed to have rediscovered a little of the famous Kelly temper. Donnie looked as if he had been slapped. "You come in here, waving a gun and expect me to go God knows where with you? I don't even know who you're working for. You might strangle me when you get me in a cab. At least Eddie brought flowers."

"You trust *him*?" Donnie protested weakly.

"Not much more than I trust you, but, given the choice…"

"I'm working for your dad. You know I am. I've always been trusted."

"You couldn't be trusted to finish *him* off properly, though, could you?" She pointed at me.

"I won't make that mistake again," he said.

"No, you won't. You're useless. You'll leave here now and fuck off out of my life. I've had enough of this, of all of you."

Donnie continued to point the gun at me. It was a big 9 mm Glock with no safety catch, large enough to take my head off with the twitch of a finger.

"Didn't you hear me, Donnie?" Sophie shouted. "I said fuck right off – now."

Perhaps it was the slug of vodka and the couple of lines

that had given Sophie the nuts for this, but her temper was up and she was taking no prisoners. Donnie seemed perplexed. Maybe, like me, he'd seen himself as an avenging angel and hadn't bargained on Sophie's reluctance to be rescued.

"I'm going to my room," she told us. She picked up the ivory box from the table. "I'm going to lock myself in, and when I come out I want both of you gone."

"You can't," Donnie said feebly.

"Watch me," she said.

"I'm going to kill him," Donnie threatened.

"Not in here, you're not. You'll make a mess on my lovely furniture and spoil some very expensive paintings. And if you do, one phone call will have you picked up outside and murdered by some very angry Russians. They will take you to a disused warehouse and cut you open so you can watch your own guts spill on the floor, before they pull your tongue out with pliers and cut your head off with a chainsaw."

Donnie looked as if he had been hit in the face with a baseball bat. Sophie had clearly inherited more of the family genes than either of us had realized.

"But, Sophie…" he bleated.

"You touch a hair on his head and you are dead, Donnie."

Some preconditioning appeared to work on Donnie: he could shoot men in cold blood, but the boss's daughter had a strong effect on him. She was to be obeyed. Sophie went into her room and slammed the door.

Donnie slumped into the armchair opposite me, still

pointing the gun. He reached for the vodka bottle on the table and took a pull. He looked beaten; I tried my luck.

"So here we are again," I said.

"Fuck off," he replied, but the anger was gone from his voice.

"Let's talk about Spain," I ventured. "About Valerie … and Juana."

He looked up, eyes like a wounded bull.

"What?"

"About Benalmádena, Bodega Jubarry; about Pedro Garcia, who worked there and saved your life when you were left for dead."

Donnie put the gun down on the glass table between us.

"What you on about?" he said.

SIXTY-THREE

It was as if the kid knew everything about his life.

He told Donnie things that he could have only known if he'd been there. He talked about Valerie, the girlfriend Donnie had hooked up with in Spain. For a month or so, Donnie had been happy in Benalmádena, feeling his life returning to some stability with a good woman.

A life that had once again become unhinged by his connection with the Kelly firm.

Eddie Savage had spoken about Valerie's beautiful daughter, Juana, with tears in his eyes. Donnie was shaken as he heard how her perfect body had been blown to pieces by a car bomb intended for Eddie, probably planted by Donnie's colleague, Terry Gadd.

There was detail upon detail about the time in Spain, about the bullfight where Donnie himself had been ordered to deliver the coup de grâce and kill Patsy Kelly, opening the way for Tommy, and whoever else, to try and get control of the business.

The kid had enough to get Donnie several life stretches, but

Donnie found himself increasingly weakened and perturbed by what he was being told. He thought he had been watching the boy, but the boy seemed to have been watching him, all-seeing, wise beyond his years. He remembered how Pedro Garcia and the girl had pulled him from the gutter and got him to hospital like guardian angels. Donnie felt the choke rise again in his throat and realized that he wouldn't be able to blow Eddie Savage's brains out any more than he could have shot Sophie Kelly. The kid was in charge, and Donnie almost felt a wave of comfort come over him as he allowed himself to relinquish control of the situation.

If he had any hope, it was here.

His travelling companion's words echoed again in his tired and troubled mind: "… a young man, lonely, like you. Look after the girl, Donnie. Look after them both … do the right thing, Donnie. Put your faith in the Lord." When Sophie came back into the room Donnie felt a huge sob rise in his chest, and feared that he was about to cry again.

"You still here?" she asked.

Sophie levelled the gun at both of us.

"'Fraid so," I answered.

"Well, if you're not leaving, I am." She grabbed her bag. Donnie left his gun on the table. My words seemed to have had an effect on him.

Her phone rang, vibrating on the glass coffee table. She waved the gun at us and reached down for the phone with her other hand.

"Yes? Hi, Mum," she said. She seemed cool – maybe the coke had placed her in a different version of the reality that Donnie Mulvaney and I were sitting in.

But her calm seemed to dissolve as she listened to Cheryl. "Where? ... Why? Of course I didn't." Her voice raised in pitch. "No..." She looked at me. "No, I'm alone... OK, OK."

She finished the call, the gun lowered by her side.

"Alexei's gone mad," she said. "He thinks *I* had something to do with Petrina being taken. Did *you*?"

"No," I said.

"No?" Donnie looked confused.

"He thinks Dad's behind it. He's sending someone round to pick me up."

"That levels the playing field a little," I said. "If we don't shoot each other, then pretty soon someone else is going to do the job for us. Like it or not, we're in this together."

"What do you mean?" Sophie shouted.

"If an angry Russian turns up and finds you here with me and Donnie, it's not going to look very good for you, or any of us. To all intents, I'm working for your dad, looking for you. Bashmakov's seen me and he'll soon find out what Donnie's job is ... it would all add up to a bit of a Kelly conspiracy."

"We need to go," Donnie said.

"Fast," I added.

SIXTY-FOUR

We made an unlikely group. A smartly dressed, preppy nineteen-year-old with a bruised face and his pretty, wired girlfriend, plus a sweating hulk – their minder? At least we were trying to get *out* of the country, because sure as hell, they wouldn't have let us in.

I texted Anna again and cc-ed Tony: belt and braces. Surely Sharp's death would bring him back into the fold?

I'm bringing them in. SK & DM. BA JFK>GTW asap. Any help gratefully rec'd. ES

I checked in at the British Airways desk. The earlier flight was only half full. I changed my ticket and bought extras for Donnie and Sophie. I looked around, paranoid that every luggage attendant, every other traveller was a potential assassin.

"Donnie, we need to use the restroom before we go through security," I said.

"I'm all right," he said. I patted my pocket and he twigged. I made sure Sophie stayed close, told her to lock herself into the ladies' and ditch any blow she might have while Donnie and I sorted ourselves out.

We crammed into a cubicle together and I told Donnie to give me his gun. He took it out of his waistband, looked at it longingly for a moment as if he was losing a friend, and handed it over. I lifted the top off the cistern and dropped both pistols into the water.

"We need to come to some kind of truce, Donnie," I said. "We've done the job and got Sophie, but we're going to have to work together."

"I'm meant to kill you," Donnie said matter-of-factly.

"I just bought you an airline ticket home, you ungrateful git," I said. "We have a couple of choices. We can fly back and, once we're through immigration, we'll walk in opposite directions and not look back. Or I can speak to my people and get you away and set you up with a false identity – but you know there'll be a pay-off. Conditions … information."

"Who gets Sophie?"

"I do," I said firmly.

"No, you don't, kid," he said. "She's the only leverage I've got."

"She's the only leverage for me, too. I can't let you take her."

"So what do we do?"

"What is it you most want, Donnie?"

"I want out, I'm tired of this. I want a fucking pension. You?"

"I'd like you to stop trying to kill me, for starters."

"It's not personal, mate. It's just business."

"So if I could get you out, you'd be off my back?"

"Like I said, it's a job."

Another scenario started to form in my mind, one that might work for both of us. I held out my hand and he shook it in his bear-like paw, crunching my knuckles as he did so, and for a moment I forgot I was shaking hands with my brother's murderer.

"We need to go," I said. We left the cubicle and went back onto the concourse to wait for Sophie.

Donnie's eyes darted around the airport. He looked edgy as the echoing calls for our flight reverberated around the hall.

"I need your help," he said finally.

Sophie emerged from the ladies and walked across to us, smiling at me.

"What?" I asked. Donnie leant in to me.

"I'm terrified of flying," he said.

SIXTY-FIVE

Belmarsh was as grim as ever – dull red brick against a grey south London sky – but after New York the scale looked more human, the route familiar.

After the usual procedure, I was taken into the interview room and I sat down at a table. A few minutes later, Tommy Kelly was brought in through another door. He looked wary, uncharacteristically nervous. He shook hands nonetheless and sat down opposite me.

"You OK?" he asked.

"I've had a bit of a bumpy ride," I said. "But I'm still alive."

"So I see."

"You surprised?"

He shrugged. "Nothing surprises me any more, especially about you. I've had a bit of a rough time myself. So what's new?"

"I've found Sophie," I said. He perked up.

"Is she OK? Where is she?"

"She's fine," I said. "She picked up a few bad habits on her travels, but nothing too serious. She's somewhere safe."

"In the country?"

"In London."

"With Cheryl?"

"No, Cheryl's in New York."

"New York? What the fuck is she doing there?"

"They were both there courtesy of Mr Bashmakov."

Tommy's face knitted in anger and he muttered a few choice expletives.

"I got Sophie away."

"Is he holding Cheryl hostage?" Tommy looked concerned.

"Not exactly," I said. "I'm not sure what the deal is, but she seems to be at liberty. Out for dinner with him and stuff; friendly."

"How friendly?"

I paused. "She appears to be with him," I said.

Tommy's face looked as if he'd been slapped. Hard.

"*With* him? What do you mean?"

"Well, I can't be certain, but I saw them together a couple of times. I had a drink with them and it was all pretty cosy. Sophie was flat-sharing with his daughter."

Tommy shook his head, uttered a few more curses under his breath.

"Someone abducted his daughter a couple of days ago," I said.

"Hope they cut her throat and send him the pictures," he smiled grimly.

"I think Sophie would have been next," I added, and the smile vanished.

"Who?"

"The Irish lot, I suspect."

He shook his head again. "There's going to be a major effing war when I get out of here. No prisoners."

"When," I said. "But I think you'll have a hard job working out whose side anyone's on."

"All I know is, they're all trying to destroy me. I'll wipe out the lot of them."

I began to feel, like some of the others, that perhaps Tommy had finally lost his grip. His threat suddenly sounded empty from inside a high-security prison.

"What about Soph?" he asked. "When do I get to see her?"

"That depends. I have her in a safe house. Donnie was with me when I found her."

"Mulvaney?"

"Yes, Donnie brought her back with me. I needed protection."

"Donnie brought her back with *you*?"

He looked at me, mystified. I tried to stop myself grinning.

"So, here's the deal. My lot can spirit Sophie away, give her a new identity and a new life and you're unlikely to see her, or me, again…"

"Or?"

"Or you take the price off my head, get Donnie off my back and put him out to pasture with a pay-off. He's a spent force."

"How much?"

"100 k."

He nodded. "And Sophie's at liberty?"

"I have to square things with my firm, but she's committed no crime. I'll keep an eye on her, of course."

"Can I trust you?"

"I'm here, aren't I? I found Sophie like you asked. Do you have a choice?"

He held out his hand across the table.

"Done," he said. "You're a right slippery little snake, Eddie Savage, but I can't help but admire you."

"Thanks," I said.

I pressed the buzzer on the desk. Seconds later a screw opened the door and Sophie walked in.

"Hello, Dad," she said.

"Hello, baby." He stood up. She walked across and hugged him tight and Tommy Kelly burst into tears.

SIXTY-SIX

"Here comes trouble," Tony said.

He looked as pleased as punch sitting back behind his desk. He was back in the Vauxhall office with Anna, who gave me a smile as I came through the door.

"Good to see you back, Tony," I said.

"I never went away, really, mate." He chuckled. "Sure, I got a disciplinary, but the shit don't stick to Teflon Tony. My stepping aside was a good move because it allowed Sharpie his head."

"Look where that got him," I commented.

Tony nodded sagely. "Out of his depth. I gave him enough rope to hang himself, so to speak."

"Who got to him?" I asked.

Anna looked at Tony. "He did it himself," she said.

"Right," I said. "Bollocks."

"That's the party line," Anna said. "We're not going to argue with it or open any other line of enquiry." She handed me a newspaper.

I scanned the headline, a photo of Sharpie and the opening paragraph – the usual stuff: *British intelligence agent found hanged … spy Simon Sharp found dead in New York Hotel … Russian-speaker, linguistic genius…* I handed the paper back.

Didn't believe a word of it.

I went to the pub for lunch with Tony.

I felt deflated now I was back. At least I'd done what I'd promised myself, and found Sophie Kelly. I'd done what Tommy Kelly had asked, even though our reunion hadn't been quite as romantic as maybe I'd have liked. I wondered if I'd have much more to do with her now. Things had changed.

Tony ordered us pints of London Pride and pie and mash. He sensed my disappointment. There was always a natural slump after the adrenaline of any mission. He did his best to fluff me up.

"You done good, mate." He took a gulp of beer and wiped froth from his lips. You drew the Irish out and you handled Sharpie well."

As far as I could remember I'd been manipulated into both situations by Tony, who'd then left me to sink or swim.

"You never wrote, you never phoned…" I said in mock Jewish mother tones. Really, I meant it. Tony looked me squarely in the eye.

"I was in a tight spot, juggling some dangerous intel. I had to keep on the down low, mate. Contact with you might just have exposed a chink in the armour."

"Your armour?"

Tony rolled his shoulders huffily.

"You might recall that I pulled out all the stops when you were up shit creek with the Irish? I had to call in some big favours there."

"Yeah. Thanks, Tony." I'd got out alive, I guess.

The things that Paul Dolan had told me about Tony stuck in my mind. Of course, he might have been making them up, but I knew enough about Tony's manoeuvres for them to have a ring of truth about them.

"Did you kill Sharpie?" I asked bluntly.

He looked surprised. "I wasn't there, was I?"

"Did you order his killing, then? Did Dolan kill him for you?"

Tony shrugged, face inscrutable.

"Suicide," he said. "He got himself in a pickle. Sharpie was a double agent. Could have been Bashmakov, couldn't it?"

"Bashmakov liked him," I said.

"So did I, until he turned me over," Tony said. "Remember the car crash, the blow-out? I had a dig around. That was no accident. I knew it wasn't. Sharpie had been seen sniffing about by one of the car-pool boys. The car was rigged. Sharpie wanted you and me out of the way. He even leaked snippets about you back to Tommy Kelly's boys. It would have been very useful for him if they'd got to you. The Russian who tried to do you in the hotel?"

"That was Sharp too? You sure?"

"Almost a hundred per cent," Tony said. "He was a busy boy. Dobbed me in over the Paul Dolan release when *I* was on the right track letting Dolan go. Napier took a view."

"Dolan did me a favour in New York," I said.

"Sure." Tony nodded. "He gave you a good steer, although you can never be completely sure with Paul. He's his own man, but he owes me a big one. Meanwhile, you turning up when Sharpie was meeting Bashmakov and Mrs Kelly rattled their bars so much they didn't suspect anything about Dolan. They were reassured by his presence: it was Sharp who suddenly looked like the rat in the kitchen."

"So did you order his killing?" I asked again.

"Makes no difference whether we did or the Russian did or he topped himself. He was going to get it one way or another."

"What about a simple kid in Northern Ireland, Christie something? Beaten to death."

Tony looked up from his pie, which had just arrived at the table.

"Don't believe everything you hear, kid. Like I told you, there are plenty of grey areas in this business, and everyone has their version of the truth."

He looked at me, impassive, and I knew deep down that Tony was capable of doing all the things I'd heard about.

I watched him tuck into his pie and mash as if he didn't have a care in the world.

My temporary safe house was Sharpie's flat in Pimlico.

It was comfortable and smart, with nondescript art on the walls. Any trace of Simon Sharp had been forensically cleared as if he'd never existed. And in some ways, he hadn't. Once a spy has gone, especially a double agent, all records are swept away and hidden somewhere dark in a vault in Beaconsfield. All that was indelible about Simon Sharp, aka Peter Pasternak, was the image of his bizarre death scarred on my mind. I would have to move somewhere else. Soon.

I turned on the lights. The flat was quiet. The bedroom door was open a chink; I went to look in. A little daylight poked through the gap in the curtains.

"You OK?" I asked.

"Still a bit jet-lagged," Sophie answered wearily. "I wondered when you were coming back."

"I'm here now," I said.

"Thanks for bringing me home, Eddie," she said.

"Wherever home is," I commented.

"Here will do for the moment." She turned back the duvet a quarter.

In the half light I saw the girl I remembered, warm and soft from sleep.

I padded across the carpet and climbed into bed.

EPILOGUE

Donnie locked up the flat in Brockley.

It was damp and smelled of mildew and loneliness.

He hadn't taken much in his bag; he was used to being light on his toes. He felt a new sense of freedom as he drove through Deptford, up and over Blackheath and out onto the A2, leaving the sprawl of south London behind him.

Driving the old Beemer at a steady 80 mph, he arrived in Dover an hour or so later. The Channel opened up in front of him, greeny-blue, and the sun shone on the four or five ferries that manoeuvred around the harbour like toys in a bath.

At the bottom of the hill, white cliffs behind him, he drove into the ferry terminal and waited in a queue.

He checked his phone. Dave, missed call. Dave, text.

Call me. D.

Donnie ignored them, but a few minutes later, Dave rang again. Donnie thought he'd answer this time. He was nearly away. He walked over to the quayside, where gulls squealed over the call.

"Wayne Drops," Donnie answered.

"Don? Dave."

"Dave?"

"What's going on, Don? Where are you? Southend?"

"I'm taking a break, Dave."

"A break from what, Don?"

"I done the job."

"You didn't finish it, did you?"

"I done a deal."

"Not with me, you didn't. When the guvnor's inside and gone soft, the only person you do a deal with is me." Dave's voice hardened.

"Whatever," Donnie said, confident of the wads of banknotes he had with him. "But I ain't going to kill him, Dave."

"I don't like your tone, Don, after all the stuff I did for you."

"You got me in the shit in the first place, mate. I'm not taking orders no more. I've had it."

"Listen, Don, you disobey orders and I'll shoot Eddie Savage my bleeding self, or find someone who will cut his throat for a monkey … and yours, an' all. And you, mate, will be personal non gratis."

"Sorry, Dave. Don't speak French. Ta-ta."

Donnie dropped his mobile phone in the Channel and drove the BMW onto the ferry bound for Calais.

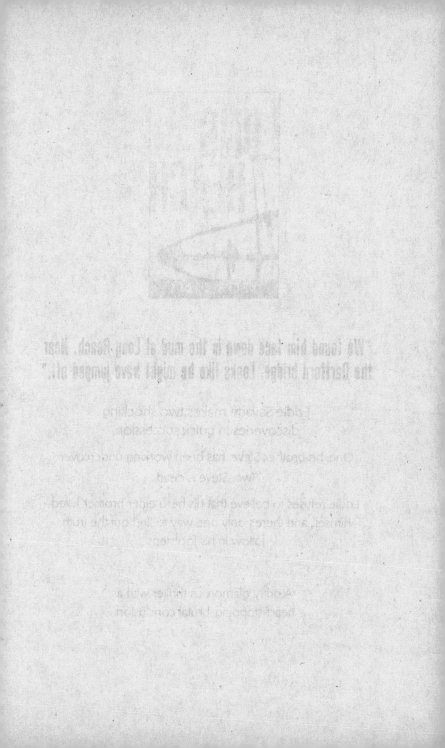

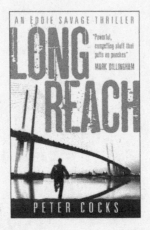

"We found him face down in the mud at Long Reach. Near
the Dartford bridge. Looks like he might have jumped off."

Eddie Savage makes two shocking
discoveries in quick succession.

One: his brother, Steve, has been working undercover.
Two: Steve is dead.

Eddie refuses to believe that his hero elder brother killed
himself, and there's only one way to find out the truth:
follow in his footsteps.

A gritty, glamorous thriller with a
heart-stopping, brutal conclusion.

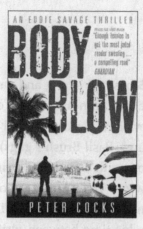

AN EDDIE SAVAGE THRILLER

BODY BLOW

"Enough tension to get the most jaded reader sweating ... a compelling read" GUARDIAN

PETER COCKS

"Well, Eddie, I'm glad to see you looking so well," Napier said. "For a dead man."

Eddie Savage is back.

While his physical scars are fading, the emotional scars are taking longer to heal.

Eddie heads for Spain on the promise of sun, sea and beautiful women – but is drawn, irrevocably, back into the criminal underworld. It appears that greater forces are at work.

A gripping, fast-paced thriller that pulls no punches.

Peter Cocks has had a long and varied career in the creative arts. He has been an interior designer, a living painting, a television performer and writer (writing, among other things, Basil Brush's gags), a hypnotist and a novelist. Along with bestselling crime author Mark Billingham he wrote *Triskellion*, a trilogy of novels for young adults, under the pseudonym Will Peterson.

Peter divides his time between writing, making pictures and producing cabaret shows on the south coast – and recently one in China. *Shadow Box* is the third in his series of Eddie Savage thrillers.